GENERATION X™

GENOGOTHS

MARVEL®

GENERATION X

GENOGOTHS

J. Steven York

ILLUSTRATIONS BY MARK BUCKINGHAM

MARVEL®

BP BOOKS, INC
NEW YORK

BERKLEY BOULEVARD BOOKS, NEW YORK

Special thanks to Ginjer Buchanan, John Morgan, Ursula Ward, Mike Thomas, and Steve Behling.

GENERATION X: GENOGOTHS

A Berkley Boulevard Book
A BP Books, Inc. Book

PRINTING HISTORY
Berkley Boulevard paperback edition / September 2000

The Penguin Putnam Inc. World Wide Web site address is
http://www.penguinputnam.com

Check out the Ace Science Fiction/Fantasy newsletter, and much more,
at Club PPI!

ISBN: 0-425-17143-4

BERKLEY BOULEVARD
Berkley Boulevard Books are published by The Berkley Publishing Group,
a division of Penguin Putnam Inc.,
375 Hudson Street, New York, New York 10014.
BERKLEY BOULEVARD and its logo
are trademarks belonging to Penguin Putnam Inc.

PRINTED IN THE UNITED STATES OF AMERICA

10 9 8 7 6 5 4 3 2 1

To Dean and Kris,
for seeing me sane through the rough times,

to my wife, Chris,
for all the on-site editorial work,

and to
George A. Johnson, patron of the arts

Acknowledgments

Thanks to Kurt Busiek for his kind permission to use his character and to ace *Generation X* comic scribe Jay Faerber for his generous cooperation in sharing information.

We also wish to acknowledge the M.O.N.S.T.E.R. Archives, and the staff and management of Little Latveria, without whose cooperation this book would not have been possible.

CHAPTER ONE

"We know, however, that many strange and strongly marked peculiarities of structure occasionally appear in our domesticated productions, and if their unknown causes were to act more uniformly, they would probably become common to all the individuals of the species. We may hope hereafter to understand something about the causes of such occasional modifications, especially through the study of monstrosities."

—Charles Darwin
The Descent of Man, 1871

"Look, kids! Mutants!"

—Walt Norman
Walt and Recall radio program

Angelo Espinosa shielded his eyes against the sun with the flat of his rubbery, putty-colored hand, and admired their creation. It had taken him, Ev, and Jono most of a week to hammer together the parts in the Xavier School for Gifted Youngsters' service garage. Then, being careful not to be seen, they'd spent better than half the night dragging the parts out into the giant greenhouse that was the school's biosphere.

Angelo glanced up at the warm, springtime sun shining through the glass panels of the ceiling. It was nearly noon. They'd spent the entire morning tacking the pieces together with screws, nails, and glue. The last step had been to apply the plywood decking, but that was finally done as well.

Ev popped out from between a pair of wooden supports with a hammer in his hand. He turned and wiped the sweat off his shaved scalp. "Behold," he said proudly, "the Danger Ramp, an extreme training challenge based on alien Shi'ar technology." He pursed his lips. "Okay, Shi'ar technology and some two-by-fours and quarter-inch ply we found in the gardener's shed."

At that moment, the top of Jono's head peeked over the far end of the ramp. Angelo glanced at him, imagining for just a second what it would have been like to know Jonothan Starsmore *before*—From the nose up he looked like what he was, a handsome upper-class English teenager. It wasn't until he climbed higher up the ramp, exposing the black leather wrap that covered his lower face and chest that there was something obviously different about him.

Before. Before a kid from the Los Angeles barrio had his skin turn into something like a cross between elephant hide and Silly Putty. Before that English kid turned into a living

3

psionic reactor and accidentally blew a hole in himself. That was a long time ago, he thought, or at least it seemed that way.

Fact was, there was something different about all of the students at Xavier's. They were mutants, born with a genetic glitch that gave them incredible extra abilities, and in some cases, incredible extra burdens.

Jono's wraps covered a gaping hole where his chest and the bottom of his face used to be, a hole filled with crackling psychokinetic energy. The injuries happened when Jono lost control of his newly developed powers. The horror and guilt of that day still haunted Jono, who'd taken the rather disturbing code-name of "Chamber." Angelo sometimes thought that the damage had been more psychological than physical. He also couldn't decide if he should feel sorry for a fellow member of the freak-show contingent, or just kick him in the butt and tell him to stop feeling sorry for himself. Most days, Angelo did a little of both.

But Jono wasn't the only one of the boys whose mutation was both gift and burden. Angelo's code-name, "Skin," was an obvious one. His gray, rubbery epidermis hung in loose folds from his face and body. Angelo could stretch and control that extra skin in incredible ways, but it required an act of will to maintain even a parody of normal appearance.

Of the three guys, only Everett Thomas's power, the ability to "synch," literally to copy another mutant's mutations and abilities, had left him unscarred. But Ev had once revealed to Angelo his deepest fear, that one day he would synch with the wrong mutant and impose some terrible change on his body that couldn't be undone. He'd synched with Jono and Angelo many times without any permanent effects, but the fear persisted.

Angelo scratched the stubble on his chin, and absently pinched a rubbery fold of skin between thumb and forefinger, pulling it out like taffy. *Can't blame him. Who'd want to end up like me?* It was just something Ev would have to learn to overcome.

That's why Ev was here, why all of them were here. This

place, Xavier's School for Gifted Youngsters, offered a hope that they, and other young mutants, could learn to control and use their powers, to live normal lives among humans who often hated and feared them.

It was not a great life, Angelo thought, but then neither were the rough streets where he'd grown up. He'd learned to live there, made some friends, had some fun, carved out a little hope among the drugs, the gangs, the guns, the hateful *anglos*. Now fate had given him a different life, and he'd have to find his place here as well.

Ev clambered up onto the narrow catwalk at the top of the left ramp, a skateboard in his hand. He held the board over his head, the sun catching the glossy black paint and the flaming biker-skull decal. "Anybody want to wrestle me for first run?"

Angelo grinned and stepped up to lean against the ramp's wooden framework. "You want to find all the loose nails for us *amigo*, be my guest."

Angelo couldn't remember whose idea it had been to build the half-pipe skateboard ramp. They'd been talking about some over-blown sports-drink commercial they'd seen on the tube and got to talking about it. Back in L.A., where half the houses, even in the bad neighborhoods, seemed to have pools, some of his friends would watch for the real estate signs to go up, then scout the back yards for empty pools. They'd trespass and turn it into a makeshift skate park until they got busted, then move to another house. Back then, it hadn't much interested him but now, well, there were moments of his old life he'd give anything to bring back. Angelo looked at the board in Ev's hand skeptically. "You sure you know how to ride that thing?"

Ev chuckled. "Me and the homies used to skate the mall parking lots until the security guards chased us off." He stood on the catwalk and dropped the board, pinning it under his right foot.

Angelo raised an eyebrow at Ev. "*Homies*. Right, Midwest boy. Get down with your corn-fed self."

Ev just stared at him. "You want it or not?"

GENERATION X

"I haven't been on a board since I was twelve and one of my boys got his first chopped Impala. Maybe I should take it slow. How about you, Jono?"

Jono put down a socket wrench and looked at him incredulously. "Ollie, upside, downside, goofy-foot, grind. It isn't even bloody English. I can't even talk it, much less do it. I'll watch you Yanks bust your butts for a while first, then maybe I'll give it a try," he said in his strange telepathic voice.

Ev brightened. "I'll teach you, Jono. It's easy. Watch." He kicked the board nose-up with his heel, twisted it over the lip of the ramp, and tipped smoothly over the edge. He shot down the half-pipe and up the other side, slowing until he was frozen for a moment standing horizontally on the far wall. Then he reversed his stance, and shot smoothly back the way he'd come, wheels rumbling over the painted plywood decking. He repeated the process, gaining speed until he became airborne at each end of the trip.

Ev started doing simple tricks: spinning his body while airborne, flipping the board, finally landing with the board's metal trucks straddling the lip of the ramp. Ev stood there for a moment, arms outstretched for balance.

"Show-off," cracked Angelo.

"Always." Ev grinned down at them. He hopped sideways onto the catwalk, flicking the board up into his waiting hand. He held up the board. "Anybody else want to try?"

"Is this a boys' club, or can anyone play?" asked a girl's voice.

Angelo turned to see Paige Guthrie peering around the end of the ramp, and Jubilation "Jubilee" Lee climbing up onto the far catwalk. It'd been Jubilee who had spoken.

Paige stepped out into full view, brushed her blonde hair back behind her right ear, and inspected the ramp skeptically. "This sure looks dangerous."

Ev chuckled. "They don't have skateboards in Kentucky," he said, "the dirt clods keep getting caught in the wheels."

Seeing the hole Ev was about to dig himself into, Angelo

flashed her his best grin. "We are mutants, *chica*, life is dangerous."

Just then a girl with flowing, black hair swooped in, flying just below the Biosphere's glass ceiling like a gorgeous brown bird. Monet "M" St. Croix dropped down and hovered over the center of the ramp. She smirked at him, something she did exceptionally well. "Here lies Angelo Espinosa, a.k.a. 'Skin,' mutant, boy, professional annoyance. He survived robotic Sentinels, marrow-sucking vampires, dragons, evil mutants, and alien invaders, only to break his fool neck falling off a skateboard in the back yard. It was natural selection at work. Darwin's will be done."

He frowned up at her. How did she make her hair blow like that when there was no wind? "I'd like to see you try it, Little Miss Perfect."

"I could, and I'd be better at it than you. But I choose not to waste my time." He looked to Ev and Jono for some sort of support, but they were just watching him, probably waiting to see what sort of trouble he'd get himself into. "Hey," complained Angelo, "Ev's insufferable too, but at least he's got the goods."

"Some of us don't find it necessary to show off our abilities."

"Then what are you doing here?"

She settled lightly down onto her feet near the center of the ramp. "If you do fall and break your neck, I wouldn't want to miss it."

Ev and Jubilee sniggered. Paige had her hand in front of her mouth, trying to disguise her smile.

Angelo scowled. "I haven't even been on a board yet, and already everyone is giving me grief. Why is that?"

Jubilee was sitting at the top of the ramp, and he noticed for the first time that she was putting on her in-line skates. "Hey, Jubes, this is a skateboard ramp. Don't you board?"

She wrinkled her nose at him. "Of course I do, and I'm not

bad either, but I'm more of a street rider." She tapped her left skate. "Besides, these are my wheels of choice."

Angelo narrowed his eyes, looking at the skates. "Is that legal?"

Monet had stepped off the ramp and was examining the construction. "The headmasters are going to have a cow when they see this monstrosity. They'll make you take it down."

Angelo brushed past her and made a show of retightening a bolt. "Have you added clairvoyance to your long list of super-powers, Monet? They don't even know about it yet, and since they're leaving today for a two-week trip to Muir Island, it's probably going to be a while anyway."

Monet just looked at him like a bug. "They're going to make you take it down."

"Ready!" announced Jubilee, brightly. She stood on the end of the catwalk, lowered her red-tinted sunglasses over her eyes, and without further hesitation launched herself into space, landing half-way down the ramp in a crouch, rising to her full height as she arched across the span of the ramp reaching the top on the far side. She lifted her feet at the top of her travel, snapped her body around in mid-air, then headed back the other way. Faster now, she reached the top of the ramp and went airborne. Instantly, she pulled her body into a tuck and somersaulted, landing smartly and then rolling down the ramp facing backwards. Just as the ramp started to flatten out, she arched her back and transitioned into a double cart-wheel that killed most of her speed. She ended up back on her skates and moving forward. She arched half-way up the ramp, turned, and rolled off the low point of the ramp to join Angelo, Monet, and Jono.

Paige and Ev applauded briskly. Jono gave her a thumbs-up. Angelo just shook his head in amazement. "Where did you learn that?"

Jubilee tossed her short, black hair and smiled. "I got moves. People forget that. Why once, when I was—"

"—with the X-Men," droned Monet, finishing her sentence.

"Actually," said Jubilee, "I was *going* to say, once when I was at the *mall*." Ev chortled, and Monet flashed him a nasty look. Ev ignored her, and jumped down from the top of the ramp. He tossed his board to Angelo. "Here you go, *compadre*, show us what you can do."

Angelo stared at the board. How long had it been since he'd ridden? This wasn't going to be pretty.

Monet's face went blank and she stared off into space for a moment. "We're wanted back in the school. Emma and Sean are getting ready to leave."

"Saved by the bell," said Angelo under his breath.

Ev looked at him. "What did you say?"

Jubilee looked at Monet. "Telepathy, I suppose?"

Monet tossed her hair and sniffed. "I'm not telepathic."

Jubilee just continued to stare her down.

Monet rolled her eyes. "Maybe a little."

"Angelo, what?" Ev repeated.

"Nothing," Angelo growled. "Let's get inside. And don't you dare synch Monet's telepathy." He looked at her. "Assuming she has any."

Xavier's School for Gifted Youngsters, nestled among the trees of Snow Valley, Massachusetts, had been built for a much larger faculty, staff, and student body than now lived there. With a large main school building, two dorms, a gymnasium, auditorium, the headmaster's cottages, the biosphere, and many other ancillary and out-buildings, space and clutter were rarely problems they encountered. Thus it was something of a shock for Paige Guthrie to step into the school's main entry and trip over a row of Italian leather suitcases.

She tried to catch herself, and succeeded only in twisting so that her elbow cracked painfully against the oak table next to the door, before she managed a soft landing in a pile of garment bags.

Paige shook her head, and saw Jubilee looking down at her. "If that had been a super-villain," she said disapprovingly, "you'd be in *big* trouble—"

Monet pushed through the door and past her, "Why when I was in the X-Men, and so on and so on."

Jubilee's limited attention span diverted, she stomped after Monet. "I was *not* going to say that!"

Paige heard someone run up the steps, and Jono skidded to a kneeling stop next to her, his strong fingers touching her arm, a look of concern in his eyes. "Are you alright, luv?"

She looked away. This was the one time she *didn't* want him to look at her. If there was one thing Paige hated, it was looking foolish. Without really realizing it, she shrugged off his touch and scrambled to her feet. Mr. Cassidy, Sean, was coming to check on her. The other students were all staring at her. She *hated* it.

Mr. Cassidy slid in next to her. "Are ye all right, lass?"

She plucked at a loose flap of skin on her elbow. "I just banged my elbow."

Sean Cassidy turned to yell over his shoulder into the other room. "Emma, I told you not to leave the luggage here!" He muttered something unintelligible under his breath, followed by, ". . . woman."

Emma Frost's voice came from the other room. "She's fine, Sean. I checked on her telepathically the instant I realized something was wrong."

Paige twitched. One more intrusion when she just wanted to turn invisible. "I'll just make sure that Artie and Leech are ready to go. Be there in a minute." Emma's voice faded into the distance.

Jubilee walked by again, going from somewhere to somewhere else, zigzagging through the rest of the luggage that was scattered around the floor of the entry hall. "Look out," she said as she went past, "Magneto's got a *suitcase*!"

Paige picked more urgently at the flap of skin on her elbow. *Invisible.* On a lark, she dug into her elbow with the fingers of her other hand and *pulled*. The skin came off her arm with a sound like the tearing of rotten burlap.

Jubilee stopped and screwed up her face. She hated when Paige used her powers, and Paige knew it. She threw the hunk of discarded skin at Jubilee, who danced and swatted it away like someone escaping a spider.

Paige looked at her hand, transparent as crystal, bending the light like a glass statue. She flexed her fingers, seeing ghostly muscle, barely visible, moving under the skin. That should gross Jubilee out even more. She grabbed the skin above her elbow and ripped again, most of the skin coming off her upper body in one big chunk.

Speaking of chunks, Jubilee was making little gagging sounds. "Oh! Gross me out! What are you doing?"

Paige smiled. "Fixing my elbow. See, just a flesh wound, and once you get rid of the flesh—"

Angelo chuckled. Even Monet cracked a slight smile. Sean just had that long-suffering expression on his face. He had that expression a lot around here.

"Oh, ew! Do me a favor, and just don't eat anything until you husk back."

"Unfortunately, I have a craving for some Choco-Sugar-Bombs."

"Ew."

"Or a cherry fruit pie."

"Ew!"

"Or some Spaghetti-Zeros with Meatballs."

"Ew, ew, ew, you win, I give."

Angelo scratched his chin thoughtfully. "A fruit pie would go pretty good right now."

A little green boy wearing a stocking cap and a South Park tee-shirt strolled into the room. "Pie," he said, wiping the spot on his face where his nose would be, if he had one, which he didn't.

"Hey," said Angelo, "Leech, my man!" He stooped down so he and the boy could slap palms with one another. "Ready for your big trip to Scotland?"

"Leech ready. Leech packed *fifteen* pairs of shorts."

Monet raised an eyebrow. "That's more information than I needed."

"Monet," Sean carefully stepped over a selection of tennis rackets to move closer to her, "is Penny on her way?"

"Gateway left with her an hour ago. They're already there by now." Monet frowned a bit. "He was rather annoyed at the intrusion. He has pressing concerns beyond our present understanding."

"Well," said Paige, "it's not like a girl with razor-blade skin can just take the Concorde, even disguised by a holographic image inducer. And this trip is for her own good. Perhaps Dr. MacTaggert will be able to help her learn to talk, or maybe enable her to touch things without slicing them to ribbons?"

"It's too bad she can't fly with the rest of them," said Jubilee. "I bet she'd like it, all the people and everything. She's shy, but I get the feeling she'd love to get out and see the bright lights and crowds."

Paige sighed. Every time you started feeling sorry for yourself, there was always somebody worse off. Penance— Penny—had to be about the most lonely person in the world. At least every once in a while Paige could "husk" into a diamond hard form and give her a hug. She bit her lip. "When you get there, tell her we miss her, okay?"

Sean nodded thoughtfully, then glanced at his watch. "Blast, it's getting late. Where are Artie and Emma, Leech?"

"They come. Miss Emma make Artie take favorite rock collection out of duffel-bag."

Mr. Cassidy hefted one of Emma's bags experimentally. "Talk about the pot calling the kettle black."

Artie and Leech, the school's youngest students, were mutants too; mutants of the type that even other mutants sometimes shied from. Leech's mutation had left him so deformed that he seemed more amphibian than human, bald headed, his greenish skin smooth and cool to the touch, his eyes featureless yellow orbs. He possessed the ability to neutralize other mutants' powers.

Artie, who was just shuffling into the room, looked a little closer to normal from the neck down, except for skin the color of a bad sunburn, but from the neck up he was different, his skull bald and oversized, covered with bumps, his eyes huge and white. Artie could link telepathically with others and project images into their minds. These images were his primary means of communication, since his mutation had also robbed him of the power of speech.

"Hey, Artie," said Jono, "word up?"

Angelo and Jubilee were definitely a bad influence on Jono's speech patterns, Paige noted. Then a clear image of a broken heart formed in Paige's mind.

Angelo took the stocking cap from the boy's small, pink hand and pulled it down over the top of his head. "Cheer up, spud, your rocks will still be here when you get back. I'll take care of them personally."

Artie lifted his eyes and smiled just a little. They were bombarded with a flash of images, candy, video games, Speed Racer cartoons, currently some of Artie's favorite things. His way of saying "thank-you."

Emma Frost entered the room carrying a pair of small suitcases, and handed them to Sean without comment. She carefully smoothed a stray stand of platinum blonde hair out of her face with a manicured fingertip, rendering herself nearly perfect. Thin, beautiful, rich, cultured, and one of the most powerful mutant telepaths on Earth, Emma literally did have everything. Maybe that explained her luggage.

Emma surveyed the room. "I think that's all."

"I bloody hope so," said Sean. "Ye didn't pack this much when we drove cross-country with the kids last summer."

"You didn't see it, Sean. We were in a motor home, I had closets. Besides, that was merely a trip through the boondocks. This time I'm packing for a trip to Europe. It's an entirely different thing."

"Scotland," corrected Sean. "Muir-bloody-Island."

"But I thought maybe we could make a side trip to the Continent, do some shopping—"

Sean looked around at all the luggage, "Shopping! For what, woman? Sure'n ye have it all already?"

Emma turned away from him sharply, her body language giving a distinct "you're dismissed" message. People around here had some very interesting ways of communicating. She looked at the assembled students. "I really don't know about this. Bishop offered to come and keep an eye on the school while we're gone."

Jubilee rolled her eyes and sighed. "Oh, *that* would be fun. Bishop is *such* a party animal."

Jono stepped between Jubilee and Emma. "What Jubes means to say is, we aren't X-Babies here, and it's spring break. We can take care of our own selves for a couple of weeks, no worries. The pantry is stocked, the satellite dish is warm, and we won't even have to leave campus."

Emma nodded. "See that you don't." She opened her purse and took out a tiny satellite phone, one of the new Reed Richards designed models that was all the rage. "Keep this with you at all times." Her eyes scanned the students one-by-one. Finally she handed the phone to Paige. "You take it. You I can trust. Mostly." She considered. "No radio call-in shows this time, okay?"

Paige felt herself blush, and hoped that it wasn't somehow visible on her now transparent skin. She'd gotten them all in a heap of trouble that way last summer in Chicago. "No call-in shows," she replied.

The front door opened and Emma's drivers started taking the bags away. The drivers were matched muscle men, identical except that one had skin of pastel pink, the other pale green. Paige had tried to get Emma to tell her if they were mutants, aliens, or had just fallen into vats of industrial-strength Easter-egg color, but she'd never gotten a straight answer. *You hang around with this bunch long enough,* she thought, *some things you learn just to not ask about. Especially when it came to Emma Frost's past.*

The last of the suitcases disappeared into the waiting limousine. "Time to go," announced Sean. Leech grabbed Artie's hand and the two of them charged down the step, Leech squealing all the way.

Emma Frost took a last look as she passed through the door and Sean followed, closing the door behind him. "Mind yourself," he said.

GENOGOTHS

The students all stared at the door silently for a while, listening up as the car drove away. Finally Angelo slumped against the door, his knees sagging slightly.

"*Dios*, I thought they'd never leave."

Jubilee did a little dance, multicolored streamers of plasma shooting from her fingers in one of the more restrained applications of her mutant power. "Ding, dong, party-on, ding, dong, the witch is gone!"

Just then, the phone in Paige's hand rang. Paige leaned over and pulled back the curtain. The limo wasn't out of the driveway yet. She sighed and held the phone out to Jubilee. "I think she heard you."

Jubilee answered the phone. She didn't say much, but she did a lot of listening for several minutes. "Yeah, bye," she said and slapped the mouthpiece closed. "Like, how does she do that?"

Angelo chuckled and slumped the rest of the way to the floor, where he sat, baggy elbows propped on the knees of his dirty, gray sweat-pants. "She says she doesn't eavesdrop on what we're thinking."

"She must not," said Jono, "or we'd never bloody get away with anything, and," he waved his hands, "we do."

Paige nodded. "You get away with plenty, that's for sure."

"What," said Jono, "about that night you got yourself drunk and puked your guts out?"

She shot him a nasty look.

His eyes smiled. He delighted in teasing her sometimes, but Paige didn't like being reminded of one of her more moronic mistakes.

He plunged ahead. "You act like the perfect student, Gel, but I can see right through you."

"So can I," quipped Angelo who bent down to peer through her transparent body.

"She just saves it for special occasions," suggested Ev, who had taken an umbrella from the stand by the door and was fencing with the coat-rack. He jabbed. "Ha! Got you right in your mittens!"

GENERATION X

There was a knock. It was the last thing any of them expected. Angelo jumped about three feet away from the door and stared at it. "Did you hear a car, *compadres*?"

They all shook their heads.

Another knock, more insistent.

Ev looked around at the others. "Somebody just ordered the pizza a little early, right? Turned off the security system, too, because they knew pizza was coming. Tell me you ordered pizza." Nobody responded. "Dang, and it was a good theory."

Paige opened the hidden panel under the stairs where the security panel was located. "The alarms are on, and show nobody outside. Either there's a ghost at the door, or they're good."

"Well," said Jubilee, "somebody answer it."

"I'll answer it," said Monet in a huff. She stepped toward the door.

Jono pushed in front of her. "*I'll* answer it." He stepped up to the door and opened the peephole. He stared through it for a while without saying anything. "Bloody hell," he finally said, scrambling to unlock and open the door. The tall, young woman standing there looked as though she'd been dragged through the woods. Her black leather pants and vest were dusty, her tank tee-shirt so dirty it was impossible to figure out which band's logo was printed on the chest. There were sticks and twigs in the shaggy green Mohawk that ran down the center of her head, and bits of grass and leaves in the close cropped hair on the sides. There were small scratches covering every bit of her exposed skin, highlighted with a few larger ones.

She and Jono stared at each other for a moment.

"Jono," she said.

"Espeth," he replied.

She blinked, looked around at the rest of them. "You've got to help them, help Chill—the rest."

Then her eyes rolled back into her head, and she collapsed in Jono's arms.

CHAPTER TWO

"Aided perhaps by others as yet undiscovered, man has been raised to his present state."

—Charles Darwin
The Descent of Man, 1871

When Xavier's was converted from its former role as a prestigious private boarding school into a distant outpost of the Xavier Institute, one of the first changes was the installation of a small, but incredibly advanced, infirmary. Though each of the students had learned basic first-aid, it was fortunate most of the infirmary's diagnostic and treatment equipment was automated.

Jono carried Espeth upstairs, and placed her on the examining table, while Ev fired up the machines and let the diagnostic scanners do their stuff. After that, there was nothing to do but wait for a while. Ev tried to shoo everyone out. "It's getting crowded in here. Give her and the machines some space. I can keep an eye on things."

"I'll stay too," said Jono, "in case she wakes up."

Paige's lips parted, but she said nothing. She stepped out into the hall and, realizing it had been long enough to allow for another "husk," started ripping at her skin, returning to normal human form. It occurred to her to wonder how she could strip off transparent flesh to find opaque skin underneath. There were things about her powers she still didn't understand.

She thought about Jonothan and sighed. There were some things maybe she'd *never* understand. She strolled down the hall and sat heavily on the top stair of the big staircase. She leaned against the banister, the oiled and polished rail cool against her cheek.

Her mind flashed back to the previous summer, when they'd first met Espeth, when *he* had first met Espeth. It happened at the beginning of their cross-country road trip from Seattle back to the school. They'd stopped at the campus of Pacific University, and the headquarters of a campus mutant support organization called M.O.N.S.T.E.R.—Mutants Only Need Sympathy, Tolerance, and Equal Rights.

They'd all made new friends there, especially the "Mutant Musketeers," Chill, Recall, and Pound, who'd paralleled their trip across country, and shared some adventures, and misadventures, with them.

At the M.O.N.S.T.E.R. house there had been a party, and a dance, and there had been a bunch of self-proclaimed mutant groupies called "Genogoths." That's where Jono had met Espeth. She was one of them.

The Genogoths had been a little rough, a little scary, but Chill had assured them the Genogoths helped mutants, especially those without the power to help themselves. They provided M.O.N.S.T.E.R. with information about anti-mutant activities, and helped keep them safe.

That's what Chill had said, but Paige wasn't so sure. With their black clothes and in-your-face attitude, they seemed to her to be posers, looking for something dangerous to attach themselves to, something that would make them look cool. Or maybe she was just rationalizing her concern. Maybe she was just worried that, by comparison, a certain little mutant girl from Kentucky had to look pretty boring, especially to a worldly older guy from England.

Jubilee appeared from down the hall and sat heavily on the other end of the step, seemingly paying no attention to Paige. She was smacking loudly on some bubble gum, pausing only to blow a large pink bubble, which she popped with a tiny firework from her fingertip. "Pretty interesting, huh?"

"What's interesting?" Paige didn't feel like talking, but she'd fallen into another conversational trap.

"Jono wanting to stay in there with her."

Paige sighed. "He's just trying to be helpful."

"Pretty conveniently helpful."

Paige frowned. Why didn't people just go away?

"They had a thing in Seattle. Doesn't that worry you?"

"They danced. Once."

"It was enough of a dance," said Monet, "to keep you two going in circles all the way from Seattle to Chicago."

Paige was startled by the voice, which came from immediately to her right. She looked over to see Monet hovering in mid-air, looking at her through the banister.

"Hey," complained Jubilee, "no flying in the school."

Monet sniffed. "No headmasters, no rules. I thought that was the whole point of the oldsters going away."

"But," said Jubilee, "I liked that rule."

"You can't fly," said Monet.

"I just said, I liked that rule."

Paige growled in frustration. *"Will you two just stop it!"*

Jubilee jerked a thumb at Paige. "She's jealous," she explained. *"I am not jealous!"*

"Who's jealous?" said Angelo, who had just strolled out of the hallway.

"Oh, Lord," said Paige, letting her head sag between her knees, "it's a conspiracy."

Angelo stood at the edge of the landing and leaned his elbows on the railing. "So what do you make of this? I mean, we see this *chica* like, once, months ago, and thousands of miles away, and she shows up on our doorstep."

"She must have missed Jono a *lot*," said Jubilee.

Paige couldn't help but let the irritation slip into her voice. "She didn't come because she missed Jono." Then she thought for a moment. "She mentioned 'Chill and the others.' That's the connection. She knows we're pals, and that we'd help them if they're in trouble. That's the connection."

"That," said Monet, "is wishful thinking. Maybe you're just hoping to see your little boyfriend, Recall."

"He had a crush on me, Monet, not the other way around. Don't you have a broom to go ride or something?"

"No," said Angelo, "she's right. That's the connection. It makes sense. So the Musketeers, they probably are in some kind of trouble."

Jubilee popped another bubble. "I think we're the ones in

trouble, you know?" She pointed at the phone still clutched in Paige's hand. "You should call the grups. Like, their plane probably hasn't even left yet."

Ev popped his head around the corner. "Hey," he said, "she's awake. You'd better hear this."

They all trotted down the hall to the infirmary, with the exception of Monet, who swooped over their heads and beat them all there.

"She's okay," explained Ev before they went in. "She's got scratches, bruises, some exposure, she's dehydrated and hasn't been eating well lately, but that's just the kind of superficial stuff that the gear in here is great at fixing. She shouldn't even need a doctor."

"Well," said Paige, "that's one less troublesome phone call I'll have to make. I should still call Ms. Frost and Mr. Cassidy though." She held up the phone and started to dial.

Jono held up his hand. "Hold off on that till you hear what she has to say."

As they entered, Espeth was trying to sit up on the bio-bed, but Jono gently put his hands on her shoulders and pushed her back down. "I came to tell you about Chill and the guys. They've been kidnapped, and they need your help. I risked a lot—I risked everything to come here."

"If they're in immediate danger," Paige asked, "why didn't you go to the police?"

Espeth shook her head. "It's not like that. They were kidnapped by the government."

Paige and Ev looked at each other. Given some of the actions taken by anti-mutant government agencies in the past, it wasn't unthinkable.

"Taken? Why?" asked Paige. "And where?"

"To a secret government laboratory in rural South Carolina. They want to experiment on them, something to do with the Hound program. You've heard of it?"

Paige nodded. "The government wants mutant trackers and hunters, ostensibly to capture mutant criminals, but more likely to round us all up into prison camps if they think they can get away with it."

"They're a lot closer to that than you think, than anyone thinks. But the Genogoths wouldn't believe me, they wouldn't help. That's why I came to you."

Paige laughed. "The Genogoths? Your bunch of mutant groupie pals? A lot of good they'd do. This sounds like a job for the X-Men, or the Avengers if they're in the mood, not a bunch of losers in Halloween costumes."

"Paige! Zip it, Gel!" Jono glared at her.

"No," interrupted Espeth. She painfully propped herself up on her elbows despite Jono's protests. "She's right to be suspicious of what I am, or how I know the things I know." She looked troubled. "You're just not going to believe me until I tell you everything, are you?" She sighed. "Okay, but look, I'm violating a sacred oath with what I'm about to tell you. You have to swear that, no matter what you decide to do, you have to swear on—on Professor Xavier and everything you hold dear, that you'll never tell another soul. Never."

The Gen Xers all looked at one another.

"Swear!" Espeth was evidently quite serious.

Paige blinked. She sounded awfully serious for somebody who was supposed to be a poser.

"We swear," said Jono.

Ev nodded, as did Angelo.

"I'm good at secrets," said Monet.

Jubilee plucked the chewing gum out of her mouth, looked at it unhappily. "Yeah. Sure."

They all looked at Paige. "I'm not so sure about this."

Jono locked eyes with her. "We don't have to do anything, luv. Just listen. How can it hurt?"

Let me count the ways. She took a deep breath. " 'Kay."

Espeth's eyes swept over them all, as though taking their measure. "At the core, the Genogoths aren't what they seem, what they're supposed to seem." Her eyes met Paige's. "You see groupies, children dressed to scare their parents, masqueraders in black with a mutant fetish. There are some of those, yes, sometimes useful to us, but not much more. They provide our cover, our smokescreen, our camouflage, and the pool from which we recruit those few worthy for our inner-circle."

Monet grinned just a little. "You should have a talk with Emma Frost some time. The White Queen has this 'inner circle' business down—"

Paige swatted at her. "Hush, Monet."

Espeth smiled slyly. "I know all about Emma Frost's past association with the inner circle of the notorious Hellfire Club. I know of Professor Charles Xavier and his X-Men as well. Would you like to hear about Sinister? Or the minions of Apocalypse, or the Morlock tunnel that your little friend Leech came from?" She looked at Paige again. "Or your mutant brother Sam, and his association with Xavier's so-called new mutants, or the latter-day X-Factor?"

"That's enough," said Paige. "You've convinced us that you and your Genogoths are more than they seem. But you haven't told us *what* they are."

"Since the time of Darwin, we've been the sworn protectors of the X-gene."

"I thought," said Jubilee, "that was us." She looked mockingly at Monet. "No, wait, that was when I was with the X-Men."

Espeth sniffed. "That's what they believe, but Xavier has never cared for the weak mutants, only the powerful ones he could use as soldiers in his cause. The X-gene is humanity's genetic legacy, the next step in its evolution, and everyone who carries it is precious, not just the powerful ones. But Xavier, Magneto, Apocalypse, all of them are the same. They build their armies, fight their squabbles, all the while drawing attention and hatred to mutants."

Paige crossed her arms over her chest and tapped her foot. "Well," she said, "you're certainly winning us over to your point of view."

"I'm giving it to you straight."

"But," said Jono, "you said that the Musketeers were in trouble, and that the Genogoths weren't going to help them."

Espeth licked her lips and looked away as though trying to reconcile the contradiction with herself. "The Genogoths believe that the preservation of the X-gene is more important than any one individual, that sometimes a few must be sacrificed for the greater good."

"Selfish genes," said Paige.

Angelo gave her a puzzled look.

"It's a theory of how evolution works," explained Monet, "that genes exist only to create other eyes. They don't care about individual organisms at all. They're just machines for producing other genes. As long as some genes of a line survive, it doesn't matter how many individuals die."

"Meaning," said Ev, "that the guys are too hot for them to rescue."

Espeth nodded reluctantly. "The government is involved, an anti-mutant arm of the government. That plus, as the result of your little excitement last summer, Recall 'outed' himself as a mutant on national radio, and has continued to appear on the radio since. That makes him one of the bad-guys as far as the Genogoths are concerned, and puts his friends Chill and Dog Pound on the expendable list by association."

"Then what," said Jono, "are you doing here if that's what you believe? Let them rot."

She swallowed. "Because—the Genogoths are wrong. This project, it's vulnerable right now. Yes, it's government, but it's a black-project secret, practically outlaw. If something happens to it, the government will just sweep it all under the rug and forget about it, but if it succeeds, then all mutants are in danger. *Especially* the weak ones."

Paige stared at her suspiciously. "You don't sound very committed to the ideals of the Genogoths. How long have you been part of the inner-circle anyway?"

Espeth frowned, but didn't answer.

Jono bent down to look her in the eyes. "Espeth?"

GENERATION X

"Nearly a year." She squirmed under their collected gaze. "Ten months. Almost ten and a half."

Alvie Walton had worked at the Snow Valley Roxxon station for a long time now, and he'd seen more than his share of tourists over the years. He thought he'd seen it all, but the guy standing by his black sports car outside gave him the creeps.

As he ran the guy's credit card through the machine, he tried to figure out exactly what caused the feeling. He peered through the dusty front window of the station. It wasn't his black wrap-around sunglasses, or his black turtleneck and crisply creased black slacks, or the strange silver pendant he wore around his neck on a chain, a pendant that looked like a stepladder that somebody had put a twist in the middle of. It wasn't the vintage black Jaguar he drove, or the thin, neatly trimmed goatee on his face. It wasn't his height, which was average, or his build, which was solid but not overly muscular, or his hair which was short, black, and came to a widow's peak in the middle of his high forehead.

Add up all the details, and he looked like one of those old jazz-type coffee shop guys. What were they called? Beatniks. The guy was maybe just old enough to be the genuine article too.

But there was something under that, some vibe, a feeling of danger and power. He remembered that movie about Patton and thought this guy had the same aura around him. He somehow, despite appearances, seemed more like a general than a beat poet.

The credit card machine beeped its approval. He glanced at the name on the card. "Black," he said quietly. No first name, no initial. Just Black. Strange. He pulled the freshly printed receipt off the machine and walked it out to the guy.

The man took the receipt and was reaching for the credit card when Alvie pulled it away. "Black," he said. "I've never seen a card with just one name before."

"That's my name." He looked slightly annoyed as he

plucked the card from Alvie's fingers and tucked it into an Italian leather wallet. He seemed to be staring at Alvie, though he couldn't tell for sure because of the glasses. It gave Alvie the willies.

"You seem to be a man," said Black, "who notices things, things that are not his business."

Alvie was caught by surprise. "No, not really—hey, just making conversation. Didn't mean to—"

Black waved for silence. "That wasn't a criticism. I'm looking for someone. A young lady not from around here. He produced a picture from somewhere, almost like magic, and handed it to Alvie.

The small snapshot showed a punk-looking girl with green hair. She was standing next to a tall boy of maybe nineteen or twenty, a boy with white hair. But, unlike hers, his didn't seem to be dyed. They were smiling, and she was holding onto his arm as they posed.

Then it hit him. Green hair. How do you forget a thing like that? He'd seen her at the station a couple of days earlier, buying a bag of salted peanuts with what seemed like her last dollar. He eyed Black suspiciously. He wondered if she was young enough to be a runaway. Could this creep be what she was running from?

Black seemed impatient. "Have you seen her?"

"Why are you looking for her?"

"We're—associates. We were supposed to meet at the Vermont ski areas to do some business, but she seems to have had car trouble. I found her car abandoned up the highway twenty miles or so. I thought perhaps she'd hitch-hiked into town."

Alvie considered. Parts of the story fit, but he wondered what kind of business they could be doing, and decided it wasn't good. He tried to remember the details of the encounter. She'd asked questions too, something about that weird boarding school outside town. If that was the place she was looking for, she'd be there already. If she'd wanted to talk to him, she could have phoned. Alvie had spotted a cellular phone sitting on the front passenger seat. "Haven't seen her. Sorry."

Black handed the picture back. "Take another look."

There was something folded under the picture. Alvie fanned it out to see the edge of a crisp one-hundred dollar bill. That was a lot of money for a guy who worked as a service station attendant. He looked at it for a moment, then pushed it back at Black. In a week the money would be spent, but a guilty conscience could last a long time. "Nope, haven't seen her."

Black tightened his lips and nodded. "Of course, thank you for your time."

Alvie watched as Black climbed back into his car and drove away. Alvie wiped his hands on a rag from his back pocket and strolled back into the office. On a whim, he pulled out the doodle-covered phone book from under the counter and opened it up. What was that school called? X something. Xavier's That was it. But Snow Valley was a small town. There were no X's listed, not one. "Must be unlisted," he said to nobody in particular. It was a shame. He had the feeling that somebody would like to know this dude was coming.

Paige made herself a peanut butter and blackberry jam sandwich and sat down at the little table in the nook off the kitchen. The jam was in an unlabeled Mason jar, part of a care-package from her mamma in Kentucky. Like Mama didn't have enough to do raising a house-full of kids by herself.

Still, Paige smacked her lips. The jam was sweet and tart, its flavor blended with the salty peanut butter. It tasted like home, and for just a moment she had the terrible urge to cry. The she reached into her pocket and pulled out the letter she'd fetched from a shoebox under her bed. It was the last letter she'd gotten from Recall, dated two weeks prior. If what Espeth said was true, it must have been sent only days before his kidnapping.

GENOGOTHS

She spread the computer printed sheet on the table and flattened it with the palm of her hand. She read.

Dear Paige and Guys,

I wish I could have come with Chill and the Pounder when they visited you guys at the school last month, but between night classes and a national radio talk-show, it's a lot for a sixteen-year-old to handle, you know? Plus, Chill was here during his spring break, and he's like the worst housekeeper in the world. Took me most of the week he was gone just to catch up the dishes. It's probably a good thing he's not here when school is in session, and I expect he'll be moving out completely after graduation.

Until then, I guess I could afford to hire a housekeeper or something, but I'm socking the radio money away in a CD to pay for grad school. This radio business is too crazy. Literally overnight I went from student nobody with a lame mutant power, to national talk show cohost, and I could be a student nobody again just as fast if the ratings take a slip or some anti-mutant sponsor gets a bee in their bonnet. It's been quite a ride though, and I owe it all to you and your Generation-X crew.

In a reckless moment that summer, Paige had gotten them all involved with an anti-mutant radio-talk-show host named Walt Norman. Through a series of misadventures, they'd all had a hand in saving Norman's life from an on-air terrorist attack. In the aftermath, Recall had been given the chance to make an impassioned plea to a national audience for tolerance toward mutants. The network had liked the volatile chemistry of pairing the mutant Recall and the anti-mutant Norman, and had offered to let him share the mike on an ongoing basis.

Since then, Recall had been in regular touch. Though he'd apparently gotten over his crush on her, his friendship with her and the group had lingered on. Unfortunately, Paige had been a less than faithful correspondent, a fact that she now regretted.

She read on.

Hey, you know, I think I'm starting to put a dent in my bone-head cohost Walt. I used to say that he sure wasn't a mutant, but he wasn't a human either, but lately our on-air debates have changed tone, more fact and less rhetoric. We still don't agree on anything, mind you, but hey, progress is progress.

Got to go. Air time in thirty minutes. See you on the radio.

Your Pal,
Recall

She folded the letter and tucked it back in her pocket. She wondered if that ingrate Norman had even noticed that Recall was missing. Maybe he was relieved to have him gone.

If she'd been listening to the show, she'd know, might even have realized weeks ago that something was wrong with Recall. After the trip, she'd listened to the "Walt and Recall" show every week, but after a while she'd slipped out of the habit. Life kept getting in the way, and Norman just infuriated her. Maybe Recall thought he was making some progress with the big parasite, but Paige just couldn't listen to him. The urge to call in and tell him what a horse's backside he was, was too strong, and it was exactly that urge that had gotten them in trouble last time.

If she'd had better control of her emotions, Recall wouldn't have gotten on the radio and become a target. Basically, this was all her fault. She looked at the half-eaten sandwich and tossed it on the table.

The kitchen door opened and Angelo walked in, followed by the rest of Gen-X. Angelo headed immediately for the peanut butter and bread, with Jubilee right behind him.

"Jubilee," said Paige sternly, "stay out of Mamma's jam."

Jubilee muttered under her breath as she and Angelo both

tried to shove butter knives into the peanut butter jar at the same time.

Jono was the last one through the door. He pulled the kitchen step-stool over and perched on the top step. "Okay, time for a war council. We've got to figure out what to do about this blinking mess."

Jubilee and Angelo finished making their sandwiches and joined the rest of them around the table.

They all stared at each other.

Finally, Paige spoke. "I think it's obvious. We call the X-Men. This is definitely a big-league problem."

Jono shook his head. "We swore we wouldn't tell anyone. That includes the X-Men, Emma, Sean, anybody. My take is we just go and do what needs to be done. We can bloody do it."

Jubilee shook her head. "No way. This is an X-Men-class problem. I say we call them. Maybe they'll let us tag along."

Monet looked at Jubilee and sniffed. "I vote against side-kick-girl."

"Monet," said Paige, "why?"

"Because I'm voting against sidekick-girl."

Paige scowled at her. "That's not much of a reason."

"It's my vote."

Paige looked at Angelo. He shrugged and leaned back in his chair. "Look, I never signed on to be a super hero, and I'm not in favor of getting us grounded till the end of time either. Call in the bad mamma-jammas."

Jono looked at Ev, seeking some sympathy in his eyes.

Ev squirmed in his seat and chewed at his bottom lip. "Our friends are in trouble, and I'm ready for action. We go."

"Bloody great," said Jono, "it's a hung jury. Looks like we fight it out or draw straws or something."

"It's a tie," complained Paige, "because Monet is voting against Jubilee, no matter what. This is too important a decision for that kind of thinking."

Jono's eyes flashed anger. "Who are you to criticize somebody's reasoning. Don't you care about your mate Recall?"

"Of course I care," she snapped. "About all of them. That's why I want to call in the X-Men. It's the best thing we can do for them. Besides, how would we get to this secret lab? The X-Men can just fire-up a Blackbird and be there in half an hour. Are we all just going to pile into Sean's Jeep?"

"The Xabago," answered Jono without hesitation.

Paige blinked. The Xabago was one of the two motor homes they'd purchased for the summer's trip. Emma and the female members of the team had traveled in a luxury motor coach, which had since been sold, but the guys had been allowed to pick their own vehicle. The Xabago was a hideous, tricked out camper with steer horns over the radiator, orange shag carpeting covering the interior, and a fighter plane's bubble cockpit on the roof.

"Jono, the Xabago blew a head gasket eighty miles from home, and had to be towed here. It's such a hunk of junk that Sean and Emma couldn't even find anybody to buy it. It's been rusting out behind the biosphere like a little slice of home."

"We fixed it," said Jono.

Paige frowned. "Who fixed it?"

"Ev, Angelo, and me," explained Jono. "We've been tinkering with it for months."

"I helped too," injected Jubilee. "None of these guys even knew how to use a torque wrench."

"She lies," said Angelo.

"About helping," asked Monet, "or the torque wrench?"

Paige threw her hands up in frustration. "Everybody just shut up! This is important!" She waited for things to quiet down. "So, we have transportation, but that still doesn't change the basic issues. We're deadlocked, I say we call in the X-Men."

Jono looked at her, his eyes intense. "You keep talking like that's an alternative. We swore to keep the Genogoths' secrets, and if we tell somebody about the Musketeers, they're going to want to know where we got the information." He tapped the side of his fist nervously against his knee. "Calling the X-Men isn't an option. Either we do the job ourselves, or we let them rot."

Black pulled into a park and found a shaded spot near a Civil War memorial. Through the trees, he could see a man in a heavy wool sweater throwing a flying disk for a dog, but otherwise, the area was deserted. He flipped open the scramble phone and dialed from memory. He never used the speed dial for security reasons.

The phone was answered on the second ring. "Night comes early," he said, giving the current code phrase. Even a scrambled phone could fall into the wrong hands.

"No moon tonight," said the voice on the other end, providing the countersign. "This is Leather."

"Black. I'm in Snow Valley, Massachusetts. She's been here, I'm certain of it. If so, she's undoubtedly at Xavier's School."

There was a pause from the other end, then, "She could compromise everything. Maybe she already has. Twenty years of staying off Xavier's radar shot in a night. I told you she wasn't ready for the Inner Circle."

Black clenched his jaw slightly, for him, an extreme display of emotion. "Remember your place, Leather. You're a field commander, but I'm the Vertex of the Circle, and I brought Espeth into the Circle myself. She's worthy, but inadequately indoctrinated, and no one could have anticipated that she would be so severely tested so soon. But I still have faith in my choice. I don't think she would casually compromise us to Xavier, not even for the lives of her friends."

"Meaning?"

"Meaning that we may still have time to cauterize this wound. Though I am loath to take direct action, we must have options available. Assemble the troops."

"How many?"

GENERATION X

"Everyone available in the region. If we must strike, we must be prepared to strike hard and do what is necessary." He watched the man playing with the dog. "Sometimes, mine is not an enviable job."

CHAPTER THREE

"Did you hear the one about the mutant that you could depend on? No? Well neither did I. [Canned laughter] As you may have guessed, my cohost, Recall, is missing in action again today. He hasn't called in or anything, so we don't know what's up. Me, I just figure he's discovered girls." [Canned laughter]

—Walt Norman
Walt and Recall radio program

J ono followed her as she speed walked toward the girls'
bathroom. "Give me the phone, Luv."

"Don't call me 'luv,' Jono, and no, I won't give you the
phone. I'm locking myself in the bathroom, turning the sink
on full-blast to drown out your noise, and I'm calling the X-
Mansion. I'm going to send the X-Men to rescue the guys,
and that's final. Yes, we swore we wouldn't tell, and we won't
any more than is necessary, but I'm not going to just sit here
on my hands while our friends are in trouble."

Espeth appeared in the infirmary doorway, leaning heavily
on the door frame, but looking much stronger than the last
time Paige had seen her. "I wouldn't do that," said Espeth.
"You can call them, but where will you send them? South
Carolina is a big state, and the lab where they're being held is
well hidden."

Paige stopped a few feet in front of her and stared. She
hadn't considered that. Espeth had been so forthcoming, it
hadn't occurred to anyone that she'd left key pieces of information out. "The X-Men have resources. Wolverine can call
some of his old intelligence budd es. Cerebro can search for
mutant biosignatures if they have to."

"This is the Hound program, remember? Mutant tracking is
their business, and if you don't think they have a way to shield
their captures from Xavier's scanning devices, you're wrong.
It can be done. The Genogoths do it all the time. And yes, your
friend Wolverine or one of the others would eventually find
where they're being held. But how long will it take? Weeks?
Months? How many times have the X-Men 'lost' someone and
been unable to find them? Even Xavier himself has disappeared on a number of occasions. Meanwhile, you can't even
imagine what sort of things they have in mind for our friends."

Paige stood her ground. "But even so, you'd deny us the information we need to save them?"

"I'll take it to my grave." Something in Espeth's facade seemed to slip for a moment, a sliver of vulnerability showing. "You don't understand the position I'm in, Guthrie, not just between the rock and the hard place, but between the unstoppable force and the immovable object. I'm trying to reach the impossible compromise here, and it can only happen on my terms."

The phone in Paige's pocket rang, and the sound made both of them jump. Paige looked at Espeth. Espeth looked back.

Paige took out the phone and opened it. "Hello." She listened for a moment. "Nothing much. We're just hanging out and watching TV." She tried to put on a brave face. "Nothing happening here at all."

Recall opened his eyes, then closed them again. It wasn't right. He opened them again. No, it didn't seem like a dream at all.

The cell walls seemed to be made out of some sort of plastic, or maybe fiberglass. Every surface of the little room—walls, floor, ceiling, the sparse furnishings that flowed into the floor and walls as though the entire thing had been molded in one piece—all were a uniform, glossy white. Two benches along the walls, one of which he was lying on, a small table, a sink, a lavatory, all melded seamlessly into the rest of the room. In fact there were no corners at all, as floor swept smoothly into wall and wall smoothly into ceiling. These were the first details that Scooter McCloud, better known by his nickname "Recall," took in as he awoke.

It also hadn't escaped him that he wasn't alone in the cell, that his two college friends and fellow mutants, Peter B. DeMulder, a.k.a. Chill, and Willy Gillis, a.k.a. Dog Pound, sat on an identical bench across the room. They were dressed in utilitarian green jumpsuits. He glanced down, and saw that he was dressed in one as well.

"We were wondering," said Chill, a look of controlled anger on his face, "if you'd ever wake up."

It took Recall a moment to realize that Chill wasn't mad at him, something totally out of character for his cool-headed friend and sometime roommate, but rather angry at their unseen captors.

"Of course," continued Chill, "you're the smallest of the three of us. It's possible whatever they doped us with hit you harder."

Recall grimaced. He didn't like being reminded of his small stature under the best of circumstances, even if it was true. Chill's beanpole frame was at least a foot taller than he, and the Pounder was not only a bit taller, he was built like a human-Rottweiler, thick and muscular. Feeling generally self-conscious, Recall tried to sit up and discovered that not only was it a difficult proposition, but it caused his head to spin.

"Hey," Pounder leaned close and put a hand on his shoulder, a frown of concern on his wide face, "take it easy, spud. That's some rough stuff they used on us. We both took it pretty hard too." He glanced over at Chill, who seemed distracted, then snapped his attention back to his cellmates.

Chill smiled nervously and ran his fingers through his close-cropped, white hair. "Sorry, short stuff. Don't mean to be cruel. This is a shock to all of us."

Recall managed to push himself into a sitting position. He slumped with his back against the wall. He turned his head, and the cool smoothness felt good against his cheek and forehead. He still felt doped up, disoriented. "Last thing I remember," he said, "I was—"

"In Chicago, taping your show," said Chill, "last we heard anyhow. And Pound and I were in Seattle, getting ready for graduation and turning over the M.O.N.S.T.E.R. chapter there to the new president. Last we remember, Pound is helping me pack up my office. We were hauling some boxes out to the car, and then it gets fuzzy."

Pound shook his head. "I don't even remember that much. I can't even remember leaving the chapter house." He put his hands on his bald scalp and let out a deep, slow breath. "Like I said, bad stuff."

Recall tried to remember. At first, even the last week in Chicago seemed a jumble. Then he focused, tapped into his mutant ability to find lost things. He'd learned early on that this ability extended to his own memories, at least when he consciously applied it. Images and memories snapped into neat piles, like the cards in a game of computer solitaire.

He remembered a marathon taping session of the Walt and Recall radio show, then the daily live broadcast, plus two taped episodes to be inventoried as fill-in while he was back at school. By the end, Walt Norman had been irritable and difficult to work with, hardly unusual.

Then Recall had gone down the elevator in the downtown building where the studio was located. His contract called for a car to take him to and from his parents' home in the suburbs, allowing him extra time for studying. The car had been there as expected. No, *a* car.

"I remember," he said. "I was going home, and I saw what I thought was my car. Then this woman gets out of the front, not one of the usual drivers. A guy gets out of the back, a big man, and holds up what looks like some kind of pistol. I'm thinking, they must be car-jackers or something, when he pulls the trigger. I don't even have time to react, but there's no bang, just a hiss and a smell kind of like honey and paint-thinner mixed. I realize that he's *sprayed* me with something. Then it's real hard to think, or stand, or anything. I fall over and he's pulling me into the car."

"I told you," said Chill to Pound, "that he'd remember more than we did. They probably nabbed us the same way and were waiting at my car." He looked back at Recall. "That all?"

Recall pondered for a moment. "No. One more thing. I woke up a little, not all the way. I felt shaking, heard voices, sounds, then that smell again." The voices had been unfamiliar, so he focused on remembering the sounds. "Jet engines, thunder, the creaking sounds a plane makes when it hits turbulence. Maybe they flew me to Seattle?"

Chill pursed his lips. "Not unless we've been out longer than we think. Meteorology is my major, you know. Jet stream was hauling all the Pacific moisture south, and a big high-pressure system was controlling the Midwest. Clear sailing all the way. Could be south though, or east." He shrugged. "What am I talking about? I just know we're not in Kansas any more, Toto. We could be in Genosha for all we know."

Pound's eyes went wide. "You don't really think—?"

"Just a joke, really. We don't know where we are really, or why." He grinned. "We should be honored. I figure, normally this kind of mystery treatment is reserved for the X-Men or the Fantastic Four." He glanced to his right, and pointed in that direction. "By the way, say hello to our viewing audience."

Recall saw that he was pointing at a small black circle high in the far wall. It was smooth and flush with the otherwise unmarked white surface.

"We think there's a camera back there," Chill explained. "Probably a microphone here somewhere too." He dropped to a stage whisper. "Don't talk in front of the toilet."

Despite himself, Recall chuckled. Cheer up the troops. It was in Chill's nature, part of why he'd made such a great chapter president these last three years.

Recall looked again at the hidden camera. Maybe there was something he could do. He stood up, reeled slightly as the blood seemed to rush from his head, then walked closer to the far wall.

"Look," he said, "whoever you are, maybe you don't know who you've got here. My name is Scooter McCloud, but my air name is Recall, of 'The Norman and Recall' radio show. We're carried on seventy stations across the country."

The black circle on the wall just stared at him. "I'm famous. People will be looking for me, not just the authorities, but the show has lots of fans."

Nothing. "The staff sends out a hundred autographed pictures of me a week. Our web page takes over a thousand hits a day."

The circle just looked at him. Suddenly something inside him seemed to shatter. He slammed his fist against the wall. "Let us out of here! I'm famous. Let us out!"

Chill was suddenly behind him, trying to calm him down.

He pounded the wall again. "Let us out! I'm famous!" His head was spinning. Suddenly it was hard to stand. He slumped against the comforting support of the wall and slid slowly down it. "I'm only sixteen years old—"

As Black drove into the parking lot of the Snow Bird Motor Court he saw that it was almost entirely full of black vehicles. They were drawing attention to themselves. Genogoths were supposed to travel alone, or in small groups. Twenty-five was considered a major gathering. Attention was inevitable in bringing such a large force to such a small town.

He found an open space and edged the Jag carefully into it. As he climbed from the car he saw an employee watching him from the door of the motel's office, a woman of fifty or so, dressed in a baggy, loud, floral-print muumuu. Rather than ignoring her, he stopped and made a point of staring back. The woman froze, like a deer in the headlights of an oncoming truck. Then finally she dashed back inside the office. As he turned away, he caught a glimpse of her peering at him through a set of blinds.

It was part of the Genogoth philosophy, to hide in plain sight. Someone attempting to conceal themselves will always be found out eventually. By not concealing themselves, by dressing strangely and acting intrusively, they became, in a strange way, invisible. The trick was not to avoid being seen. It was to be seen, and then make the watcher turn away.

Doubtless the locals would talk, rumors would circulate, of cultists, Hollywood people scouting for a movie location, traveling rock bands, and a thousand other things, none of which would remotely resemble the truth. The Genogoths, each and every one of them, were soldiers; trained, determined, dedicated, and ruthless. He had assembled a small army under the townspeople's very noses, and they would never know it.

He stepped up to the door of room sixty-six and tapped on the door, two soft, two hard, one soft, two hard. The door opened and Black stepped inside without a word.

The room was like a thousand others of similar vintage that Black had seen. There were two beds, a small table with two chairs, a combination dresser and writing desk, an end table between the beds, a cracked mirror on the wall over the desk, and a few ugly lamps. An ancient window air conditioner was mounted in a box near the door at the front of the room. The wallpaper peeled in the corners, and in some places had been stuck down with cellophane tape. The carpet was avocado green where the original color showed through the stains.

There were two men in the room, sitting in the chairs by the table. One was in his late twenties, tall, slender, muscular. He wore no shirt under his black leather vest, and displayed an impressive assortment of tattoos and body piercings. His blonde hair was shaved on the sides exposing more tattoos. The hair in the center of his head was long, pulled back in a ponytail. He also had a single tattoo on his right cheek, a tiny, stylized section of a DNA molecule. It exactly matched the silhouette of the silver pendant that Black wore around his neck. The man paused just a second too long, then stood and offered Black his chair.

Black took the chair. "Thank you, Leather."

The man who sat across the table from him was older, and much more massively built. He was muscled, the build of someone who did heavy work on a regular basis, not someone who honed themselves in a gym. His hands were rough and calloused, the fingers thick and strong. His hair was red, streaked with gray, and hung half-way down the back of his black Van Halen tour shirt. His jeans were torn in places, and his sandals were heavily worn. On his right wrist, he wore a hand-made pewter bracelet. Woven into the design of the bracelet was the same double-helix design that Leather and Black wore. He would have looked at home as the head roadie on any concert tour in the country.

"You," said Black, "I don't know."

"Name's Styx. East coast head of Covert Information and Surveillance."

"What happened to Pit?"

"Took a bullet from a rogue Genosian Magistrate, protecting a mutant in Florida." He shrugged. "Not his job, ya know, but he was in the right place at the right time."

Black nodded. "He was a good man, Pit. We all do what we must." He looked up at Leather, who stood with his arms crossed over his chest. "Status?"

"We'll have patrols along all the roads and in the woods around the school by nightfall. If they attempt to leave by air, we have modified Gulfstream interceptors stationed strategically at three nearby airports."

Styx continued the report. "We've got an RF monitoring and jamming van in place, and my roadies are working to tap the incoming phone and data lines. We'll shortly be able to monitor communications in or out, and to cut the lines at a moment's notice."

Black leaned his elbows in the table and pressed his fingertips together. The gesture was at once thoughtful, and an opportunity to engage in isometric exercise. Black liked everything to do double-duty whenever possible. "So, we have them contained, and when we're ready, isolated. Young Espeth has been quite resourceful in evading us so far, but in coming here for help, she's created her own trap. All we need do is slam it shut on her."

Scattered around the western part of South Carolina are the various patches of woodlands, hills, and low mountains that collectively make up Sumter National Forest. Within the boundaries of one of these patches, at the edge of the Blue

Ridge Mountains, was a separate plot of government land not listed on any map.

Originally, it was the home of a secret radar site guarding against missile attack by Soviet submarines in the Atlantic. A huge tunnel had been drilled into side of the mountain, visible from the outside only as a huge concrete portal sealed with steel doors. Passages were drilled out into the mountain and expanded into chambers, where a dozen men could live and work, and where tons of bulky radar and communications could be stored and operated against the threat of nuclear attack. But the technology on which the station was based had become obsolete long before the Cold War ended, and it had been gutted and sealed.

The locals took little notice when the site was years later leased to a "mining operation" which began to haul in unmarked trucks full of heavy equipment, and haul out truck-loads of rock. Nor did the fences and signs, warning hikers and hunters who might consider trespassing against the possible danger of lost explosives and blasting caps, cause much disturbance. When, in time, the flow of trucks turned into a trickle, most assumed that the mining venture had been unsuccessful, or that whatever vein of whatever ore it had been mining had merely played out.

None of them could have suspected that the "mining company" was actually the cover for a secret government operation, or that the trucks had been hauling away not ore, but the tailings resulting from a massive expansion of the underground tunnels and galleries of the original installation. Nor did the trucks coming in carry mining equipment, but rather advanced equipment once associated with a now-defunct black operation known only as "Project Homegrown."

Project Homegrown had been under the direction of General Macauley Sharpe, an effort to study, and replicate in humans, the powers of non-mutant super-humans. Mistakes had been made. The super-human vigilante "Spider-Man" and the government-sanctioned mutant group X-Factor had become involved. The project's primary laboratory, known as "Shadowbase" had been destroyed.

Sharpe had been made the scapegoat, court-martialed, and stripped of his rank and honor. Then, quietly, the very people who had taken everything from him offered him a new position, one with even less sanction, one for which he was ideally suited.

And so it was that, Mister, not general, Macauley Sharpe sat in a control room nearly a hundred feet under the South Carolina countryside. Rather than a general's stars, he wore another kind of uniform, the suit of a corporate warrior. In front of him, a bank of monitors allowed him to observe every corner of the hidden installation called "the Foxhole." His attention was focused on one screen in particular, showing the interior of a holding cell and the three young males housed within. Though it wasn't much evident from the picture on the screen, each of these young men was a mutant, hand-picked as an experimental subject by Sharpe himself.

In front of him, two men worked at a sweeping horseshoe-shaped console, overseeing the operation of the Foxhole. One of these men, Happersen, had served under him at Shadowbase. "Are the test results in, Happersen?"

Happersen spun around in his chair. Light reflected off the lenses of the horn-rimmed glasses hiding his eyes. Though he wore coveralls bearing the logo of the fictional "Canus Mining Company," his erect posture and short haircut clearly marked him as a former military man. "All but the final genetic profiling, Mr. Sharpe. Everything looks positive. They seem to be ideal subjects for the program."

"Begin the prep work then. Have the bionetics lab begin tuning the power amplifiers to their mutant auras. Have the armorers adapt the field gear to complement their individual mutant abilities. And of course, tell the behavior modification lab that we're ready to begin conditioning our subjects immediately."

Happersen nodded and smiled slightly. "Eager to begin trials, sir?"

GENOGOTHS

Sharpe nodded. "You know me, Happersen. I believe that a new weapon can only be truly proven in the field. It won't be long before our guests are changed into obedient hounds, eager to help us hunt down their fellow mutants in the service of humanity."

CHAPTER FOUR

"Ignorance more frequently begets confidence than does knowledge: it is those who know little, and not those who know much, who so positively assert that this or that problem will never be solved—"

—Charles Darwin
The Descent of Man, 1871

Jono had escorted Espeth back to the bio-bed to complete her treatment while the students made preparations for the journey. Fortunately, the school had its own gas pumps, so they were able to top up the Xabago's tanks before leaving. A raid on the school's pantry stocked the vehicle's kitchen.

The biggest problem was cash. They'd been caught off guard by Espeth's announcement that they'd be unable to use plastic of any kind, credit cards, debit cards, ATM cards. The Genogoths would be looking for such transactions and would use them to track their travels.

"You mean," said Paige, after she'd made this proclamation from her infirmary bed, "that the Genogoths aren't just unwilling to help, they're actively trying to *stop* you?"

Espeth nodded. "I thought that was obvious. It's what made my journey here so arduous. I had to hitch, jump freight-trains, and walk more miles than I can count, often cross country. I did my best to throw them off the trail, but they can't be far behind. We have to get out of here just as soon as we can." She turned her attention back to Jono. "So, this Xabago of yours, it's some kind of aircraft?"

Paige and Jono stared at each other in surprise.

Finally, Jono said, "No, luv, it's not exactly a bloody aircraft, but it's transportation."

Espeth looked concerned. She pushed back the monitoring console that hovered over her midsection and sat up. "What kind of vehicle is it?"

"You'll see," said Jono.

Espeth looked at Paige, demanding an answer.

"It's a motor home."

"What?"

"The Xabago," repeated Paige, "is a motor home. A cara-van. A camper van. Not a very pretty one, either."

Espeth's eyes were wide. "You're Xavier's pups! You're supposed to have resources!"

Paige turned to leave. "We do have resources, but we're at Xavier's *school*. Consider yourself lucky we don't have a big, yellow bus."

Jono got Espeth settled back in the bio-bed, then followed Paige down to the service garage where the Xabago was parked. They arrived there at the same time as Ev, and fol-lowed him inside. There, Monet and Jubilee were loading the last of the food and supplies that they'd scrounged from around the school. Ev and Angelo had been given their own assignments.

"I've finished rerouting the phones," Ev announced. "If I did things right, any call to any of the incoming phone lines at the school should be routed out through another of the lines and into your satellite phone. If Emma, or anyone else calls, they shouldn't be the wiser."

The Xabago, Paige observed, wasn't getting any better looking after several months of sitting out in the harsh, winter weather. The paint was even more streaked. The spray-painted red X's that Angelo had "tagged" the sides and front of the vehicle with were now dull and faded, chipping in a few places where the paint hadn't properly adhered. The bubble cockpit grafted onto the roof looked slightly milky and crazed from exposure. Even the chrome women reclined on the cus-tom mud-flaps looked tarnished. "You sure this thing runs?"

Jubilee emerged from the Xabago's door and sat on its step. "Like a champ. Runs as good as it ever did."

Paige was skeptical. "That isn't saying much."

"It'll get us there," said Jono.

The door in the side of the garage opened and Angelo strolled in, a big grin on his face. "Mission accomplished." He held out a stack of bills and fanned them for show. It wasn't a huge stack, and the bills were only twenties, but it was far greater than the sum total of money they'd been able to pool between them.

Paige looked at him. "Where did you get it?"

"The headmaster's offices. All it took was a bent paper clip and certain unwholesome skills I learned from my gang days to get into the strongbox where they keep the petty cash." Angelo saw the look on Paige's face and responded. "We'll pay it back when we return, *chica*. This is just a cash flow problem. I didn't even scratch the lock."

Jono examined the haul. "Bloody good thing too. The Xabago doesn't exactly sip the petrol. We'll need every bit of it."

Monet emerged to stand behind Jubilee in the doorway. "It's going to be very crowded in here. You only had the three guys and Sean in here last trip. This time there will be seven of us."

"We'll sleep in shifts," said Jono, "take turns keeping watch. This is a combat mission, not a pleasure cruise."

Preparations complete, the group returned to the infirmary to fetch Espeth. But when they entered the room, the bed was empty. Paige called her name, but there was no answer. They all stared at one another.

Paige saved an especially angry stare for Jono. "You and Angelo search the room, the rest of us will fan out and see if she's still in the building."

Angelo picked up the pillow off the bed and threw it angrily at the door. "*Madre de dios*, she's run out on us!" He shook his finger at Jono. "You see, I knew this would happen. I know something about loyalties, and that *chica* is conflicted."

Jono checked in the bathroom, but emerged, obviously having found nothing. "If that's the way you felt, Angelo, why didn't you say something earlier?"

"I voted my way, I kept my suspicions to myself. I figured I could trust the rest of my *compadres* to be smart enough to figure it out for themselves. But some people weren't thinking with their brains."

Jono glared at him. "What's that bloody supposed to mean?"

Just then they heard Paige call from down the hall. They both ran out to join the others standing outside a janitor's closet.

"The door," explained Paige, "was ajar."

Angelo smirked grimly. "I wish I was in a punning mood." He saw Jono glaring at him. "I know, '*shut-up, Angelo.*' Shutting up now."

Paige looked from Jono to Angelo, trying to figure out what was going on between them, then turned her attention back to the interior of the closet. Among the mops, buckets, brooms and bottles of cleaning supplies, a ladder was bolted to one wall of the small room. "Roof access," she explained.

"So," said Jubilee, sarcastically, "she's using her mutant powers to fly away." She looked mockingly surprised. "Wait! Not a mutant. Well, duh." Her mask dropped, and she frowned at them all. "Cut her some slack. Maybe she just needed some air, you know?"

The phone rang. Paige muttered under her breath. She tossed the phone to Angelo. "It's the old people. Take this out of earshot and handle them."

Angelo looked perplexed.

"Do it," she hissed.

He flipped a sloppy salute and trotted back to the infirmary.

"I could fly up," suggested Monet, "and look for her."

The hatch above them flopped open. "Not necessary," said Espeth. She stepped onto an upper rung of the ladder, then slid down the outside of the side rails gripping them with her hands and the sides of her feet, in the manner of a sailor from some old submarine movie.

"Where have you been?" Paige demanded angrily.

"Well, duh, again," said Jubilee.

Espeth didn't seem to hear either one of them. Her expression was grave. "Are you ready to travel?"

"Yes," said Paige, "we're ready. We were coming to get you. *What did you think you were doing?*"

"You don't understand," she said, "I was on the roof scouting. There are people in the woods all around the school. The Genogoths have us surrounded. We've got to leave, *now*." She started walking toward the garage, and the rest just naturally started following her.

Paige looked puzzled. "What? The security system hasn't picked up any—"

"It didn't pick me up either, did it? And these people have better equipment and vastly more experience than I do. These aren't amateurs you're dealing with here, they're *Genogoths*."

As they passed the door to the infirmary, Angelo emerged from the door and fell in step with the rest of them. His eyes widened slightly as he spotted Espeth.

"She was watching our backs for us," said Jono.

Angelo smirked. "Watching her back, at least." He handed the phone to Paige. "Sean says 'hi,' and to be sure to put away the croquet set when we're through. The wire hoops are hell if they get caught in the lawn mower."

He followed them all silently for a few yards as Espeth broke into a trot, and the rest kept in step. "Somebody want to tell me what's happening?"

Jubilee's eyes remained fixed straight ahead. "Genogoths. Surrounded. Imminent danger. Gotta split."

"Oh," he said, "sorry I asked."

The conference room was in one of the chambers that had been used for the radar base that preceded the Foxhole. Though the conference table, chairs, podium, lighting fixtures, and flat screen computer monitors on the rock walls were all relatively new, someone, either out of whimsy or frugality, had left a pair of early 60s vintage ceiling fans hanging over the table. They whirred quietly over the assembled staff meeting, adding a faint whiff of ozone to the air.

Sharpe stood at the head of the table, and all eyes were on him. He let the moment linger. He liked attention, liked to wield authority. He missed his uniform, the stars, the brass buttons, the medals and ribbons representing his service in covert actions in South America and the Mid East, and his two years on the staff of General Thunderbolt Ross at Hulkbuster Base. Despite his continued service to the government, his continued authority at this project, he missed the power, authority, and respect that only a military officer could truly command.

That had been taken from him forever. It was something he could never truly forgive, never forget. His time with General Ross had given him little sympathy for super-humans, and now, after his encounter with X-Factor, he had even less for mutants. They were vermin, suitable only for use as experimental animals. Nothing more, nothing less.

He scanned the faces in front of him, men and women, mostly former military or intelligence personnel. Most were wash-outs from their former organizations, expelled for the very ruthlessness that Sharpe coveted for his organization. Fortunately, his shadowy employers had made a list of such people available to him. There were a few new faces, needed technical specialists that had only recently made it through their convoluted recruitment and relocation.

"Before we begin, I want to review our project's methods and goals for our newest staff-members. Most of you are familiar with 'Project Homegrown.' The objective of Homegrown was to analyze so-called superhumans in order to duplicate their powers in normal humans. For our purposes, we were allowed the use of convicts as experimental subjects on which to test our methods. We were successful, not only in temporarily inducing powers in these subjects, but in developing the rudiments of mind-control technology that allowed us to use our subjects in field trials."

He touched a control on the podium, and an image of the Shadow Force, the test subjects from Homegrown, flashed on the big screen behind him. He turned to look at the six men and women dressed in similar green uniforms, topped with power inducing yokes and their prototype mind-control head-pieces.

"Unfortunately, our project ran afoul super-human intervention. Several of our subjects were terminated, our project exposed, and our installation, Shadowbase, was destroyed. I willingly sacrificed my military career, as did some of the others in this room, to provide plausible deniability for my superiors, persons at the highest level of government."

He scanned the room, paying particular attention to the new troops, without making it obvious that he was doing so. They were lapping it up. The "noble sacrifice" thing always got them, even if it wasn't exactly true. It didn't matter. Truth was what your superior said it was. He'd learned that a long time ago.

"It is publicly believed that all the equipment and data from Project Homegrown was destroyed with Shadowbase. Given the ongoing threat of super-human involvement, we've worked hard to maintain that impression and to remove ourselves from those areas frequented by super-humans.

"In fact, much of the equipment and data from Homegrown survived in off-site storage facilities and our super-human data acquisition stations in Manhattan. These formed the basis of our current program. In recent months, we've made great progress in improving our mind-control technology, and adapting our shadow-agent technology for use on mutants."

He pushed another button on the podium, cutting live to the camera in the holding cell. Though the sound was off, one of the subjects, the most recent capture, seemed quite agitated, not an unusual after-effect of the sleep-gas used. He smiled. He wanted them disoriented. That was part of the plan.

"In the last day we've obtained our first three mutant subjects. Obviously, they are not volunteers. They have been designated code-names for the purposes of our project. The stocky one is an animal telepath with minor physical mutations. His designation is 'Top Dog.' The small one is a telepathic locator, designation 'Bloodhound.' The tall one is a negative-thermomorph, code-name 'Three Dog Night.' "

One of the new people, a rather striking woman with long, blonde hair raised her hand. "Fortuna Bouille, Mr. Sharp. My understanding of Homegrown was that the technology was used to give powers to subjects without any special abilities. These are mutants, they should already have powers, shouldn't they?"

"A reasonable question, but not all mutants are in the power class of Magneto or X-Factor's Havok, Bouille. Some have minor mutations of limited power, sometimes effectively useless. But all mutants carry the X-gene, and our research has shown that this gene gives them an enhanced bio-signature, an 'aura' for lack of a better word, one that allows them the potential to tap vast energies in a way we don't understand. The Homegrown technology also worked by enhancing and altering the normal human bio-signature, but there were drawbacks that came out in field-testing."

He pushed another control, and a picture of a large and advanced power reactor appeared on the screen. "The biggest was a dependence on a centralized broadcast power, much of which was wasted simply maintaining the altered bio-signature. It's ironic that accidental readings taken of the mutant Havok during the destruction of Shadowbase were ultimately responsible for our breakthrough.

"As you said, mutants already have special abilities, no matter how weak, and we have also discovered that they all have the potential, even if they can't directly access it, to tap into vast energies."

He turned and smiled at Bouille. "Therefore we don't need to impose an altered bio-signature, nor do we need to supply power. All we need do is enhance what is already latent in any subject carrying the X-gene, then *control* that subject for our purposes. Our job is actually simpler by an order of magnitude."

"So," said Bouille, "we're here to perform dangerous biogenic experiments on unwilling, mind-controlled, human-mutant subjects?"

Sharpe raised an eyebrow. "You have a problem with that?"

She grinned and shifted in her chair. "No, it's pretty much my dream job."

Black sat in his car, parked beside the road near Xavier's school. About a mile ahead, there was a cutoff to a private road leading to the school itself. He held an unfolded road map in front of his face for show, but in fact, all his attention was focused on the nearly invisible radio receiver in his left ear.

A voice said, "I'm picking up motor noise on my shotgun mike. Heavy diesel, coming from the service garage. No sign of movement."

Another voice, "Do you have visual on any activity there?"

The first voice again. "Negative, the doors are closed, and the rear access to that building is not visible from beyond the compound."

Black felt himself tense. This was a critical moment, and there were decisions to be made, not only when to move, but *how* to move. He took a deep breath, let it out slowly, and turned his wrist so that he could talk into the disguised microphone in the clasp of the watchband. "Leather, this is Black."

"Go ahead," said Leather, "we're ready to move in on your authorization."

"Your orders are that the mutants are not be harmed. That is the priority. They are to be captured unharmed if possible. Only Espeth is expendable. And no firearms." The latter instruction should have been unnecessary, the philosophy of the Genogoths called for use of minimal force where possible. In theory, if the operatives were good enough, guns should be necessary in only the most dire circumstances, and the Genogoths were good.

But he had noticed in Leather a tendency to overkill that he found disturbing. A certain ruthlessness was necessary to the job, but it was important not to lose sight of the greater goals.

There was a moment of silence on the radio. "That limits our options, Black."

"Options are always limited. It's only a matter of degree. We need to interrogate the mutants to learn what they know and who they may have told. We hope to contain the situation, but first we have to learn if it *can* be contained. In any case, I'm hopeful that they can be salvaged somehow. There are methods of inducing amnesia, or they might be relocated to a containment camp so that we can maintain their genetic stock."

"It places my people at risk, Black."

"That risk is the duty of any Genogoth, Leather. You have your orders. Now, move in when ready."

Jono sat in the driver's seat of the Xabago, listening to the motor rumble. The air smelled strongly of soot and diesel exhaust, but powerful fans in the roof of the garage kept them from becoming a real danger. "I wish," he said idly, "that we had some kind of diversion."

The door opened, and Espeth climbed into the motorhome. "They're out there. As I expected, the motor noise has caused them to become careless."

Angelo raised an eyebrow. "So, what's the word?"

Espeth looked grim. "Not good. They'll charge the vehicle before we get off the grounds, and they've undoubtedly got a roadblock planned."

Paige and Monet looked at each other, and for once, seemed to be on the same wavelength.

"Earlier," said Paige, "you said something about the Xabago being an aircraft."

"How much," said Monet, "do you think the Xabago weighs?"

Ev nodded. "Maybe too much for one, but maybe not too much for two."

"Never mind that," said Jubilee, "has anybody seen my skates?"

GENOGOTHS

• • •

Leather lay on his belly in a ditch at the bottom of the drive-way. It had taken him more than an hour to creep this close to the school without being seen. If he twisted and looked back over his left shoulder, he could just make out one of their peo-ple sitting on a platform attached to the trunk of a tree, thirty feet in the air, and pointing a sensitive microphone at the garage.

"Activity," said the voice in his ear, a voice he knew was being transmitted from the watcher in the tree.

Leather watched the garage intently as one of the big doors rolled up with a motorized whir. The motor noise was louder now, but he could see only darkness inside the door. Then something small and yellow, rolling out of the darkness and down the driveway. A girl in a yellow raincoat. A girl on skates. *A girl on skates.*

"Something's wrong," he said into his radio. "We may have misjudged the situation."

"The girl is identified as Jubilation Lee," said the voice from the tree, "mutant plasma/energy caster of great reported potential, but limited ability. Threat factor is minimal."

The girl rolled slowly down the gentle slope of the drive-way, seemingly unaware of any danger. Then she bent sharply forward, placed her palms on the ground, and went into a graceful handstand. The bottom of her coat fell down around her shoulders. Leather noticed that her hands were placed over a large crack in the sidewalk, as though it had somehow been her target. None of it made any sense.

The girl continued her handstand for several more seconds, then tucked and rolled, ending in a sitting position with her knees raised. She wore red tinted glasses, but he could swear she was looking right at him. He pushed himself farther down into the ditch.

Then the ground began to rumble, and the soil around him seemed to boil with glowing streamers of plasma, coming out of the ground like earthworms after a heavy rain. *The girl.* She had done this somehow, sending the plasma into the ground during her handstand, then guiding it underground. There was a bang, like a gunshot next to his ear, and the streamers began to explode all around them.

Despite himself, Leather jumped to a crouch as one of the streamers exploded inches from his face. It took him a moment to regain his composure, at which point he realized two things. First, he had exposed himself to anyone watching from the school compound. Second, the other door of the garage was open, and a bizarre looking camper van of some kind was advancing down the driveway.

Furious at himself for become distracted, he held his microphone up and shouted, "They're on the move by vehicle! All units inside the perimeter attack! I want a roadblock by the inner gate! Go! Go!"

Jono sat in the driver's seat of the Xabago, Paige in the passenger seat to his right. Espeth stood behind them, looking anxiously out the windshield. One moment, the grounds and driveway in front of them were empty, then a virtual carnival of Genogoths boiled from every possible hiding place converging on their position. Farther down the driveway, Jono saw a large, black pickup and an equally black SUV appear from either side of the decorative gate, sliding to a stop nose to nose, blocking the drive.

He felt strangely calm.

He turned to Paige. "Tell me, luv, ever see the film *Flubber*?"

"No," she said, "but I saw *The Absent-Minded Professor*."

"Never heard of it," he said.

As the Xabago rolled past, Jubilee jumped up onto her skates and skated furiously after it. She had almost caught it, her hand reaching for the roof-access ladder above the back bumper, when a bearded young Genogoth, head down, charged out of the shrubbery next to the drive headed directly for her.

She swerved, jumped, hit him on the head with her skate

and rolled right down his spine. She used the increased height to spring herself into a flip that took her clear over a woman in biking leathers. Jubilee hit the ground rolling, but she was headed away from the Xabago. She jumped, changing direction in the process, pumping all-out to catch up with it.

Then a man in a sniper's camouflage suit popped out of the landscaping and grabbed her around the ankles. She went down hard on the concrete, thanking whoever had put the dorky-looking knee and elbow pads onto their training uniforms.

Then there were more, and more, grabbing her arms and legs, holding her up like a puppet, unable to get leverage. She watched as the Xabago rolled away.

Leather watched the camper roll past. It wouldn't get far with the road-block just ahead of it, and he could see a group of about a dozen people who seemed to have the skating girl well in hand. She struggled, showing no evidence of her mutant powers. Perhaps she had exhausted herself creating the impressive diversionary display.

He stepped up to look at the girl who had humiliated him. She was beaten now, fear marking her Asian features. "Put her down," he ordered.

His people holding her lowered her feet to the ground, but continued to grip her arms. Despite appearances, she had exhibited the strength, grace, and speed of a professional athlete. But now she was humbled, like a cheetah in a cage, struggling only weakly.

Suddenly, one of the people in the group pointed behind him and shouted. He turned and realized something was wrong, though he couldn't immediately tell what. Then he saw the front of the camper lift off the ground as though by an invisible jack. Then the rear. To his horror, it passed just beyond the reach of the group assembled on the driveway to intercept it. Underneath the frame he could see two of the mutant teens, flying, *carrying* the motor-home, literally on their backs.

It was thirty feet off the ground as it passed over the road-block. Below, he saw Black's small sports car slipping between the bumpers of the stopped vehicles. Black was here to witness his humiliation, and they *were getting away!*

At least they had the girl. "Your friends," he said, "are leaving without you. Or was that the plan all along? Self sac-rifice is a noble impulse when not wasted." He reached his fin-gers under her chin and gently raised her eyes to meet his. "Perhaps we can use you as bait."

The girl looked shocked. "You can't do that!"

He chuckled. "What's to stop us, little mutant?"

Suddenly her expression changed, from supposed terror to a broad smile, and the knot in Leather's stomach told him that somehow he'd just been had.

"Because," she said, "to do that, you'd have to keep me." She gestured upwards with her eyes and whispered, "Incom-ing."

He turned. The sun was suddenly blotted out by the Xabago, angling down out of the sky exactly like a hunting hawk, if hawks weighed six thousand pounds and were made of corrugated metal. As he dived for the ground, he heard more of the mutant girl's fireworks, saw her break free and start running. He hit, rolled, saw the vehicle swoop by just above him, saw the side door open and a young man with putty-gray skin lean out.

Angelo gripped a towel bar under the Xabago's sink with the extended skin of his right toes, then leaned out the door. The Xabago was tilted nose-down at about a forty-five degree angle. Things were shifting noisily inside all the cabinets and closets. Somewhere he heard glass breaking, and the frame of the vehicle itself groaned ominously. Things rolled down the center aisle of the vehicle from front to rear. He *oofed* as a rolling duffel bag hit him in the belly.

"Thank the Blessed Mother," he whispered, "that we didn't have time to fill the water bed."

Below him, he saw the Genogoths ducking for cover, saw

Jubilee using her fireworks to blast herself free of her captors. He stretched out the skin of his left arm forming a huge caricature of his normal hand. Jubilee flashed by below, and he caught her like a baseball in a catcher's mitt.

Leather watched as the flying motor-home lifted away, the girl dangling underneath. Enraged, he reached into the hidden pocket under his vest and drew the automatic pistol hidden there. A press of a stud, and the extended barrel and pop-up site of the S.H.I.E.L.D. covert-ops model snapped into position. He squinted, drew a bead on the rear of the flying vehicle. He held his breath, felt his own pulse. For a moment, nothing existed but him and the target. He squeezed off a round, heard the slug hit metal.

A powerful hand grabbed his wrist, pushed the gun up, away from the target, then expertly twisted it from his hand. He shook his injured fingers and turned to face his attacker. *Black.*

He grunted and wedged the skin of his other foot between the stove and the kitchen cabinets. "Have you gained weight, *chica*?"

Jubilee looked up from where she dangled. "Just watch where you put your fingers, smart-guy!"

"Did someone," yelled Ev from under the vehicle, "hear a shot?"

Angelo ducked his head down, looked under the Xabago. "You're imagining things," he called, then turned to wink at Monet. "Word up, pretty lady?"

She scowled at him. "This thing is getting heavy. I hope somebody has a plan."

Jubilee was climbing up his extended arm, hand over hand. He pulled his head back and yelled toward the cab, "Does anyone know where we're going?"

Espeth ran back to give him and Jubilee a hand. "Head for the river," she yelled. "If we cross it before we land, it's twenty miles by road for them to catch up."

"She said—" started Angelo.

"I heard," said Monet. The Xabago turned slowly toward the river.

"Does anyone," yelled Ev, "smell gas?"

"It wasn't me," replied Angelo.

"Not that kind," he said.

Jubilee was crawling up over Angelo's shoulder, and Espeth was pulling her inside. "You're just being paranoid," he called.

Then the propane tank on the back of the Xabago burst into flame.

Black flicked the clip from Leather's pistol with his thumb. He put it in one pocket of his black sports-coat, clicked the barrel and sight to their closed positions, then put the gun in another. "You could have hit one of the mutants," he said. "If you'd hit one of the flying ones, you might have killed them all."

Leather watched the motor-home, girl still dangling beneath, as it vanished beyond the tree-line. The truck and van that had formed the roadblock were already rolling out in pursuit. "I was aiming for their fuel tank. They can't get far that way. I thought if I could disable their vehicle—"

Black got directly in his face. "That was a stupid move, Leather. I don't want any more mistakes like that."

Leather growled. "If you hadn't tied our hands, they might never have gotten away!"

"Our duty," said Black, coldly, "is to protect the X-gene whenever possible. Remember that." He turned and trotted back to his car, to join the pursuit.

Leather glared after him. "Don't worry," he said under his breath, "I have a long memory."

Angelo gave Paige a questioning look as she pushed past him into the open doorway. "Hold your breath," she said, "and give me a boost up." She ripped a hunk of skin away from her shoulder, revealing a gray, shiny, fibrous material underneath. "Asbestos," she said.

Angelo's eyes went wide. He held his breath, cupped his hands for her to step into, and hoisted her up over the top of the door.

Black tried to drive the Jag on the twisting forest roads and read the map at the same time. As the tires squealed around a curve and the map tried to refold itself, it was one of those rare times that he wished he'd availed himself of the full-time aide that his position in the Genogoths afforded him.

The feeling would pass. Getting close to people was only trouble. People were only trouble, as Leather had proved today. Black preferred to travel alone. He would have done the whole job alone if he could, but it was far too much for one man, or even one generation.

The map flopped open again, and the road straightened again. Espeth and the escaped mutant children were headed for the river. He needed to know where the closest crossing was. His finger traced a blue line on the map, glancing up to steer the car back into the middle of the road.

He groaned. The closest bridge was almost back to Snow Valley, miles in the wrong direction. A horn sounded, and he looked up and swerved just in time to avoid running head-on into a red pick-up truck.

"Leather," he said into his radio mike, "how long till we get a 'copter on-scene?"

Silence. Then, "We don't have any in the area. Xavier's people are known for their fast jets. Nobody expected them to attempt escape in—*Chitty Chitty Bang Bang.*"

Black bristled. "We're going to lose them," he growled into the radio. The trees parted. He leaned over the wheel and looked up. His eyes went wide. "Then, perhaps not," he said. He kept the flying vehicle in sight for only a moment, but long enough to see the flames.

He turned off the transmitter, cursed under his breath, and pressed the accelerator.

Paige Guthrie climbed across the roof hand-over hand, ripping off chunks of skin as she moved. She wasn't sure if the synthetic asbestos she'd turned her body into was as toxic as the real thing, but she hadn't wanted to take chances inside. She only hoped it was as flame resistant.

The wind whipped past as she swung herself over the back of the Xabago and climbed down the ladder. Asbestos was a rock, basically, and she was strong in this form. That helped. She was also heavy. That didn't. Treetops flew by under her feet.

To her relief, the flame was still limited to the tank, and hadn't spread to the rear of the vehicle. She could see where a bullet had nicked the tank, causing a tiny fracture which jetted gas and flame. The bad news was, there was plenty of gas in the tank, enough to turn it into a bomb at any moment.

She climbed down onto the rear bumper. Blue flames jetted over her belly as she slid past the tank. It tickled. Once she was on the other side of the tank, she could see that it was held into its bracket by a metal strap, and there was a buckle holding it closed.

She reached in, flame playing through her fingers and making it hard to see. She shifted her grip on the frame of the back window, and gasped as she almost lost it. Her asbestos fingers were slippery.

She pulled at the buckle which was rusted and layered with paint. At first it wouldn't budge, then it came open with a snap.

The strap sprung open. The tank fell out of the bracket. It hung from the copper tubing that connected the tank to the Xabago, spinning. The jet of flame played over the thin, corrugated metal of the vehicle, blistering paint like a blowtorch. In moments it might cut through.

She kicked at the tank. It turned, more flames against the

vehicle. Again. Something on top of the tank snapped. There was a loud hiss, and flame enveloped her.

She kicked blindly. Another snap, and the tank fell free.

Then her fingers slipped completely from their handhold.

Black rounded another curve and the road paralleled the river. He tried to catch some glimpse of their escaped quarry, looking up just in time to see something like a flaming comet coming straight at him.

Instinctively he reached for the door handle, and rolled from the car.

Impact. Pain. Spinning. Noise. A terrible heat.

Then he stopped, lying in wet grass along a ditch. He heard the roar of flames, and, after stopping just long enough to make sure that nothing major seemed to be broken, sat up. He watched as his car coasted off the road and rolled down the embankment into the river, already a burned-out hulk before it hit the water.

Sharpe studied the young man slumped in the examination chair, the harsh overhead spotlight casting dark shadows on his unconscious face. As Sharpe watched, a technician stepped between them, adjusted an arm-mounted remote scanner, nodded at Sharpe, and then slipped back into the shadows at the edge of the room. Sharpe leaned closer. The boy didn't *look* dangerous. He was the youngest of the three, with what seemed, on the surface, to be the least useful mutant ability.

Sharpe stood and removed a small headset which he clipped over his right ear. He smiled. Appearances could be deceiving. "Status," he said almost inaudibly. Sensors in the headset picked up the minute sounds conducted through the bones in his head and transmitted them to the next room, where half-a-dozen technicians invisibly monitored the session.

"Subject is approaching awareness," said a woman's voice in his ear. *Bouille.* "Shall we hit him with more sonics?"

Here in the controlled environment of the Foxhole they could use beamed sonic stunners to subdue the subjects rather than the cruder sleep-gas used on them in the field. "No," he replied, "not if you're ready. We can begin."

"Shall we wake him then?"

"Good to go," he said.

The boy—the *subject*—twitched as a mild electric tingle was directed through the wrist shackles that bound him to the chair. His head rolled groggily, then he snapped upright as someone zapped him with a second charge.

The subject looked around, confused, tugged ineffectively at his bonds, and finally slumped back in the chair. "Not again," he said.

Sharpe stepped into the pool of light, so that the subject could get a good look at him. "Again," he said. "And again, and again, as necessary."

The subject's eyes narrowed. Sharpe knew his face would be the first stranger that the subject had seen since his capture.

"Let me go," said the subject. "Let us all go."

He smiled grimly. "So predictable. I'd have expected something more original from a radio professional."

The subject looked surprised. "You know who I am, then?"

"Oh, yes, even if I hadn't watched your rather pathetic display for our cameras on taped replay." He stepped closer, the smile melting like ice in a fire. "That's why I picked you— *mutant*."

Again surprise. *Good. Keep him off balance.* "Oh, yes, I've listened to your program. I listened to Walt Norman before you came along, with your pro-mutant propaganda. It was the ruin of a perfectly good program. But then, without it, I never would have found *you*."

The subject said nothing. He just stared at Sharpe.

Sharpe clasped his hands behind his back and walked slowly around the chair. In the other room, complex devices were recording not only every word said, every movement made, but every aspect of the subject's physiology as he responded to Sharpe's prodding. Sensors mapped the electrical and chemical pathways of his brain, how consciously and unconsciously he accessed the power inherent in his X-gene. With every breath, every thought, the subject betrayed himself further. Sharpe had only to provoke a reaction from him.

"A few years ago I cared nothing for mutants, one way or the other. Then a group of mutants called X-Factor—you've heard of them? Yes, I see you have. X-Factor took everything from me, my rank, my career, my public honor. Only then did I fully understand the threat that mutants posed to the world, to *Homo sapiens*. Only then did it became *personal*. Fortunately, circumstances have offered me an opportunity to contribute to the ultimate downfall of mutant-kind."

"Good data," said the voice in his ear, "see if you can get his heart rate up."

"You are not," continued Sharpe, "a celebrity here. You are not a man. You are nothing. You are an experimental subject, code-name Bloodhound, nothing more. Some of my superiors said it was a mistake to take such a public figure for our project, but I simply wanted to silence you. End your prattling. And—," he smiled, the irony was so sweet, "your program has made you many enemies in Washington, powerful enemies. Some people work their whole lives to earn such notoriety. You achieved it well before reaching drinking age. Congratulations."

"What about my friends? They didn't do anything to you."

Get the heart rate up? This should do it. "No, but we've been observing you for some time, and you brought them to our attention. It's fortunate that their mutant abilities dovetailed so nicely with our project." He smiled as he saw the dismay on the subject's face. "Oh, yes, it's your fault that they're here. They'll suffer just for knowing you. They'll get their turn being studied as we're studying you."

The subject was agitated, pulling at the bonds that held him to the chair.

"Good data," said the voice in Sharpe's ear.

The subject glared at him. "What are you going to do to us?"

Sharpe raised his eyebrows and looked at the subject. *Keep them wondering. Keep them fearing.* "Right now," he said, "we will study you, learn to understand you, every nerve, every cell, every molecule. We need to understand you, because what you don't understand, you can't control." He suddenly leaned close to the subject's face. "And you," he said, "are mine."

The ebony-colored van rolled to a stop on the highway next to Black. He opened the door and slid into the front passenger seat. At the wheel, Leather's eyes were locked on the road ahead. He said nothing as he put the vehicle in gear and roared off in the direction of Snow Valley.

In a moment they were traveling fifty, then sixty, miles per hour on the narrow, curvy road, but Leather's face showed no emotion. He had the casual indifference of someone circling the parking lot looking for an open space.

Black finally broke the silence. "They've gotten away, haven't they?"

Leather still didn't look at him. "We think so, for the moment."

The van shot along the road, the sun flashing through the canopy of trees like a strobe light. More silence.

"You hamstring us, Black. I need full authority to act. We can't keep a lid on this with our hands tied."

"You're mixing your metaphors, and making excuses. When we find them again, and we will, I don't want any more mistakes." Black leaned back in his seat and watched the trees go by. "In some ways this is better. They've lost the protection of their school, they're contained, isolated, and we know exactly where they're going."

They passed the service station he'd stopped at only yesterday. He wondered if they'd be the ones sent to tow his wrecked car. He wondered what they'd think. "Stop at the motel," he said. "I want time to pack, make a few phone calls."

Leather looked at him incredulously. "They're getting

away. Even if we do know where they're going, you're just giving them more of a head start."

He dismissed Leather with a wave of his hand. "We have people watching all the roads south. Let them put some distance between us and the excitement we've caused here. Besides, I want to give young Espeth some time to consider what she's done. She's never had to face her own kind on the battlefield before, never looked at their faces. She may yet return to the fold."

CHAPTER FIVE

"All animals living in a body, which defend themselves or attack their enemies in concert, must indeed be in some degree faithful to one another; and those that follow a leader must be in some degree obedient."

—Charles Darwin

The Descent of Man, 1871

The Xabago's engine labored, and since their emergency flight from the school Jono had to keep the steering wheel well to the right just to keep them centered on the road. Under his feet, something scraped with every rotation of the wheel. The dash lights flicked on and off, even though the headlights were off, and the fuel-gauge had dropped suddenly from full to empty almost an hour before, though fuel supply seemed to be the least of their current problems.

Angelo and Ev were plastered to the back window watching for pursuit that never came. Likewise, Paige had climbed into the seat under the Xabago's roof-top bubble, using it as a crow's nest. She had also seen nothing, other than startled motorists gawking at the bizarre vehicle that shared the road with them.

Jubilee sat uneasily in the passenger seat to his right.

"Hey, Gel," he said to her. "What you did back there at the school, that took guts."

Jubilee immediately perked up and smiled. "You think so? Get out!" She thought for a while, unable to suppress her smile. "Like, I totally didn't know if that trick with sending my plasma underground like that would work."

Jono glanced at her. "What if it hadn't?"

She shrugged. "Then it would have been a really nice hand-stand I guess. Then on to plan B. Wolverine used to tell me there's always a plan B. Like, if you guys hadn't come back to rescue me, on to plan B!"

He was puzzled. "So, what's plan B?"

She grinned. "Whatever you do when plan A doesn't work. Wolvie was never big on planning when you could just do the deed."

If he'd still had a mouth, Jono would have grinned back. "Just about that whole escape was bloody plan B."

Since they'd landed, Espeth had paced back and forth, from front to back of the vehicle, checking with every look-out, peering through every window. Finally she perched on the lounge chair behind Jubilee. "We've lost them," she announced, "for now."

Jono glanced back over his shoulder. Espeth didn't look happy, leaning forward on her elbows. "And—?"

"And, they'll give us some time. They don't like attention, and they'll have attracted a lot of it back at Snow Valley. They'll want some time and distance to cool things off. Then they'll be back."

Angelo slid in from the rear of the vehicle and sprawled on the couch behind Jono. "That's just great. And how do we lose them next time?" He glared suspiciously at Espeth. "Maybe we don't lose them at all. I didn't see you doing much to help us against your Genogoth buddies."

Jono waited for Espeth to say something in her own defense, but she stared silently off at nothing.

"Ease off, mate," he said. "She was in the 'bago with us. Not much she could do."

"Yeah," said Angelo, obviously unconvinced, "not much."

Jubilee squirmed in her seat, then reached down behind the cushion. She pulled out a CD in a cracked jewel-box, *The Best of Devo*.

Seeing the CD, Monet immediately moved forward to lean between the seats. "Princess found a pea," she said. "I was wondering where that went after our trip. Give."

Monet reached for the CD, but Jubilee snatched it away.

"Hey," complained Monet, "that's mine. I got it at the M.O.N.S.T.E.R. chapter last summer."

Jubilee smirked. "Yeah, because some grungy deejay liked the way your tee-shirt fit and gave it to you." She opened the box and took out the disk. "I want to listen."

Monet frowned, but didn't interfere as Jubilee slipped the CD into the dash-mounted player. They listened to *We're*

Through Being Cool. When it was over, Jubilee paused it and said, "You know, this was recorded like, what, a hundred years ago, right? So, like who gave these guys cosmic awareness so they could write songs about *us*? It's—"

"Uncanny," suggested Angelo.

She nodded. "It's like that Nostradamus special on FOX last month."

Angelo absently rearranged the skin on his face. "I thought it was more like *When Monsters Attack III*."

Jubilee frowned. "Shut-up, Angelo. I'm serious."

He snorted. "Nostradamus, serious. Yeah, got it. I got some of my mamma's old Menudo albums somewhere. You can listen to them for hidden mutant messages too."

Jubilee glared at him. "I'll tell you where you can put your Menudo—"

"Guys," said Paige from the crow's nest, "we got company on our tail."

Angelo glared at Espeth. "Well, that was quick, wasn't it *chica*?"

Espeth ignored him and climbed onto the tubular metal frame that supported the crow's nest seat for a better look.

Jono leaned over and peeked into the side mirrors. He could see a vintage Z-car coming up on them fast. While he was watching, a black Lincoln Continental came down an on-ramp and pulled in with it.

"Scouts," she said. "They just found us. If they had an ambush set, there'd be more of them. They'll bring company soon though. We've got to ditch them and get off the freeway."

Jono put the gas pedal to the floor. With a moan, the Xabago sluggishly responded. "How do you propose we do that, Gel? We've got a Japanese muscle car and some heavy Detroit iron on our boot, and we're having trouble doing fifty-five."

"I could blind them with some fireworks," suggested Jubilee.

Espeth shook her head. "That would only blind them for a minute or two. If we do it and we're on the freeway, there's no time to get away. If we get off the freeway and do it, they'll have phoned in the exit, and every Genogoth in the state will converge to track us down."

"We could do the flying trick again," said Paige.

"Captain," said Ev, imitating a Scottish brogue, "she won't take any more of that." He dropped back into his natural voice. "Serious. You see the problems we're having. I think the frame could just snap in two. For sure it'd never drive again."

Jubilee socked her right fist into her left palm nervously. "Ev's on the right track. What we need is, like, warp drive."

"I can do that," said Monet.

Angelo looked at her skeptically. "What up? You got some antimatter in your purse or something?"

She pushed her way to the front of the vehicle and started exploring the dash and the front floor with her fingers. She found a solid beam under the dash that seemed to meet with her satisfaction. She rapped it with her fist, and it made a clang like a bell. "Jono, you sure you can drive this thing?"

He nodded.

"I mean *drive*," she said. "Well, get ready. Jubilee, go do your fireworks thing."

Jubilee looked puzzled, but shrugged and climbed back to the side door.

Ev seemed to understand what she was up to. "You need some help down there?"

"It's a tight squeeze. No room to get you down here. Without something solid to push against, you'd go right through the Xabago's nose."

Jono looked down as Monet put her hands against the beam she'd found, stretched out, and was suddenly *floating* above the floor. Then he realized, she was *flying* inside the Xabago.

There was a blast of cool air and a roar of wind as Jubilee pushed the door open a few inches with her shoulder. She yelled, "You ready?"

"Go, girl," Monet yelled back.

Jono shielded his eyes against what he knew was coming. Through his fingers there was a brilliant flash, as though lightning had struck immediately behind them.

He glanced down. There was a look of determination on Monet's face, her arms flexed.

The headrest came up and slapped him in the back of the head. Everyone not sitting down was suddenly thrown backward, Paige and Ev falling into a heap in front of the couch, Jubilee holding onto the door frame for dear life.

The speedometer needle surged and he wrestled the wheel to keep them from veering off the road. Ahead, the road was clear. He dared a glance at the rearview, but the two cars were almost lost, both having run off into the median strip.

His eyes went wide as he glanced at the speedometer again. It read to one hundred miles per hour, and the needle was pegged. They were still accelerating. The tires screamed. Something big and green flashed by. "Either the Hulk is hitchhiking or the exit is coming up," he said.

Espeth pulled herself up next to him. "Skip it. That's what they'll be expecting. Go for the next one."

The whole vehicle was shuddering. The wheel rattled so hard that his hands were going numb. "Aye, aye," he said grimly. "Steady as she goes." He watched the lines in the road going by in a blur and wrestled the wheel to follow them. "I hope."

The same old woman that Black had observed earlier stood in the open motel office door watching the flurry of activity as the Genogoths packed out. Every hotel door was open, every vehicle in the parking lot being loaded. From the expression on her face, he knew that later she would be counting all the towels, checking the end-tables for Bibles, and inventorying the lamp shades.

The side door of Leather's van rolled open and Leather stepped out. He closed the door quickly behind him, so that nobody would see the complex communications and surveillance gear installed inside. He looked at Black and frowned.

"Two of our scouts picked them up over in New York state, but they managed to escape again."

Black was unshaken. "Two points make a line. They're headed south. We suspected as much, but now they've confirmed it. We'll find them again." He considered for a moment. "Have a plane waiting at the local airport to take me to Philadelphia, and have an appropriately-equipped car waiting for me there."

Leather said nothing, but the scowl on his face made it clear that he didn't like being used as a lackey.

Good, thought Black. Then his attention was drawn to the sound of a heavy vehicle pulling to a stop behind the van. A car door opened, but the engine remained at fast idle.

A man in a blue uniform shirt, badge, and police hat stepped around the back of the van and approached Black, his hand casually, but conspicuously, resting on the hilt of his holstered pistol.

He stopped and looked at the two of them suspiciously. "Chief Authier, Snow Valley Police. I'd like to ask you gentlemen some questions."

Dog Pound had been strapped into the chair for what seemed like hours as the machines poked and prodded and the tall, angular-faced man named Sharpe pestered him with questions and vague threats. Recall had warned him what would happen, but it didn't make it any easier. He was hungry, he was thirsty, he was tired, and he was, admit it or not, afraid.

Sharpe had disappeared into the gloom that surrounded the examining chair for a while, but he returned, a sly smile on his bloodless lips. It made Pound's skin crawl. "So," he said, in a tone as though he were discussing the weather, "you're a telepath."

"I told you, Sharpe, I'm not saying anything. Name, rank, and serial number."

He laughed harshly. "Oh, please. Anything I want to know, I probably already know. Anything I don't know, I'll soon find out. I'm just passing the time here, making pleasantries, something that's not especially in keeping with my nature. I'm sorry you don't appreciate the effort."

He waited to see if Pound would respond. When he didn't, Sharpe continued. "Of course you're a telepath, of a limited nature, but a telepath just the same. You can communicate telepathically with animals. You find this—useful?"

The boy frowned. He'd learned early on that animals didn't have much to say that an attentive observer couldn't figure out anyway, and as for talking to the animals, most of them just weren't inclined to listen. "Not especially," he said.

Sharpe crossed his arms over his chest and nodded knowingly. "It must be frustrating, to be born with such a unique ability, and then discover that it really wasn't good for much of anything. At least your friends, they can find a lost library book or keep their ice-cream from melting on the way home from the store. Not fantastic abilities, but of at least minor utility."

Pound studied the man. He was leading up to something. What?

"My people here have done a great deal of research on so-called super heroes. You've heard of the famous Avengers, I'm sure. They have an android member known as the Vision. You've seen him?"

"I've seen him on the news, yeah."

"Did you know he has the patterns of a human mind super-imposed on his synthetic brain? I'm afraid I don't understand the process, but my people have had some luck in experiments with animals."

Pound started. It was bad enough what they were doing to his friends and him. What could they be doing to animals?

"Dogs, actually." He saw the expression on Pound's face. "Oh, don't worry, they haven't been harmed. We've just used them as templates, copied their mental patterns onto synthetic brains housed in powerful robot bodies." He glanced off into the darkness. "Would you like to see one of the results?" He paused only for a moment, then shrugged. "Send it in."

Pound heard a door open invisibly, heard the sound of

metal claws clicking on the concrete floor. Then he saw two glowing, red eyes. They focused, mechanical irises widening with a slight whir. Only then did it occur to him to be afraid.

Then something incredible happened. He saw himself sitting in the examining chair, saw Sharpe's back. In the blackness behind him he saw walls and hidden machines, colors shifted strangely as though he were seeing in infrared. He saw a large mirror on the wall behind him, then a shift, and he saw *through* the mirror, to the hidden control room behind, half-a-dozen people inside, busy as ants, oblivious to his attention.

The dog. He was seeing through the robot dog's eyes. And if he could see through its eyes—*Step forward.*

He saw through his own eyes again, as the dog stepped into the light. It was huge, sleek, deadly looking. Highlights glared from its chrome-plated mechanical muscles as they shifted in its broad shoulders. Jaws parted to show rows of shark-like metal teeth. The eyes glowed red, even against the room's illumination.

He looked at Sharpe, fear melting. "You've made a big mistake, Sharpe."

He looked at the dog. *Attack!*

The dog trotted rapidly toward Sharpe, who to Pound's surprise, didn't move. The dog stopped a few yards short of Sharpe's position, its terrible jaws open, crouched, powerful metal legs coiled to leap. Then nothing.

The fear was returning, and with it, a knot in the pit of his stomach. "Attack!"

The dog didn't move.

Sharpe laughed. He walked up to the dog, rapped his knuckle against its inert skull. "Just a little safeguard I had built in. This was the test of that safeguard. Believe me, if there had been any problem, a technician would have powered down the cyber-hound instantly."

He stepped around the dog and came closer to the chair. "You're a telepath, but interestingly enough, that only makes you that much more vulnerable to certain kinds of mind-control. I think you'll be the first to respond to our control, and when you do, you're in turn going to command an entire pack of cyber-hounds against your fellow mutants."

Pound shuddered at the utter confidence in Sharpe's voice. Even if he could resist Sharpe's mind-control, he'd be helpless against him. A moment before, he couldn't wait to move on, to get out of this chair, to get on to the next thing. But now—

Now the future held only dread.

Black stared at the police officer for just a moment before breaking into a practiced smile. "Hey, officer, what can I do you for?" He waved his arms, being careful not to move in a threatening fashion, and to keep his hands in plain sight. "No problem here. Just checkin' out."

Chief Authier didn't seem impressed. "There's a lot of that going around," he said dryly. "You gents got business in the area?"

Black glanced casually back at Leather, who looked far too tense. *Don't do anything stupid.* He turned back to the chief. "Just passing through, Officer. Can I—" He sidled a little closer, leaned over, and whispered conspiratorially. "Can I trust you with a little secret. We're all *roadies* here. For the *Stones*. You like the Stones, officer?"

The Chief pursed his lips and adjusted his mirror-shades. "I think they're getting a little old for the 'angry teenager' bit. Not that I heard they were anywhere within a thousand miles."

Black snickered, as though he enjoyed his secrets a lot. "We don't want word to get out. They're shooting a video out on the reservoir. Something with, like, jet-skis, explosions, babes in bikinis, like that."

"Like I said, they're getting kind of old for this stuff." His hand drifted away from his gun. "I listen to rap, myself." He didn't move. "Listen, Mr. Black, I get the feeling that the one bit of truth in what you're saying is that you're *leaving*. Fortunately for you, that's the part I really care about. Normally I'd check your I.D.'s and run all these vehicle plates, but that would slow down your *leaving*." He turned and started back for his car. "The last thing you see in town," he said, "will be me in your rear-view mirror. You think on that," he cracked a tiny smile, "and have a nice day."

Black looked back at Leather, whose eyes were wide with alarm. "Give me my gun back. I'll take care of him."

"What?"

"He isn't what he seems to be. He knew your name. You never gave him your name."

Black watched as the police car pulled out of the parking lot of the motel. "But I did give it to the man at the gas station. They may have talked. But you're right. He probably didn't, and he isn't what he looks like."

Leather continued to look at him.

"I am *not* giving you your gun back."

Leather scuffed his feet on the asphalt in annoyance.

Black frowned at him. "If you read your field reports, you know that man is most probably a mutant."

Leather blinked. "What?"

"We haven't been able to run a genetic scan to confirm it, but he's on our 'probable' list. He's a demonstrated low-level telepath. That's how he knew my name, knew I was lying about our identity, and telling the truth about leaving. That," he paused for emphasis, "is what the Genogoths were created to protect." He opened the door of the van and climbed in. "Drive me to the airport, Leather. I have work to do."

The Xabago pulled into the alley behind a grocery store. They slipped between two semi-trucks, and Jono shut down the engine. He slumped back into his seat. He'd never before appreciated the simple joy of being *stopped*.

Angelo looked out the window. "Is it just me," he asked, "or are the tires smoking?"

"That," said Jubilee, "was an E-ticket ride."

Monet floated into the air, then set her feet down lightly. "What, is an 'E-ticket'?"

Jubilee shrugged. "Just something Wolvie used to say.

Speaking of which—" She peered out of the windshield. "Do you *know* where we are?"

Monet brushed at a bit of lint on her sweater and wrinkled her nose. "Judging from the smell of rotten eggs and over-ripe bananas, alarmingly close to the Dumpster."

"Yeah, but. Check it out." She pointed at the company name stenciled on the Dumpster. "We're in Salem Center. New York. Like, practically at the X-Mansion. Like, if there was an off-ramp for the X-Men, a sign that read XAVIER INSTITUTE, a sign that read SERVICES THIS EXIT: BLACKBIRDS, CEREBRO, DANGER ROOM, a sign that read MUTANTS NEXT RIGHT, that would have been the sign for this exit. We are *here*. It's fate."

Espeth stared at her. "No," she said.

Paige came over and watched the exchange. It was obvious which side she was on, but she said nothing.

Jubilee held up her hand, index finger and thumb held just slightly apart. "Couldn't we pick up just a couple of X-Men? Maybe just one. Maybe a *small* one. Somebody with *claws*."

"No," said Espeth firmly.

"We could just drop in," suggested Jubilee. "So, I'm like, *Just in the neighborhood. Don't mind if we borrow a Blackbird, do you? It's for a—field trip. Yeah. A field trip. Take the Blackbird and see how cheese is made, in modern, clean, efficient factories.*"

"No," said Espeth. "No X-Men. None. We don't go near the place, or I walk, flag down the first Genogoth I find or who finds me, and you never see me again. I mean it."

Jubilee sagged in her seat. "Like, so close, and yet so far."

CHAPTER SIX

"A good number of you listeners have called to ask about my missing co-host, Recall. Well, I have some slightly alarming news to report. I've been informed that his family doesn't know his whereabouts, and have filed a missing persons report as a precaution. Now, I'm sure you all remember being young and flighty. I never was, but I remember you. [Canned laughter] I'm sure Recall has simply left on one of his frequent school-related trips and neglected to tell anyone. So if you're listening out there, Recall—Get back here, slacker!" [Canned laughter]

—Walt Norman
Walt and Recall radio program

"As a struggle may sometimes be seen going on between the various instincts of the lower animals, it is not surprising that there should be a struggle in man between his social instincts, with their derived virtues, and his lower, though momentarily stronger impulses or desires."

—Charles Darwin
The Descent of Man, 1871

ono pulled the sleeping bag tighter around him and watched the headlights of oncoming trucks project an ever-changing pattern of light and shadow on the headliner of the Xabago's cab. He was curled on the floor between the front seats while Paige took her turn at the wheel. The radio was turned low, tuned to some country station, her choice, not his. Angelo was sprawled on the couch, snoring softly. Everyone else seemed to be asleep as well.

He rolled over on his back and looked up at Paige, her long, blonde hair bobbing with the motion of the 'bago, raindrops from the windshield projected onto her cheeks. She looked beautiful and mysterious, tired and vulnerable. He blinked and turned away. "Hey, Paige. You doing okay up there, Gel?"

"Nothing a gallon of coffee wouldn't help. Of course, thanks to me, we've got no stove, no hot water, no nothing."

"Not your fault, luv. We'd all have been fish and chips if you hadn't kicked that tank loose." He listened to the road noise for a while. He couldn't hear water on the pavement any more. They must have driven beyond the rain clouds that had shadowed them since midnight.

"You know, I didn't say so, but that was a brave thing, climbing up on the roof, going after that burning tank."

"You told Jubilee she was brave."

"She needs it more than you, Gel. You know you're good. She had to keep reminding herself, and it helps when somebody else joins in." He looked up in time to see a hint of a smile curl the edge her lips. Headlights played over her features. *Yes, there's that hint of a dimple*. He looked away again.

"Just so you know, Mr. Starsmore, my mamma taught me that a compliment to a lady is always appropriate."

"Point taken, Gel." He thought for a while. "I know I've been hard on you this time out. You don't think we're doing the right thing going with Espeth."

"Going to rescue our friends? It's not that we're doing the wrong thing, Jono, it's just that we're not doing the *best* right thing. We just drove within a few miles of the X-Mansion this afternoon, and didn't go for help. That's not right. Of course, she didn't give us much choice."

"You don't like Espeth very much, do you?" She said nothing. "I think she's a better person than you or Angelo give her credit for. She's just in a really bad place right now."

Paige frowned. "Yeah, and our friends are paying the price. This whole Genogoth thing gives me the creeps, Jono. I don't want humans hating us, but I don't want them—lusting after us either."

"This isn't still about that dance, is it?"

"No!" A pause. "Yes." Another pause. "No—I don't know, Jono. It's hard to keep my head and heart straight on this business."

"If that's what it's about," he said, "shouldn't I be the one worried that we're running off to rescue your boyfriend, Recall?"

"Jono!"

"Hero of Chicago. Big media personality. Lower face pretty much intact, except for a few zits. I should be worried."

"Jono, stop! I like Recall, but he's just a kid who had a crush on me. Plus, he's over it. I think."

"Well, if it's any comfort, Espeth gave me the creeps a little too, at first. I mean, the attention was flattering and all. It's been a long time since a girl came at me like that."

Paige shot him a dirty look.

"You know what I mean. Anyway, it's not like you have that problem. A looker like you could have any boy she wants."

She snorted. "Long as I don't start shedding on our first date. Let's face it, Jono, it's been a long time since anybody understood us, accepted us, *except* us. I can see how it would be right nice to have somebody without wings or antennae on their head who was interested in you for just being yourself."

Silence for a while. There was a sad song on the radio. Had to be sad, Jono reasoned, based on all the wailing.

"She's still wrong," Paige finally said, "and she's wrong to impose this on us."

"Remember last summer, when you started calling the Walt Norman show, and asked us all to keep it a secret from the headmasters? Was that wrong too?"

Paige licked her lips nervously. "I don't know, Jono. Maybe not. But I took my lumps for it, just like I'll probably take my lumps on this one too, and it *seemed* right at the time."

"I imagine Espeth is just doing what seems right too. We may not agree, but sometimes you just hold on and go for the ride."

"Mmm," Paige said.

Jono closed his eyes and listened to the hypnotic rumble of the Xabago's engine. The uncomfortable silence dragged on until Jono figured the conversation was over. Then the road noise changed. One of the tires crunched into gravel. The Xabago lurched slightly.

"Paige?" He looked up in time to see the wheel spin out of Paige's hands, and then he and his sleeping bag went airborne.

Chill sat up and groaned. The Pounder was back, looking only a little worse for the wear. "I wish they didn't knock us all out every time they took one of us in or out of this box."

"That," said Pound, "was bad. That guy Sharpe is crazy."

Recall nodded. "Yeah, I'll buy that assessment."

Chill rubbed his scalp and looked at them. "I'll have to take your word for it. I haven't had the pleasure yet."

"I have the feeling," said Recall grimly, "that your time is coming."

"Hey," said Pound, brightening, "your power is to find things. Why can't you just find us a way out of here?"

Recall pulled his knees up to his chest, and put his hands over his eyes. The lights in their cell never seemed to go out or to dim. After a while, the glare got to them all. "I've tried. I know there's not supposed to be such a thing as an inescapable cell, but this one has got to be close. Without tools, weapons, or equipment of some kind, we're stuck. If there's a way out, it has to be in the form of an opportunity we haven't seen yet."

Recall uncovered his eyes and looked around the room. "No loose furniture, no seams, no vents, openings, or pipes even remotely big enough to get through. We don't even know how they get us in or out. For all we know, they cut a hole in the wall and patch it back each time."

Chill sighed. "I hate to be the one to break the news, but we're in trouble, guys."

Recall chortled, but the gloom was quick to reassert itself. "That guy Sharpe thinks he's going to brainwash us, turn us into some kind of mutant hunters or something. He can't do that."

Pound chewed on a thumbnail, his eyes fixed on the far wall. "I don't know. I think maybe they can."

Chill leaned closer and put a hand on Pounder's arm. The big guy was really afraid, like they all weren't. "Hang in there, pard. What's up?"

"He showed me some kind of robot dog, a 'cyber-hound' he called it. I could command it telepathically, just like I can communicate with real animals. I could command it, and I could see what it saw. Only it was rigged so I couldn't use it against Sharpe."

Chill grinned. "Which means you tried." He slapped Pound on the arm. "Good job!"

But Pound didn't look reassured. "He knew what I'd do before I did. He knows my powers inside and out, knows everything about me. He says he's going to turn us against our friends, and he means it." He took a big breath. "We're screwed man. We're not getting out of this one."

Recall tried to put on a brave face, but it was obviously an effort. "Pound, you say the same thing every exam week. We're the good guys. There's always a way out, we just haven't found it yet. Or—" he paused, seemingly unsure if he should go on. "Or, we could get rescued."

Chill raised an eyebrow. "You know something. Spill."

"You remember last year, when I used my power to track Paige and the gang cross-country. I was sitting here and started wondering where our friends were, what they were doing and stuff. So I think about Paige, and I can *feel* her. It makes me feel better, so a while later, I do it again, and it seems like she's getting closer."

Chill leaned forward, suddenly very interested. "Go on."

"So I didn't want to say anything unless I was sure. I've only used my power that way a couple times, and only with Paige. But I decided to see if I could get it to work with any of the rest of the Gen X gang. It seems like they're *all* getting closer. So, just for a control, I try thinking about some of our other buds. So I try Espeth."

"Espeth," said Chill, suddenly very interested. "What about her?"

"She's getting closer, too. I think maybe they're together, all of them. They're still far away, but they've been feeling closer for, I dunno, I'm guessing a day now." He shrugged. "It's hard to keep track of time here."

Pound's mood seemed to improve. "Rescue? We could get rescued?"

Chill was suddenly aware of the camera, the hidden microphones. It didn't seem like anyone was especially monitoring their every word, but you could never be sure. Anyway, Recall wasn't looking very happy for somebody who expected to get rescued. "So," he said, "what's the problem then?"

Recall chewed his bottom lip and sighed. "They've stopped. Very suddenly, they've stopped."

Jono was half-standing on his head, feet on the dashboard, still tangled in his sleeping bag. Angelo was on the floor next to him, along with an avalanche of canned goods that had rolled forward from the kitchen area.

Paige was hunched over the wheel, shaking her head to clear it.

Jono slid down until he was lying on his back, and began to climb out of the sleeping bag.

Angelo pulled himself to his feet and dusted himself off. "Everybody okay?" The others were all awake, of course, with the exception of Monet, who had been sleeping in the back. Her nearly invulnerable body seemed to have shrugged off being slammed into a bulkhead without her waking up. There were nods and affirmative murmurs all around.

Jono looked up at Paige. "What in blazes happened, Gel?"

Paige looked away and rubbed her eyes. "I guess—I guess I dozed off at the wheel."

Jubilee pulled the side door open and stepped outside into the grass, creating a little ball of glowing plasma in her hand to light her way. Jono looked out the window. He could see traffic passing on the freeway just a dozen or so yards away. They'd evidently gone off the road, run through the right-of-way fence, and come to a stop among some bushes.

Angelo glared at Jono. "I thought you were going to stay awake and keep her company?"

"I did!" He looked over at Paige. Her head was down, hair in her face. She looked miserable. He reached out and put his hand on hers. "It could have happened to anyone, luv. We're all exhausted." He glanced at the clock on the radio. At least it still worked. "It's four A.M. Look, we aren't going to bloody rescue anybody if we kill ourselves first. Let's get this beast back on the road and look for a rest stop or campground or something."

"Guys," Jubilee's voice called from outside, "you'd better come look at this."

They all piled out of the Xabago. Stiff as they all were from the cramped and uncomfortable sleeping arrangements, it was a welcome chance to stretch. But Jono was more interested in Jubilee, who led them to the front of the Xabago.

Jono groaned. "A flat tire."

Jubilee bobbed her head sideways. "Try *two* flat tires. The one on the other side is out too. Looks like that fence we hammered through did a job on them."

"I don't suppose," said Jono, "that we have a spare?"

"On the back," said Angelo. "I checked it when we last stopped for gas. The propane tank burned a hole in it."

Jono threw his arms up. "Well, *that* does it then. We're here for the night, what little is left of it. Paige, get on that phone of yours and call the auto club. We'll get somebody out here in the morning to patch those tires. Meanwhile, let's get some sleep."

The others were shuffling back inside. Paige looked at the phone unhappily. "Jono, I'm sorry." She walked off to place the call.

Jono watched her go, and wished he was absolutely, one hundred percent, completely sure that this had been an accident.

Despite its luxurious exterior, the interior of the Gulfstream jet was Spartan, a cramped metal pipe full of electronic gear, equipment racks, and ammo boxes for the retractable, wing-mounted guns. Outside, it looked just like any other corporate business jet. Inside was where the *real* business went on.

Black sat in one of a quadrangle of otherwise unoccupied seats in the middle of the plane, reading scouting reports as they came off the printer. Despite several reports of possible sightings, none of the scouts had turned up anything concrete. It was frustrating, but not alarming. It only meant that, after slipping the patrols last time, their targets had either spent a lot of time on back roads, or they'd simply found some place to lay low. It made them more difficult to find, but it also slowed them down. Eventually they'd make a mistake, and when they did, the Genogoths would be waiting.

A telephone mounted on the bulkhead next to him rang. Somehow, as he picked it up, he knew it was another break. "Black," he answered.

It was Leather. "One of our scouts has picked up a tow truck dispatch on their scanner. The vehicle fits the description, no mistake."

"Where?"

"North of Baltimore."

He leaned forward and tossed the reports aside. "Confer with my pilot and have a car waiting at the closest possible airport. Move your people into position and delay the tow truck if necessary. I want to be there when we close in."

There was a pause. When Leather spoke, there was annoyance in his voice. "If we delay, we risk losing them again."

"There's more chance of that if you go after them in the dark. If they need a tow truck, they'll stay put until we're ready to make our move."

Just beyond the trees and brush where the disabled Xabago sat, a small creek flowed over an abandoned beaver dam, around a tight bend lined with flood-deposited sandbars, under a small steel bridge that carried a single-lane farm road, and finally disappeared through a freeway culvert. Even in the moonlight it was picturesque, but Angelo Espinosa had never considered himself a poet. As he settled himself cross-legged on a sandbar to wait for the coming dawn, he told himself that he just came here to escape the crowded interior of the Xabago and to have a few minutes alone with his own thoughts.

Thus, he frowned when he heard the Xabago's door squeak open and somebody walking through the brush toward him.

He expected possibly Jubilee, who was also a night-owl, or maybe Paige, who had ample reason to be restless this night. He was surprised when instead he heard Espeth's voice speaking to him.

"Aren't you sleepy, Espinosa?"

He glanced back at her, but didn't change his position on the sand. "I could say the same of you. Going somewhere?"

She seemed surprised at the question. "Where would I go? I've betrayed almost everyone I know to put this fiasco together. I finally found a place I belonged, a mission in life, people who accepted me, a chance to change the world for the better. That's all gone now. All I want now is for my friends not to get hurt. *None* of my friends."

"I'd play you a song, but my little violin is busted." He clenched his jaw and watched a patch of clouds drift across the face of the Moon. Espeth made a little sound. He couldn't see her clearly in the sudden darkness, but she made a little sound. *Was she crying? Miss Leather Amazon?* "Look," he said, "maybe this men-in-black routine isn't for you. Head home, sign up for Junior College, learn a trade. I hear that blacksmiths could be back in any day now."

That sound again. If she wasn't crying, she was doing a darned good job of messing with his head. "You got family somewhere, right?"

It took her a moment to answer. She seemed to be pulling herself together. "I ran away when I was sixteen, hitchhiked to Seattle and met up with the 'Goths after a year on the street."

"Ran away? Where from?"

"Boise, Idaho."

Idaho? Well, everybody had to be from somewhere.

"So, you could go back. Why'd you leave anyway?"

Things got very quiet for a while, and when she spoke again, the tears seemed to have dried like spit on a hot sidewalk. "I had my reasons," her voice was as hard as he'd ever heard it, "and I'm never going back."

"Whoa, sorry." He thought about his own estranged family in Los Angeles. "Guess I can understand that 'you can't go home again' gig."

"I think," her voice softened just a little, "that maybe you can. I wish you liked me better, Espinosa. A little genetic quirk aside, I think we're maybe more alike than you think."

"That," said Angelo with a chuckle, "is what worries me, *chica*. It's why I will continue to check my back for any projecting knife handles. Besides, no matter how much alike we are, you will *always* look better in a tank top."

She didn't laugh, but when she spoke again, he heard a trace of a smile in her voice. "That truck will be here in an hour or so. I'm going to try for forty-winks, or at least twenty-five. You coming?"

"Nah," he said. "I'm gonna sit here and watch the sun come up. Father Mendoza back at the old parish used to say that when you watched the sun come up, it was God scanning you like a can of tomato soup at the supermarket checkout. Father Mendoza, he was a character. Sure could play b-ball though—"

Espeth didn't seem to be listening. "Scanning," she said. "We've made a terrible mistake. C'mon," she yelled as she started sprinting back to the Xabago, "we have to get out of here. *Now!*"

Chill clenched his fists, tugging at the shackles that held his wrists to the chair. It didn't do any good, but it made him feel better.

"I want to show you something." Sharpe's voice came from the shadows. He stepped into the light pushing a pedestal on which a suit of futuristic armor stood inside a support gantry. Various thick cables and umbilicals snaked away from the suit into the darkness. Chill was reminded of a space-shuttle sitting on the launch pad.

The armor was perhaps six and a half-feet tall, pale metallic blue, dozens of overlapping plates cunningly designed to mimic all the movements of the human body. The primary material seemed to be some kind of plastic composite. Chill had seem similar stuff in the university's science labs, bulletproof, light as balsa, and stronger than steel. Pound was right. These guys were for real.

Sharpe smiled. "This armor is the end product of years of work. You might say that my entire career is tied up in this suit. Here, let me show you." He pointed at the arms. "Carbon-nanotube reinforced composite armor. Thin as an eggshell, but nothing short of a cannon shot will penetrate. Under that, a layer of linear micro-motor 'muscle' that will amplify the wearer's strength ten-fold." He pointed the helmet. "This incorporates a real-time satellite data uplink, and full sensory feed with global positioning. We'll be in constant communication with the wearer, see what they see, hear what they hear, and know, to the inch, where they are at all times."

Chill sneered at him. "Nice mecha, Sharpe. Why don't you just strap one of the goons I keep hearing in the dark out there into it and go hunt some mutants, or maybe beat up some old ladies, if it's more your speed."

There was a look of mock surprise on his face. "No, you don't understand. The armor is for you. *You* are going to be my mutant hunter."

"So I've heard," said Chill, dryly. "When hell freezes over, not to make a pun."

Sharpe laughed. "Interesting you should put it that way." He pointed at the heavy yoke that covered the shoulders of the armor. "This," he explained, "is what we call the power amplification system. We've tuned it specifically to you and your mutant abilities. It taps into the energy generating abilities dormant in all mutants and uses this energy to amplify your mutant aura."

"I'm not," said Chill, "really into that whole New Age, crystal, pagan thing, but if you'd like to leave some of your literature—"

"Joke if you want." A harsh edge crept into Sharpe's voice. "I'm talking about an invisible energy field that all mutants generate, one tied to their special abilities. Perhaps you've been jealous of other mutants' greater powers, the well-known 'Iceman,' for-instance. Well, with this suit, you'll have your chance to equal him, perhaps even ultimately surpass him." His eyes narrowed. "You're going to become a living weapon, a soldier, *my* soldier."

"See," said Chill, "there you go with that again. We are not going to work for you Sharpe, none of us. We'll fight you with our last breath."

Sharpe's fingers traced a flat, blade-like antenna on the side of the helmet, then its twin on the other side. "That would be a formidable threat, assuming fighting would do a bit of good. This is the mind control unit. We've spent years developing the technology. Despite some earlier problems, I'm convinced we've got it right this time. We picked up some very useful tidbits from a super-criminal called 'the Controller,' who is currently in government custody.

"In fact," Sharpe continued, "we were just about to give it a try."

To Chill's alarm, a headpiece lowered over his brow with an electric whir. He struggled against his bonds with all his strength, but it was useless.

"I had in mind a very simple test. I'm going to come over there, and give you the opportunity to spit in my face. You'd like that, I'm sure." He turned to someone out in the darkness and nodded. "Let's give it a try."

He moved and positioned his face only a few inches from Chill's. "Wouldn't want you to miss," he said.

A wave of hate washed over Chill. Well, Sharpe had asked for it.

He didn't move.

He couldn't move.

He didn't feel anything. In fact, it was as though he suddenly *couldn't* feel anything at all. Hate, anger, rebellion, initiative, he observed them pass through his mind and disappear in the distance, like the lonesome whistle of a night train. He observed this, recorded it, and felt nothing. Like a robot. Like a machine.

He couldn't even feel the horror.

Sharpe stared into the subject's eyes, and watched them go flat and cold. Satisfied, he stood and smiled with delight. Dozens of technicians appeared out of the darkness and began to work on the armor and on the subject.

Happersen walked up and handed him a digital clipboard. "I imagine you can sign off on this phase now."

Sharpe nodded, took the clipboard, signed, and handed it back.

"That seemed to go well," said Happersen, adjusting his glasses.

Sharpe chuckled. "Fortunately for you. The penalty for failing that particular test could have been quite harsh." He watched Bouille as she positioned the virtual reality training goggles over the subject's eyes. This done, she turned to him. "We should get this started with the others. It will take about twelve hours to imprint the basic command protocols on them. After that, we can downlink new modules and commands in the field using the armor's satellite link."

"Excellent." Sharpe walked over and put his hand on the armor's chest. "When can we have them suited up for field-trials?"

Bouille frowned. "I'd like a few weeks to do tests and drills here before we take them on a real mission."

Happersen just chuckled and shook his head. "Boss doesn't work that way. Better get used to it."

She looked nervously from Sharpe to Happersen and back again. "Twenty-four hours," she said, "maybe twenty if we do double shifts and cut some corners."

"Do it," said Sharpe. "I want to see what our new hounds can do." He turned back to Happersen. "Which brings me to another matter. We need a target. Find me a mutant, Happersen. Nothing too ambitious this time out. We'll save Magneto for another day." Then he smiled wistfully. "But once we have a full platoon of Mutant Hounds at our disposal, who knows? No mutant will be safe, and each new captive will just be cannon fodder to throw against the rest."

"Scanners," Espeth explained to the groggy Gen Xers. "The scouts have radio scanners. I always think of them in terms of police calls, but of course they could pick up a tow-truck dispatch. I just wasn't thinking."

"Nope," said Angelo sarcastically, "you weren't."

"Look," she said, "I told you as soon as I thought of it."

Ev and Monet came swooping out of the sky like a pair of hawks and landed softly next to the group.

"Either, this place is ground zero for a mortician's car rally," Ev said, "or we've got Genogoths coming north and south. Lots of them. I figure we've got four or five minutes to get out of here."

"And all we are," said Jubilee, "is surrounded, outnumbered, and running on two flat tires. *Lots* of time."

Ev looked at the Xabago's front tires. "Monet, this thing might fall apart if we tried to lift it in one piece, but what if we each grab a wheel hub and just keep the front end off the ground?"

Monet looked exasperated. "We're the heavy hitters on the team, and we get used as a pair of spare tires."

Jubilee also looked exasperated. "*Who* are the heavy hitters on the team?"

"I wouldn't say that I carry your weight," said Monet, "except that it looks like I'm about to do it again."

Angelo shoved Jubilee through the door into the Xabago. "You drive," he called after her. Then he turned back to the others. "Didn't have the heart to tell her that no steering was involved. Look," he said, "if we could get across this little patch of rough ground to the farm road, we might have a chance of giving them the slip up in the hills."

"We'll do it," said Ev, "if we have to drag the blasted thing."

Paige sighed. "And we'll leave tracks that the Mole Man could follow." She looked at the stream.

Jono leaned over to meet her eyes. "Is that a plan I see cooking, luv? If so, out with it."

"Plan," she said, urging Angelo and Espeth into the Xabago. "They get away. We stay behind to cover their escape."

"That," said Jono, "is a plan?"

Paige shrugged. "Only one I've got, old-son."

GENOGOTHS

They watched as Ev and Monet dragged the Xabago along, leaving deep furrows, torn grass, and crushed underbrush. Finally they got it onto the road and made pretty good time getting away, the front end hovering while the wheels pushed.

Jono turned to Paige. "You ever see *Butch Cassidy and the Sundance Kid*?"

"No, Butch, but I've seen *Flubber*."

Leather squinted against the rising sun and wished that he'd taken the time to wash the windshield at his last gas stop. As his van roared down the freeway, he was at least thankful that he didn't have Black as a passenger this time. The "old man" had flown into Raleigh, and was with the group that was closing in from the south.

He growled and slammed the wheel with one hand as he thought about it. What business did that fossil have putting himself in the middle of a field operation? "If I wanted a ball and chain," he muttered, "I know a club in Manhattan—" Thanks to Black's interference, he'd lost these—these *kids*, twice already.

"It's because of his little pet, Espeth," he said. Leather had heard how he'd found her on the streets of Seattle, guided her into the public Genogoths, then groomed her for membership in the inner circle. "Nobody made it easy for me," he said. "I worked my way up through the ranks. Didn't let anyone stand in my way." He wasn't going to let anyone stand in his way this time, either. Maybe it was time for the Genogoths to have a new leader. Maybe it was time to see how that would work out.

He carefully leaned down and pulled out the machine-pistol stuffed under his seat. He held the gun between his knees while he slapped in a magazine one-handed, then hefted it. "Oh, yeah," he said, "this one is going down Leather style."

Paige dragged Jono by the arm up the slope and onto the little wooden bridge, "husking" as she ran into a metallic form. "I don't want to get a splinter," she yelled. They ran out onto the bridge deck, wooden planks thumping under their feet until

Paige stopped them near the middle. "I've got the plan," she said, "but you're the man." She pointed at the beaver dam which although it was deteriorating, still held back a sizable pond. "Blast it," she said, "give it everything you've got."

He looked at her doubtfully.

"A busted beaver dam once flooded out two acres of our garden back home. That should be enough water to cover the Xabago's tracks. Even if they figure it out, it should slow them down a little."

Jono reached up and hooked his index fingers over the wraps that covered what used to be the bottom of his face. He tugged them down, and tendrils of scarlet colored energy danced through the air, seeking escape. He granted their wish, clenching his fists as he focused all that energy into a column of sheer, destructive power.

What took beavers years to build simply ceased to exist, instantly transformed into an expanding ball of debris that enveloped the little bridge. Paige jumped in front of Jono, using herself as a human shield, chunks of wood and rock bouncing harmlessly off her metal skin. Jono ducked low, arms crossed over his head.

Then a roar, a blast of air, and the little bridge shook as though in the grip of a giant hand. He looked up to see the wall of water as it lashed through the little stream's channel, pounding the bridge abutments and surging just a meter or so under their feet.

Paige yelled something, but he couldn't hear her over the din. He could see her pointing though. A dozen black cars and trucks were sliding to a stop near where the Xabago had only moments before rested.

Leather slid to a stop just in time to watch the huge mass of water and debris swallow the culvert below the roadway and sweep up the bank toward him, lapping at the edges of the pavement before slowly withdrawing.

"What was that?" it was Black's voice in his ear-piece. He and his group had pulled up just shortly after Leather. He saw them on the other side of the median strip, several of the off-road-capable vehicles poised to cross the median strip if so ordered.

"They've slipped away again," he answered. "Maybe they took that thing airborne again. We should have helicopters—"

"Out in the country like this helicopters draw attention," Black snapped back, "but I'll take it under advisement."

"The main groups should head north and south and fan out from the next couple of exits." He looked at the surging water. He still didn't see how that piece of the puzzle fit. "I'll stay here and see if I can pick up any clues."

"Sounds reasonable. Keep in touch." Black's car accelerated north and the rest of his group followed. The rest of Leather's group headed out as well.

Leather pulled off onto the shoulder. He could see a bridge through the trees. Railroad? No, there was a narrow gravel track hidden back there. He pulled forward for a better look at the bridge. Then he saw two figures run out from behind a bridge support, one a boy with some kind of energy flaming from his chest, the other a girl who seemed to be made out of quicksilver. *Two of the Xavier mutants!*

He looked desperately for a way across to the road, but even with four wheel-drive, the overflowing stream and thick trees had every obvious route blocked. They were going to get away. *Unless . . .*

He pulled forward about twenty yards and hit the button that opened the sunroof. Setting the brake, he grabbed the machine pistol and climbed up to stand straddling the two front seats.

He took aim, then hesitated for a moment. These were *mutants* he was shooting at. But he reminded himself that they were Xavier's pups, public mutants that put all others in jeopardy. They knew secrets that could destroy the Genogoths, and they were his only lead to capturing the rogue Espeth. They *had* to be stopped.

His finger tightened on the trigger.

• • •

Paige and Jono hid themselves behind the narrow metal support beams of the bridge. They tried to make themselves very small. Unfortunately, that was a mutant power that neither of them possessed.

"Oh, Gel," Jono projected his telepathic voice into Paige's head, so there was no danger of being overheard, "you take me to the best parties."

Paige, who was standing with her back pressed against the next beam, gave him a nasty look, but said nothing. Carefully she balled her left hand into a fist, held it out, back toward her, and stared at it intently. It took him a moment to realize that she was using her own metallic skin as a crude mirror to check on the Genogoths.

He could hear a mass of idling motors stopped along the freeway. Jono wished he'd remember to put the wraps back over his face after blasting the dam. It would be difficult to do now without waving his elbows around where they could be seen. He was trying to figure out another way when he heard, first one, then more of the vehicles drive away.

He made eye contact with Paige, who nodded. *They were leaving!* Finally, there was only one motor, and Jono waited for it to leave. And waited.

Paige was frowning. They could wait here all day, but eventually, the straggler was going to spot them. "I say we make a run for it. The Xabago went that way," he nodded toward the road to their right, "so we go left. If he sees us, we lead him away from the others. If not, we can find a place to hide and double back."

Paige nodded, held up three fingers, and began a countdown. *Three. Two. One. Go!*

They sprinted, and Jono immediately groaned to himself. He'd forgotten how much noise their feet made on the bridge timbers. The watcher was sure to hear them.

He heard the vehicle suddenly start moving. It rolled along the highway only a few car lengths, then slid to a stop. Paige was just in front of him. Jono pushed his pace, and pulled up even with her.

He risked a glance over at the watcher. Somebody was poking out through a hole in the roof. He wanted to look again, see what he'd been holding.

Something zinged around them like angry bees. It hit Paige hard enough to make her stumble, and cause her metal body to ring like a bell.

"Bloody hell, what was that?"

Suddenly she grabbed him and pushed him to the side of the road, shielding her with his body. "They're *shooting* at us," she yelled.

Jono was suddenly very, very conscious of how *small* she was. Then he heard a pair of whistling noises coming out of the sky. His eyes went wide.

He said, "Artillery—"

Then a cruise missile hit him in the back. He was instantly flying through the air at blinding speed, air ripping through his hair.

When Jono recovered from the shock, he realized the cruise missile's name was Everett Thomas and he was being carried through the air at fantastic speed. He looked over to see that Monet was likewise carrying a startled Paige.

"Welcome to Air Monet," yelled Ev, "this is your co-pilot Synch, and I hope you enjoy today's flight. We'll be traveling at an altitude of—," suddenly they all dived through a hole in the tree canopy and were zooming along *under* the trees, their speed not having diminished a bit. "—and altitude of about two feet!"

"You know," yelled Paige, "the first time I saw this part of *Return of the Jedi*, I ralphed." She held her hand over her mouth. "But I'm a big girl now. I think."

Suddenly they hooked a sharp U-turn around a large oak tree and were headed back the way they came.

"Lead the blighters off track and then double back," said Jono. "That was *our* plan!"

"We do it quicker," said Ev.

"Do we have to go this fast?" complained Paige, as they zigzagged through an especially dense stand of trees.

Monet smiled. "When you've been a piece of auxiliary equipment on a motor home as long as we have, it's *good* to finally cut loose."

Quickly they sailed over the top of an overgrown, split-rail fence, across a weedy field free of trees, past a burned-out farm house, and toward an old barn. Suddenly they swooped skyward, traveling straight up for a hundred feet or so, slowing until they seemed to be in free-fall. Then they went down, through the open top of the barn's silo. As they touched down gently at the bottom, they could see the Xabago through a rectangular opening to their right.

Jono shook himself free of Ev's grasp. "We left my bloody stomach about two klicks back."

Ev grinned. "We could go back for it."

"Hell, no," said Jono.

Ev shrugged. "Suit yourself. Me and Monet have to go back out anyway. We've got some tracks to cover." The two of them disappeared back into the silo.

"Hey," Jono called after Ev, "is there any reason we couldn't have come in through the front door?" Then he noticed Paige inspecting her arm. "You okay, luv?"

She looked up and nodded. "Just a few dents. Nothing fatal."

They walked into the barn, and Jubilee and Angelo trotted out to meet them.

Angelo held his arms wide and grinned broadly. "Jono, Paige! Our heroes have returned!"

Jono and Paige looked at each other. "Just call me Butch," he said. "That okay with you, Sundance?"

She grinned and nodded.

Angelo looked puzzled. "What's up with that?"

Jono and Paige laughed.

Leather parked his van in the middle of the little bridge and climbed out. The flood had run its course, and he looked down on the debris-littered creek bed and the remains of what looked like a beaver dam. It had taken him forty-five minutes to find his way off the freeway, double back across country, and return to this spot.

He saw now that the flood had been a ruse to cover their escape onto the back roads. He'd hoped there might be tire tracks or some other useful clue, but a dead tree, pulled up by the roots, now lay by the stream under the bridge. It hadn't been there when he left, and it didn't appear to have been pulled up anywhere nearby. From the looks of it, somebody had used it as a giant whisk broom, dragging it down the road to erase any tracks.

Leather slammed the van's door in anger and kicked the tire. They could be a mile from here, or all the way in South Carolina by now. Even the satisfaction of shooting off a few rounds had been fleeting. What this situation needed was not a little more firepower, it was a *lot* more firepower.

He climbed back into the van, plucked his phone from its pocket on the dash, and dialed. "Jet," he said, "round up as many of the chieftains as you can for a conference call. In one hour. Just the ones that are loyal to me. Yeah. Pick them carefully. It's time to make some changes, and Black's in the way."

CHAPTER SEVEN

"*As man gradually advanced in intellectual power, and was enabled to trace the more remote consequences of his actions—his sympathies became more tender and widely diffused, extending to men of all races, to the imbecile, maimed, and other useless members of society.*"

—Charles Darwin

The Descent of Man, 1871

Jono found Paige sitting alone in the barn's hayloft, sitting on a pile of baled hay. She'd husked back to her normal form and was dressed in her training uniform. Jono looked at her shyly. "Wassup," he said.

"Pull up a bale," she said, "sit a spell." She leaned back against a beam and sighed. "This reminds me so much of home. Just for a minute, anyway, I can forget what a mess we're in."

Jono sat on a hay bale. It was harder than it looked, smelled funny, and the ends of the straw poked him in the butt. It didn't feel near as comfortable as Paige made it look. It was all a matter of perspective, he guessed. "I guess that's no small part my fault."

She waved a hand at him in annoyance. "Could we not talk about it? Give me my five minutes of vacation here."

She was quiet for a while, then a faint smile crossed her face. She looked at him, a little wicked glint in her eye. "You know, for a girl from Kentucky, a hayloft is a seriously romantic setting."

Jono blinked. "What?"

She laughed at him. "I wasn't trying to start anything, Jono. It's just that, well, I think there are some Kentucky counties where being alone in a hayloft with a guy is just about as legally binding as a ring and a preacher."

Jono squirmed. "Meaning?"

She laughed again, just thinking about it. "Meaning, if you value your life, you will *never* tell my brother Cannonball about this."

The humor of it finally hit him, and he laughed too, or as close as he could come in his present condition. "I'll keep that in mind next time I see him. Guess that gives you some pretty good blackmail on me." His humor faded. "I hope you're not going to want to use it."

Her smile dimmed. "Uh, oh. Why do I have the feeling that that patented Starsmore *cloud-o-doom* is going to descend on us both?"

He looked away. "Don't be like that, luv. It's just, I have a confession to make. Last night, when we ran off the road, well—it's just that—I harbored just a little suspicion that you might have done it on purpose."

She stood and looked at him in amazement. "What? Jono, how could you?"

He shrugged. "I was tired. It was a moment of weakness. Like that." He met her eyes. "And it made sense. You don't like the mission. A little sabotage. Nobody gets hurt. Maybe Espeth sees things your way and we call in the big leagues."

She glared at him. "Is that still what you think?"

"No," he said weakly.

She put her hands on her hips. "Good, because listen up. We are a *team* here. We might disagree, but I would never sabotage you or anybody else on that team. Not you, not anybody, not even M, much as I might like to introduce her face to my boot some days."

"But," he said, "that doesn't extend to Espeth."

She looked thoughtful. "No," she said, "it doesn't. But this isn't Espeth's mission, its yours, it's the team's. I'm not calling the shots this time, but I can be a good little soldier if you'll let me."

Jono looked down at the barn floor, where Espeth was helping Angelo roll one of the flat tires over to a workbench. "Yeah, well, it's just sometimes hard to know who to trust."

Paige looked indignant and tapped her finger over her heart. "Trust *me*, Jono."

He nodded.

Just then, a roar of rage and frustration came from below. It was Espeth.

Jono looked at Paige, who nodded, and the two of them climbed down from the loft to join the others who gathered from various corners of the barn and the Xabago to see what the commotion was about.

The tire was lying on its side on a rickety bench half covered with pieces of old farm machinery. A spot on the bench had been cleared next to the tire. There, Espeth had spread a tire patch kit she'd found in one of the Xabago's dustier storage compartments, obviously left over from some previous owner.

Jubilee leaned over and made eye contact with her. "You growled, O gothic one?"

"This isn't going to work," she snapped back. She pounded her fist against the bench repeatedly. "This just isn't going to work. What was I thinking? I know. I was thinking you'd have Blackbirds or pogo-planes or quinjets or something." She spotted a corn cob on the floor of the barn, grabbed it and flung it at the Xabago. "This is *hopeless*. Even if we can fix it, it'll just break again, or they'll catch us again. They just keep finding us. It's a miracle they haven't gotten us yet, and the closer we get, the easier it gets for them to find us. We can't even begin to worry about what we'll find when we get there, because odds are, we'll never make it that far!"

Angelo stepped in, his face angry. "Listen, *chica*, we aren't the X-Men or the Avengers. We aren't super heroes. We're just a bunch of students with funny genes doing what we can do. I *told* you that when you first showed up at the school, but it went in one body piercing and out the other! We're going to bust our *amigos* out of the slam." He turned and stomped away to the Xabago. "You do what you want," he said.

Espeth watched him go, her mouth open.

"Man-o," sneered Paige, "and I thought Jonothan was negative! We'll cope. They'll throw things in our way, and we'll cope with it. We have so far, haven't we?"

"Plan B," said Jubilee, giving Paige a high five.

"Plan B," said Paige.

Espeth glared at them. "They've been coddling us so far. Time and space have been on their side, but we keep raising the stakes. Somebody is going to get hurt."

"Then," said Paige evenly, "somebody gets hurt. Those are the risks." She stepped closer to the bench. "Now, how do we fix this thing?"

Espeth sighed. "I can patch the tires, but we can't inflate them without an air compressor."

"I," volunteered Monet, "can blow up a tire."

Ev's eyes narrowed. "I am *not* even going to go near that one."

"You'd *better* not," said Jubilee.

"So," said Jono, "we fix the tires, get back on the road."

"Back," said Paige, "to the status quo." She looked at Espeth. "You've set the rules here, Espeth. We're going to rescue our buds. Are you in or out?"

The door of the Xabago opened, and Angelo leaned out with the satellite phone in his hand. "Hey, Paige," he yelled, "Emma on line one!"

Paige stared into Espeth's eyes.

"What choice have I got?" asked Espeth.

"There's always a choice," said Paige. "If you stop taking the alternatives out of consideration." She turned and headed for the Xabago.

Espeth made eye contact with Jono. She didn't say anything, but it seemed like she'd made some kind of decision. She shrugged. "There are always choices," she said, then went back to work on the tire.

The town of Muddy Gap, Kentucky, had one of the highest poverty rates in the state. Located in an isolated valley deep in the Appalachian Mountains, its primary attractions were two churches, a post office, a gas station, a tiny grocery store that also rented videos, a café that served up some pretty good barbecue on Sunday, and three blocks of empty and boarded storefronts. Towering above it all was the rusting, steel gantry that topped the old Faerber Mine #50.

At one time, all of the town's prosperity had come out of that hole. Now all that came out was an occasional cloud of black smoke from the underground coal fire that had burned out of control since 1989, killing twenty four of the town's menfolk, closing the mine, and condemning the town itself to a slow death.

Sometimes, when business was slow, storekeep Beelo McComb would limp out into the street, his artificial foot making a hollow *clop* with each step, and put his hand on the asphalt. He'd squat there, feeling the heat of the fires still smoldering far underground, thinking of better times and lost friends. Some days he'd just stay there until he cried. Other days, someone would come along first and rescue him from himself.

This was one of those days. The beep of an approaching truck's horn brought him back to the present. Beelo looked up to see a big four-wheel drive pickup coming up the street. It slowed, stopped in front of him, and backed in to park in front of the store. Beelo didn't have to look to see who was in the truck. Only one truck like that in town, and only one man that drove it.

People moved out on a regular basis, but nobody had moved *to* Muddy Gap since the mine closed. Nobody except Smokey Ashe. Beelo watched as he climbed down out of the truck. Smokey didn't make a lick of sense, with his big black trucks, his handlebar moustache, his black rodeo shirts and his Garth Brooks hats.

Where his money came from, nobody could say. When people asked, Smokey made vague references to an inheritance. When asked why he'd moved to such a God-forsaken place, he'd talk about how he liked the country, the quiet, and the cheap real estate. If he liked the smell of coal smoke, he didn't say so.

All that was sure was that he showed up four months after the mine disaster, bought up the old Kerny place near the lake, and put up some kind of big ham radio antenna. He didn't work, didn't do much of anything except pal around with his neighbor and long-time friend, "Catfish" Quincy. Beelo watched as the passenger door of the truck opened and a man who looked for all the world like a fish stuffed into a pair of coveralls stepped out.

Catfish's daddy had been down in the mine that night, and was still down there to this very day. It was ironic that he'd been working double shifts to pay for doctors for Catfish. He'd have done anything to give his son a normal life. Instead, he only succeeded in having him grow up without a daddy. His mamma, Bess, had been broken-hearted, and died the winter after Catfish's eighteenth birthday. Beelo didn't know what Catfish would have done without Smokey, but the two of them were near inseparable.

"Hey, Beelo," Catfish waved. He reached into the truck, pulled out a plastic squeeze-bottle of water, and squirted a bit of it over his hairless head. It trickled in rivulets down over his flat, nose-less face and the gill slits in his broad neck. He put the bottle back into the truck, topped his head with a John Deere baseball cap, and wiped the fleshy feelers that hung on either side of his wide mouth with the back of a webbed hand.

"Hey, Catfish, Smokey."

Smokey nodded in greeting. The big man wasn't a big talker. That was okay, Catfish talked enough for both of them. As Catfish walked over, Beelo saw that he was carrying a little Styrofoam cooler. He pulled off the lid and showed it to Beelo.

"Brought you a mess of bluegill," said Catfish. "Caught 'em myself up at the lake this morning." He made some grabbing motions with his free hand, the webs between his fingers making a wet, slapping sound.

Beelo smiled and took the cooler. "That's right nice of you, Catfish. You know how I like a good mess of fried bluegill. I'll have them for supper. You boys wouldn't want to join me, would you? Plenty for three."

Catfish laughed. "Nah, but thanks, Beelo. Some other time. Me and Smokey was going to rent us a movie. You got any new space pictures?"

Catfish loved monster pictures and that sci-fi stuff. Beelo

figured it was because the critters in it looked even stranger than Catfish did. Beelo nodded and led them inside. "We got in that new Warlock movie last week." He went behind the counter and started looking through the rack of milky, plastic, video cases. "That short guy from *Taxi* plays Pip the Troll. You like *Taxi*? That short guy kills me." He pulled out a box and checked the label. "This is the one." He handed it to Catfish, whose round, black eyes gleamed with delight.

"This is gonna be a good one. I read all about it in *Starlog*." He held it up for Smokey to see. "This is gonna be a good one."

An old Chevy coupe with a crease in the front-bumper pulled up outside the store, and the bell on the door rang as a heavy-set woman in her sixties came inside. "Afternoon, Beelo. Need me some creamed corn and coffee. Afternoon, Catfish, Mr. Ashe."

Catfish beamed and trotted over to meet her. "Afternoon, Mrs. Mills. Want me to get those things for you? You just stay here and visit, and I'll get those for you."

She smiled and nodded. "Thank you, Catfish. I surely appreciate it." She watched as he trotted off into the canned goods aisle, then waved after him. "Percolator grind, Catfish, you know the kind."

Catfish was always helpful like that. He looked funny, but you couldn't help but like the boy.

Betty Mills put her purse on the counter and leaned against it heavily. "You know what's going on up the street?"

Beelo saw Smokey's eyebrow go up with interest. The man didn't say much, but he didn't miss a lick.

"No, ma'am," said Beelo, "don't know a thing."

"There's cars stopped up the road, and some contraption blocking the way."

Beelo shrugged. "Contraption? Like a combine?"

The door tinkled again, and Billy Thorton, a teenager whose mother ran the Café, leaned in. "You should come out and see. They's a gov'ment helicopter landed right in the middle of the street! They's some men dressed in armor-like. They says they's hunting for—," he paused to think of the word, "mutants." His eyes were wide. "I didn't even know we had those here."

Catfish returned with a can of coffee.

Billy smiled. "Hey, Catfish."

Suddenly Smokey was moving. He snatched the coffee out of Catfish's hand, handed it to a startled Betty Mills, and started pushing Catfish toward the back door of the store. "Don't you ask questions, Catfish. I want you to head for the lake. Head for the lake and make for the bottom and you stay there. You just settle down in the muck, and you take a little nap and you stay down there till I come for you. You hear?"

Beelo was shocked. He'd never heard Smokey put that many words together in a string, not in all the years he'd lived in Muddy Gap.

Catfish seemed just about as surprised. He just stood there, staring at his friend.

"You go," insisted Smokey, "and you go fast. If you see them fellers she was talking about, you do whatever it takes to hide or get away. *Go!*"

Catfish finally seemed to be convinced. He ran out the back without another word.

Smokey turned to the rest of them. "You care about Catfish, no matter what happens, no matter what anybody says to you, you didn't see that, never heard of him, and you *sure* don't know where he is. Understand?"

Though confused, they all agreed. "You wait here. I'm gonna go see if I can slow them down."

They watched as Smokey stepped outside, paused for a moment to get something from his truck, and walked off up the highway. Mrs. Mills suddenly clutched at Beelo's hand.

She'd seen the same thing Beelo had seen as Smokey walked away. In all the years he'd lived there, they'd never seen Smokey Ashe turn a violent hand toward any man, nor seen him with a firearm of any kind. But right now was carrying a pump shotgun, and he was holding it like he meant to use it.

• • •

GENOGOTHS

Black pulled his borrowed Thunderbird into the parking lot of the Dog N' Suds Drive-in and parked under the shelter. Only a few customers parked under the old-fashioned corrugated steel roof, ordering burgers and root-beer from speakers mounted over fluorescent-lit menus. The place smelled of french-fry grease and malt. Behind the parking lot, almost overgrown with weeds and small saplings, he could see the remains of an old drive-in theater, half the screen collapsed and fallen forward, as though taking a bow. Nearer the highway he located the theater's rusted old sign, a few letters still clinging tenaciously to the marquee.

L ST NIGHT!

ROG R MO RE

AG NT OF SHI LD

T E MAN WI H THE GOLD N CL W

And below that, in a different color lettering:

CLOS D FO W NTER

Evidently it had been a *very* long winter. Black sighed, and scanned the menu in a vain search for espresso. He wondered why Leather had chosen this as a meeting place. Had he picked it at random, or was it a not-so-subtle suggestion that he was a fossil, that his time was past? Well, he thought, as he eyed the menu, at least there were some places where he was still ahead of the coffee curve. He pressed the button on the menu and ordered a black coffee and onion rings.

He noticed a couple of concrete picnic tables under an oak tree at the rear of the property. He pressed the button again and told them he'd take his food there. He locked the T-Bird and strolled past a teenager couple parked in a Chevy sedan as old as both of them put together. They were laughing and feeding each other french fries. He thought of simpler, happier times, sighed and continued on his way. Maybe he *was* getting old.

Black brushed dry leaves off the picnic bench, sat down, and looked at his watch. As he was trying to compute how late Leather was, he saw the black van pull around the back of the building and park a few yards away.

Leather emerged and sat across the table from him. He didn't bother to clean the seat, and the leaves crunched as he sat down.

Black lowered his Foster Grants and eyed the younger man over the top of them. "I'm here, Leather, at your insistence. What do you want?"

Leather seemed to be in no hurry. He spent some time taking in their surroundings before going on. "How long have I known you, Black?"

He thought. "Third year I was chieftain of the Seattle 'Goths. You came up from the Bay Area Rovers to study martial arts under Master Panda. I was told you were trouble, and to keep an eye on you."

He smiled wistfully. "I am often misunderstood by my superiors, but I get the job done—when I'm allowed."

Black pushed his dark glasses back up on his nose. "These are mutants, Leather, not much more than children, and Espeth, one of our own."

"Espeth has betrayed us. These mutants endanger everything the Genogoths have worked for, back to the time of Darwin. Traitors have to be brought down *hard*. We have to serve the greater good."

"Espeth is an idealist, young and inexperienced. She thinks she can have her cake and eat it too. She doesn't know the—sacrifices—that some of us have had to make." He frowned. *We're so much alike. She doesn't know*. "I'm not," he continued, "going to let you turn this operation into a bloodbath."

Leather pulled a switchblade knife from inside his boot, snapped it open, and began to use the point of the blade to clean under his fingernails. "It would have been much easier if you'd done this my way from the beginning. They're getting close to a confrontation with the government. The situation grows desperate, and desperate times, to quote the cliché, call for desperate measures."

"No bloodbath," Black repeated forcefully.

"My people need helicopter gunships, weapons."

A girl in a crisp, blue uniform put a tray in front of Black. Her eyes never left Leather's switchblade as she took Black's money and made a hasty retreat.

Black stared silently at Leather.

Leather smiled and shook his head sadly. "Your position in the Genogoths isn't as strong as you think it is, old man."

Black squared his jaw. "And maybe it isn't as weak as you think it is, Leather. Not all of your friends are your friends. I know about your conference call."

Leather seemed momentarily surprised, but quickly covered it with bravado. "So? I knew you'd find out. It doesn't matter, Black. Your days are growing short."

"Indeed," he said, "that may be the case, but I can kick your skinny ass before lunch and still have time to read the morning paper." He took a sip of the coffee. It tasted like rust. He emptied the cup into the parking lot with a toss of his wrist and spit the rest out. He stood and looked down at Leather. "You'll have non-lethal weapons, kept in reserve, and helicopters operating under visibility restrictions. This comes over my objections, and everyone is going to know that. Any mistakes are now directly on your head." He pushed the untouched onion rings at Leather and turned back towards his car. "You're in charge of this operation for now, Leather. Enjoy the benefits of authority."

As Smokey Ashe walked down the yellow line in the middle of the road he noted two things about the scene in front of him. One: The helicopter was black. Two: It wasn't one of theirs, a Genogoth ship. There were no numbers on the flat-black airframe of the chopper, which perched in the middle of town like a giant mosquito. The words UNITED STATES GOVERNMENT, stenciled in gray paint down the tail-boom, were the only signs of ownership. There was nothing more specific which might only mean, Smokey thought grimly, that it came from an agency without any name, the worst kind.

Half the town's population was already there, crowded together, yet maintaining a respectable distance from the three strangers who stood in their midst. One was tall and thin, one small, one broad. They wore glittering armor, similar in general design, different in details and color; pale blue for the tall one, purple for the wide one, red for the small one. Faceplates hid their features, adding to their air of mystery and menace. They stood in a neat row in front of the helicopter, their bodies rigid, at perfect military attention.

The locals saw him coming, and their eyes went wide at the sight of the shotgun. They parted to let him through. The tall one stood in the middle, and Smokey aimed the gun squarely at the middle of his chest. "State your business," he demanded.

"Official United States Government business," said the one in blue, his voice cold and metallic. "Specified: the apprehension for questioning of one Samuel Leon Quincy."

"Catfish," Fred Tavish, the Postmaster, said.

Smokey shot him a poisoned look, but the damage was done.

Tavish shrugged apologetically, and pointed to the embroidered flag on his uniform jacket.

The small one in red stepped up to Tavish. "Locate, Samuel Leon Quincy."

Tavish squirmed uncomfortably, seemingly regretting his words.

The one in red suddenly reached up and put his hand against the side of Tavish's head.

Tavish looked startled, but didn't move.

"Locate," the red one said, more firmly this time, "Samuel Leon Quincy."

Tavish's eyes went wide. "He lives—He lives out on—"

Smokey pumped the shotgun, and the sound silenced

Tavish and made everyone scatter for cover. Tavish hesitated only a moment before running after the rest of them.

Red didn't pursue. He turned toward the others. "Subject Samuel Leon Quincy is not at that location."

Smokey raised the gun and squinted down the barrel at the intruders. They all turned to look at him, but said nothing. "Get back in your vehicle and leave. I'm not going to say it again." A cold wind blew up suddenly, and something white fluttered down between gun and target. Then another. And another. *Snow. How could there be snow?*

He was still puzzling over that when a sudden movement caught his eye. A small door had opened on a pod that hung under the belly of the 'copter. While that was registering, six sleek forms shot out one-by-one. Dogs? Robots? *Robot dogs!*

The red one suddenly reached for something on his belt, *a weapon.* Smokey pulled the trigger. Red staggered back. He pumped the gun, aimed at blue. Fired.

Something flew in front of him and the gun was ripped from his hands. One of the robot dogs slid to a stop a few yards away, the gun in his mouth. There was a squeal of metal, a crunch, and the gun fell to the ground in two pieces.

Smokey tried to run, but his feet wouldn't move. He looked down to see that his boots were, literally, frozen in their tracks. Purple and blue stepped up on either side of him. Each grabbed a wrist, and they pulled his arms behind his back. Red stepped up and put his hand beside Smokey's head. *He had to be some kind of telepath.* He remembered his training, bracing for a straight-forward psychic probe that never seemed to come.

"This one," said Red, "knows the subject Samuel Leon Quincy very well." His head turned, as though he were listening for a distant sound. "I have a track on the subject. He is moving, on foot."

"We will pursue," said Blue.

The three of them, and four of the dogs, trotted in the direction of the store. The dog that had destroyed his gun remained, its glowing, quartz eyes focused intently on his every move.

Slowly, he reached up, lifted his hat, and with a soft tearing of Velcro, removed the satellite phone hidden inside. He and the robo-dog eyed each other warily as he dialed Black.

Jubilee and Paige sat on the floor of the Xabago counting their dwindling funds. Ev was taking a turn playing lookout in the crow's nest, Monet was zoned out on the couch, while Angelo drove and Jono rode shotgun in the front. After a hundred or so miles on the back-roads, they'd returned to the freeway. "You'll get better mileage," Espeth had told them, "plus, if you can keep in traffic and crowded places, the 'Goths are more likely to keep their distance. They don't like attention."

Angelo peeked at the girls in the rearview mirror. "What up on the budget situation, ladies? It's hard to tell with this screwy gas gauge, but I think we're on fumes, and there's a mega-truck stop coming up soon. If we have to wake up Monet and have her push again, we are *never* gonna hear the end of it."

Paige swept all the bills into a little pile and wrapped them together with a maroon hair scrunchie. "Do it," she said.

"Daddy needs a new tank of gas," cracked Jubilee.

"I don't suppose," said Angelo, "there's enough there for another burger run, is there? Cold Beanie Weenies and Spam sandwiches are getting old."

"Not to worry," said Paige, "the Beanie Weenies are running low, and we ate the last of the Spam for breakfast."

Angelo groaned. "A simple 'no' would have done the job." He lapsed into a mock-announcer voice. "Come on down to Mr. Fixit's World-O-Trucks for the Beer Nuts and tree-shaped air fresheners, but be sure to bring your Visa, 'cuz they can't drive fifty-five and they don't take Avengers' Identicard!"

Paige snickered.

"Like," said Juiblee, "the Avengers would ever let you in, Angelo."

"Hey," he said, "they let the Beast in didn't they? There's got to be some flaw in the membership process. Me, I figure you just have to slip Jarvis a C-note or something."

"Well," said Paige, scrutinizing their kitty, "that leaves you a couple of twenties short. We should just about get there, but I have no idea how we're getting home."

"The way I figure it," said Jono, "once we get in there and rescue the guys, the Genogoths have no reason to bother us. As long as they don't have a grudge, we should be able to fire up the old charge cards and ride the plastic surf-board home."

"They won't hold a grudge, will they?" Jubilee seemed doubtful.

Angelo shrugged. "Ask Leather Lass," he squinted into the mirror looking for Espeth, "assuming you can find her."

"She's been brooding in the back ever since we got the tires fixed," said Monet, without opening her eyes.

"Hey," said Jubilee, "I thought you were sleeping!"

"Sometimes," replied Monet, "I like to see if you're any less annoying when you think I'm not listening." She opened her eyes. "So far, it hasn't worked."

"I know you are," said Jubilee, "but what am I?"

Monet sat up and straightened her long black hair with a sweep of her fingers. "Sticks and stones may break my—" She gave a look of mock realization. "Oh, wait, they won't."

"Exit coming up," said Angelo. "I'm going for it."

"At least," said Jubilee, "the hot water in the restrooms is free."

"Hot water," said Angelo, as he put on the turn signal, "the other white meat!"

Suddenly Ev shifted violently in the crow's-nest seat. He yelled, "Heads up!" Then he relaxed and slumped back into his seat. "Sorry, false alarm."

Jubilee wrinkled her nose at him. "Huh?"

"To paraphrase Sigmund Freud, sometimes a black Volkswagen is just a black Volkswagen."

The Xabago slowed and pulled into one of the diesel

pumps among endless rows of much larger semi-trucks. "Could be our last stop for a while," said Angelo. "Everybody out for stretch and pottie break."

"Just keep it short," said Paige, "and don't pick any fights with truckers."

Espeth appeared from the back bedroom. She avoided eye contact and slipped silently past them.

Angelo scratched his nose idly. "What did we do this time?"

The boredom of the North Carolina interstate was broken as Black's phone rang. He snatched it up off the passenger seat, expecting news of the missing mutants. Instead, it was Smokey Ashe, a friend from his earliest days as a Genogoth in Phoenix. Ashe had spent the last twenty plus years on a deep-cover guardian assignment, screening an isolated mutant from detection.

"We got bad trouble here," said Smokey. "Some kind of government super-troops after my boy Catfish. I'm pinned down and can't help him. The jamming tower was working fine when I checked it two hours ago. I don't know how they found us."

Black cursed under his breath. He had a guess how they'd bypassed the screen that protected mutants from scanning devices like Xavier's Cerebro, but he hoped he was wrong. "Troops, Smokey? How many? This is important."

"Three. One of them is a tracker, one freezes things somehow, and the other has a pack of robot dogs. One here ready to rip my throat out if I make a wrong move. I need backup. Lots of it."

A knot tightened in Black's stomach. "I'm in North Carolina right now, Smokey. Most of our east-coast rover-packs have been pulled south of here. It'll take hours to get help there. You'll have to hold out."

"With my last breath, Black, for all the good it will do Catfish. This dog is looking at me funny. I think it's figured out what my phone is for. It's—"

GENOGOTHS

Black shook the phone and tapped it against his steering wheel, but the problem wasn't on his end. The phone had gone dead.

Heart pounding, gills gasping, Catfish Quincy ran through the Kentucky woods like his life depended on it, and just possibly it did. Behind him he could hear something a little like the baying of hounds, and yet different enough to make his leathery skin crawl.

He didn't know who the strangers from the helicopter were, or what they wanted, but Smokey had said they were bad, and that was enough for him. Smokey was his best friend in the entire world, like a big brother to him, and he'd never, ever, steered Catfish wrong. If Smokey said run, he'd run.

The hounds, or whatever they were, were closer now, but so was the lake. It was a big, sprawling man-made thing, nestled between two hills and held back by a huge earthen dike that the WPA had built back in the 30s. The water was green, murky, and as much as fifty feet deep in places. Catfish knew every inch of it, not just the surface and the shoreline, but the bottom as well, even to the location of a limestone cavern in the deepest part.

If he got into the water, he could shuck off his boots and coveralls and just stay down there, for months if he had to. They'd never find him, even if they came back with submarines and sonar. He'd just be the Loch Ness monster of Muddy Gap, Kentucky.

He groaned as he slid down an especially steep bank covered with a thick layer of dead leaves. His webbed feet didn't fit into boots that well, and they were no danged good for running on the best of days. He'd be glad to get in the water and shuck them off.

This was the last hill. Once he topped this rise, cut through that thick stand of trees, and slid down the bank, he'd be in the water, free and clear. *Up, over, down.* Even as he slid down the bank, he could see that something looked wrong about the lake. Then he landed with a syrupy splash, and found himself waist deep in—slush.

It startled him, but it wasn't much of a problem. Cold, even freezing cold, had never hurt him, just made him sluggish. He dived under the slush with no more hesitation, and began swimming with powerful strokes down for the deep water. Then he ran face first into a wall of ice. He recoiled. His eyes were especially sensitive, but he couldn't see much. He relied on his incredible sense of touch, and the feelers on either side of his mouth. He couldn't find a way through the wall. He turned 90 degrees and started swimming again. Ten yards later, he hit the ice again. He doubled back the other way. Maybe fifteen yards. Back the other way again, maybe he'd missed something.

Ten yards. How was that possible? Not only had the pond never frozen completely in all the years he'd been coming here, it was *spring*. When he'd swam here catching fish this morning—well—it hadn't been like bathwater, but it had been nowhere near freezing. Now it all seemed to be frozen except the little bit he was swimming in, and even that was getting smaller.

Cautiously, he poked his eyes above the surface. White flakes were falling all around him. He'd seen snow before, but never like this. There were three men on the bank, looking right at him. They wore some kind of armor, like the hardsuits the girls in *The Bubblegum Crisis* video wore. He quickly ducked under the surface—and his feet ran into the ice coming up underneath him. In a panic, he reached out. The ice was closing in from all sides, close enough to touch!

He shoved his head above the slush, just in time to feel it freeze solid around his shoulders. He struggled, but the ice held him solid, sapping his strength, till even his brain seemed to work in slow motion. "Who are you?"

The one in the blue armor spoke, though apparently not to him. "Hound units Three-dog-night, Top Dog, and Bloodhound reporting. Mission successful. Mutant target located and immobilized. Calling for air pickup."

"Who are you?" wailed Catfish. "What did you do with my buddy, Smokey? Why are you doing this to me? *I never hurt nobody!*"

"Cease struggle, mutant," said Blue. "You are now the property of the United States Government Hound Program."

"Let me go," cried Catfish. "Mutants ain't real," he sobbed, "they're only in the movies!"

The students filed back into the Xabago. Angelo handed Paige the thin stack of bills left as change after he'd paid for filling the tanks. In return, she handed him a small, plastic bag with a cartoon pig printed on the front. He looked at it, puzzled.

"I took pity on you," she explained. "There was some pork jerky in the double-discount, close-out bin."

Angelo held it at arm's length, between thumb and forefinger. "Yum," he said without enthusiasm.

Jono looked around, puzzled. "Where's Espeth?"

Paige looked surprised. "She's not here. She left the ladies' room while we were washing up, and said she was headed straight back here. That was ten minutes ago. Ev, look in the back."

Ev disappeared for a moment, then returned. "No joy," he said. "We better spread out and look for her."

"You won't find her," said Angelo, "if she doesn't want to be found."

Jono glared at him. "What's that bloody supposed to mean?"

Angelo smirked. "Isn't it obvious. Leather-lass has skipped out on us."

"No," said Jubilee, "she couldn't have."

"Ev," asked Angelo, "was her bag in there?"

He shrugged. "I didn't notice. I'll go check."

He ducked into the bedroom, then came out with a folded fast-food napkin in his hand. Somebody had written on it "JONO" in felt pen. "Her stuff is gone," said Ev, "and this was on the bed." He handed the paper to Jono, who unfolded it, read, then groaned and closed his eyes.

GENERATION X

"What?" demanded Paige. "What?"

Jono held out the napkin so the rest of them could see. There were two words written there. "TRUST ME." It was signed, "Espeth."

CHAPTER EIGHT

"In recent days, you've heard me joke about my missing cohost, Recall, Scooter McCloud is his real name, one you don't hear him use very much. Well, I've made light of his absence, in large part because I just couldn't believe anything serious had happened to him. It had to be some kind of misunderstanding. [Pause] I'm not so sure of that now. Now, Recall has been a thorn in my side since he joined this program last summer. More than once I've wanted to—[Nervous laughter] But I've come to respect his intelligence and his devotion to his cause, no matter how much I personally think he's full of hot air. Things just aren't the same around here—[Pause] I miss him, the little pain-in-the-butt. Look, I read the ratings, I know how many of you out there are listening. Lots of you already know what Recall looks like. If not, check our web site for a picture and description, or call and we'll send it to you. But somebody out there must know something. So this is old Walt Norman asking you—[Pause] No, I'm begging you, send an e-mail or call us, we'll have operators on duty around the clock till this is over, or call your local police—[Pause] If you think you can trust them with a—[Pause] He may be a mutant, but he's just a boy for God's sake. [Pause] I need to go to a commercial here."

—Walt Norman
Walt and Recall radio program

P aige was the last one to meet back at the coffee shop. The vinyl cushions made a rude noise as she slid heavily down into the booth with the others.

"I take it," said Angelo, who was warming his hands with a heavy china cup of joe, "that you found her. Probably got her in your back pocket so we don't lose her again."

She frowned. "No, Angelo, I didn't find her. I take it nobody else did either?"

The all looked glumly at her, and that was answer enough.

"Well," said Paige, "here we are, broke, six-hundred miles from home, our friends are in mortal trouble, we've told more lies than a Roxxon 'environmental spokesman' at a Greenpeace conference, and we don't even know where we're going."

Angelo grabbed a salt shaker to use as a microphone. "That was last week on 'Mutant Teenagers In Trouble.' We join today's episode, already in progress." Angelo noticed a rough looking trucker a few tables over staring at them, and tugged his lower lip up over the bottom of his nose.

Jubilee pulled the collar of her coat up to hide her face and tried to slide under the table. "Gross me out, Skin. Like things aren't bad enough, you're going to start a riot."

Angelo let his lip snap down to its normal position, revealing a big frown. "Yeah, well right about now, getting to bust some heads would be a big improvement as far as I'm concerned."

Jubilee sighed. "Ang, this wasn't a fun routine when Wolvie used to pull it, and he had way more couth than you do."

"Let's face it," interjected Paige, "she probably hitched a

ride out of here on a truck. She could be sixty or a hundred miles away by now."

Angelo was looking indignant. "She disrespected my couth."

Paige ignored him and continued. "I think we need to move. In case she, intentionally or not, leads the Genogoths back here."

"Where I come from," said Angelo, "a man's couth is his castle. Now, I will walk down the street, and they will shake their heads and say, 'there is a man with a disrespected couth.' "

Paige slapped her hand on the table. "Shut up, Angelo!"

Angelo suddenly looked very serious. "*Chica*, I was just trying not to say 'I told you so.' "

Her anger faded. "Point taken."

"Look," said Jono, "we still don't know what this is about. She could be back."

Angelo shook his head. "So we can just sit here on our hands, waiting for her buddies in black to come and collect us? No way. I'll hitch out of here on my own first."

Jubilee straightened her back and put her elbows on the table. "But where do we go? Back to the school? She never told us where the guys were being held."

"Sure she did," said Jono.

"Huh?" Paige stared at him curiously. "Since when?"

"South Carolina," he answered. "I'm a Brit, and even *I* can find that on the map."

"That," said Monet dryly, "narrows it down to only thirty-thousand, one-hundred and eleven square miles. That's only five-thousand, eighteen-point-five square miles each."

Jono looked indignant. "It's a bloody start. We might find some clues when we get there."

Jubilee seemed to be thinking about something intently.

"Gosh, Scoob," mocked Angelo, "let's get back to the Mystery Machine."

Paige glared at him. "You got a better idea?"

Angelo shrugged. "I would have gotten away with it too, if not for you meddling kids." He rolled his eyes. "Let's go."

"Wait," said Jubilee. She put out her hand, "Give me the phone."

Paige handed it over, a puzzled look on her face. "What are you going to do?"

Jubilee was already dialing. "I'm calling the X-Mansion."

Jono tried to grab the phone, but Jubilee snatched it away. "Hey, Sparky, trust me, okay?" Someone answered. "Hey, Rogue, this is Jubilee. Can I talk to Logan?"

They all stared at her as she slipped out of the booth. "I'm gonna take this outside."

The helicopter was gone for perhaps ten minutes before it returned to land briefly in the middle of Muddy Gap. The big door opened in the side and the mutant-hunter in the purple armor jumped out. He had only to look at the robot-dog for it to drop the crushed phone from its mouth and dash back into the pod in the 'copter's belly.

Smokey Ashe muttered a curse under his breath as he looked into the aircraft's rear compartment. The other two armored men sat on a bench seat on either side of Catfish. The poor fellow was a sight, shivering, one boot missing, his coveralls torn, wet, and icy, his hands and feet bound with some kind of high-tech shackles.

As soon as the dog disappeared, the townspeople began to appear from their hiding places. They slowly advanced on the 'copter. Several of them saw Catfish chained in the back. One of those was the postmaster, Tavish. His mouth hung open. He looked pale, and sick. He seemed to come to some decision and trotted up to the armored man. "Let him go," he yelled over the helicopter's din. "He didn't do anything!"

The others began to gather around Tavish, joining him in the protest. The man in armor just stood there. Somebody picked up the broken phone and threw it at him. He didn't flinch as it bounced harmlessly off his helmet.

Smokey struggled, and one of his boots came free of the pavement with a wet crunch. It took him a minute, but he freed the other one as well, and ran forward to join the group. He didn't yell at the man in armor, who was now climbing back into the helicopter. Smokey locked eyes with Catfish. "Don't you worry, pard'na! I'll come get you out of there!" The door started to close. He pushed forward. "No matter where they take you, Catfish, I'm coming to get you, boy!"

Then the door closed. The rotor sound changed pitch, the engine spooling up to speed. They all ran back, shielding themselves from the down-blast as the big black machine lifted off and disappeared over the roof of the post-office. The flag whipped in the rotor wash.

Tavish came up to him, an apologetic look on his face. "I'm sorry," he said, "I didn't know. I didn't know." He held up the paper. "One of them slipped me this. It says Catfish has been legally detained for questioning by the United States Government. It says that complaints or inquiries can be directed to the proper authorities." His eyes looked wide and lost. "But, it doesn't say who the proper authorities are!"

Jubilee wandered out into the parking lot of the truck plaza and sat on the chromed running board of a parked semi. Rogue had told her that Logan was working out in the X-Men's Danger Room, and that it would take a few minutes for him to get to the phone.

Logan, better known to the world as the ferocious X-Man, Wolverine, liked to tell people that he was completely self-reliant, that the X-Men needed him more than he needed the X-Men, that he didn't need anybody for anything. Usually, maybe 99.9 percent of the time, that was true. But on those rare occasions when he had needed someone, one or more of the X-Men were usually there for him. He didn't talk about those times much, but he was fiercely loyal to them because of it.

Jubilee had often said the same thing about herself, that she didn't need anything from anybody, that she could take care of herself. Then one day fate had thrown the two of them together. Her parents were dead, she was lost, alone in a distant land. Logan, Wolverine, had just taken the beating of his life, and lay close to death. She'd saved him. And he'd saved her.

After that time, Logan was many things to her, friend, protector, mentor, father figure. There was nobody in the world she trusted more than Logan. No one. She hoped he trusted her half as much.

"Jubilee," his voice came from the phone. She could still hear that danger-room edge to his tone. "I was slicing up Sentinels when you called, but Rogue said it wouldn't wait."

"I wish I could be there with you, team up, give them the old plasma bombs like we used to."

"You didn't call to chat, Darlin', I can tell."

She sighed. "I need a favor, Wolvie, like, a big one. I need some information about a guy. You still have lots of cloak-and-dagger friends you could call, don't you?"

"You know I do, but something tells me this don't have nothing to do with one of Emma Frost's class projects."

"I need to know anything you can find out about a guy named Sharpe. All I know is, he used to be a general, and he went up against X-Factor once."

"Need ta know what?"

"Like what he's up to now, where he hangs his hat, like that. And this isn't the kind of guy you can look up in the yellow pages."

A truck rumbled by.

Logan heard it. "You aren't at the school, Jubilation. Where are you? Do you need help?"

She sighed. "Wolvie, you know how you used to tell me, and I quote, 'sometimes there are things a man has got to do—alone.' "

There was silence from the phone for a while. "It's like that, is it?"

"It's like that," she said firmly.

"Darlin', I was always afraid you'd grow up to be just like

me. Now it looks like my worst nightmares are coming true."
A pause. "I'll make some calls, get back to you."

She gave him the number for their phone.

He didn't have to say it. "I'll be careful," she said.

The Genogoth safehouse was a nondescript farm house outside Fayetteville, North Carolina. From the outside, the only thing that differentiated it from a dozen other similar houses on the same two-lane blacktop road was a thirty-foot antenna mast topped with a huge television antenna which was hooked to nothing, and a much smaller cone-shaped antenna that was the real reason for the mast. The small antenna was attached to a special jamming transmitter located in the house's attic.

The signals transmitted by the antenna would interfere with any mutant locator device, such as Professor Xavier's Cerebro machine, or other similar, but less sophisticated, devices used by government agencies and independent organizations like the Hellfire Club. While it was operating, any mutant within a fifty mile radius of the antenna might be detected, but their genetic signature would be impossible to localize and pinpoint. If the mutant were very close to the antenna, or if the detector were much less sensitive, they might not be detected at all.

It was just such a jamming device that had, for twenty years, protected the mutant Catfish Quincy, and had just as abruptly failed to protect him at all. Perhaps fortunately, there were no mutants currently present in the safehouse, only a handful of human Genogoths.

Espeth sat in the middle of a sway-backed couch covered in textured, avocado-colored fabric. The room smelled unpleasantly of cigarettes and stale beer. Leather sat in a chair near the door, picking rocks out of his boots with a switchblade, and carefully avoiding making eye contact. That was good, because she had no intention of talking to him anyway.

Another of Leather's troops, a tall, muscular woman named Inky, stood by the front window on lookout. She watched closely as a car crunched up the gravel driveway outside and a car door opened and closed. She turned to Leather and nodded. She walked over and opened the door for Black.

Leather didn't get up. "She called us from a diner near the ninety-five, forty interchange. She demanded to talk to you, and nobody else."

Black nodded, walked over, and sat down in a brown easy chair across from her. "Where are your friends, Espeth?"

"Locked up in a secret government installation, last I heard."

Black frowned at her. "You know what I mean, child. Where are the Xavier School mutants?"

"I don't know. They don't check in with me."

"Where did you leave them?"

"Can't remember."

He sighed and leaned forward in the chair. "What then, Espeth? Did you simply call me here to taunt me? Act as a distraction while your friends attempt a rescue? It won't work. We'll still catch them before they even get close. It will be even easier without you to help them."

"You might be surprised," she said. "Let them rescue the guys. The Genogoths don't have to be involved at all."

"Thanks to you, we already are. They know too much to be allowed to escape, Espeth, much less to risk their falling into government hands. It could be a disaster, the end of everything we've worked for—"

"—since the time of Darwin," she sneered. "I know the speech. Black, do the right thing. Let them do what they came to do, or at least let them go. You'll never catch them at this point anyway."

"We know where they're going, Espeth."

"*They* don't know where they're going. I never told them where Sharpe's base was."

His eyes widened. He hadn't expected this.

"They don't know anything, really. Let them go."

"I can't do that, Espeth. They have to be captured, taken to a relocation center." He studied her face. "Don't look at me like that, Espeth. They weren't involved at all until you brought them in. You've created this situation, now others must pay the price for your mistakes. I feel for your three friends who were taken, I really do, but this is for the greater good."

He stood and turned to Leather. "I think she's trying to throw us off their trail. They've gone west to bypass our search. Concentrate your people on a line north and south of Charlotte." He glanced at Espeth. "You, are coming with me. *Now*."

Espeth slowly stood.

Leather looked suspicious. "Where are you taking her?"

"I'm sending her back to Washington state," he said firmly, "to the Abbey, for reeducation. Perhaps a few years of simple living, hard work, and meditation on the principles of the Genogoths can salvage her spirit. If not, at least she will be contained. Come on, Espeth, I'm going to have a plane waiting for you."

She followed him reluctantly. Leather smiled evilly as she walked past. "We'll get your little friends. Don't you doubt it for a minute."

She said nothing, and followed Black out to his car. Perhaps there would be an opportunity for escape later.

"Don't look back," Black said quietly as they approached the car. "The situation has changed."

She climbed into the car with Black. She stared straight ahead, careful to maintain the unhappy expression on her face.

He started the car, backed out, and drove off up the highway. Only when they were several miles from the farmhouse, did he speak again. "The situation has changed radically in the last few hours. I had to put on a show for Leather. He's building a power-base independent of my own, and he can't be trusted."

"I could have told you that," she said sarcastically.

"That's enough of that," he said angrily. "The situation has changed, but you were still wrong in what you did." He stared grimly at the road. "You remind me of myself when I was your age, Espeth, angry, headstrong, convinced that you can right all the world's wrongs single-handedly. But some wrongs can't be righted, some sacrifices must be made. That is the hard truth of what we do. The genes must survive, and nature doesn't play favorites."

She watched as they drove past a row of hothouses, some sort of agricultural station, tall stalks of corn growing under glass, never feeling the rain or the caress of a summer's breeze. "If you really feel that way, why aren't you putting me on that plane back to Seattle?"

"Who says I'm not?"

"I know you too well. Besides, you wouldn't have thrown Leather off the trail if something wasn't up. Something has changed. What?"

"I have to talk to your friends, meet with them. Perhaps I can negotiate some sort of settlement so that nobody else gets hurt. You can contact them?"

"I have a phone number."

He plucked his phone from its pocket and handed it to her. "I know a place we can meet, someplace public and along their route. I'll make a reservation for them at the hotel there."

"They're short of money," she said.

"It'll be taken care of. Tell them that. Anything for their comfort."

She looked at him.

"The phone won't be traced. This isn't a trap. You, me, and them. We'll have a talk."

She didn't dial. "What happened? I won't call unless you tell me."

His frown deepened. "This morning a mutant under Genogoth protection was taken from his home in eastern Kentucky. He was hunted down and taken by three armored individuals who identified themselves as government agents." He let that sink in for a moment. "The agents wore face masks, but judging from the physical descriptions, and the special abilities they demonstrated, we believe them to be your missing friends, Chill, Dog Pound, and Recall."

• • •

Leather wandered onto the safehouse's front porch and sat down in one of the old-fashioned metal lawn chairs. It squeaked under his weight, but it was surprisingly comfortable. A soft breeze blew through the trees that shaded the front yard and driveway. Birds chattered out their territorial disputes, and he could hear the faint sound of a tractor plowing a distant field.

By now, most of his forces were headed north to intercept the young mutants, and he knew he should get into his van and drive to join them, but something didn't seem right. Oh, things seemed to be going well enough. Though he was disappointed that Black had failed to provoke a direct confrontation, he had bowed, at least a bit, to Leather's demands. The traitor, Espeth, was in custody and would soon be sent where she could do the Genogoths no further harm.

Still, something didn't seem right. Black was old, but he was a fighter. Did he know something that Leather didn't about the situation, or rather, was there something he didn't *want* Leather to know?

Leather stood and locked the safehouse's front door, then flipped the sequence of hidden switches that activated its intruder alarm and emergency self-destruct systems. That done, he climbed into his van and fished out his palmtop computer.

One of the Genogoths' most valuable resources was a deep-cover operative known as "Visor." Visor worked somewhere in the financial industry, and provided information to the Genogoths on banking and credit transactions. Black had recently charged him with locating all bank accounts, debit cards, and credit cards belonging to Espeth or any of the students of Xavier's school, and further, informing them instantly of any transactions on those accounts. Unfortunately, Espeth seemed to have anticipated this, as none of their accounts had been accessed since the beginning of their flight from Massachusetts.

Leather had never met Visor, never even talked to him by

phone. Visor could be reached only by an encrypted internet mailbox. That didn't mean that Leather hadn't made it a point to be in regular touch with Visor, or that he hadn't had a chance to plumb the operative's opinions on Black and various issues in dispute. Thus, he had a certain confidence that Visor would be receptive to what he was about to ask.

He opened the computer and began to finger a message into the little keyboard:

> REQUEST YOU ACQUIRE, MONITOR, AND REPORT ACTIVITY OF ALL ACCOUNTS UNDER CONTROL OF BLACK. REPORT IMMEDIATELY, FOR MY EYES ONLY.
>
> ——LEATHER

He pushed the send key. He was just about to put the computer away when it beeped to notify him of incoming mail. He looked at the screen and smiled.

> REQUEST RECEIVED. ACCOUNTS IDENTIFIED AND MONITORED. STAND BY FOR CONFIDENTIAL REPORTS AS NECESSARY
>
> ——VISOR

He closed the computer and slipped it into a pocket inside his vest. He chuckled to himself. "Whatever you're up to, Black, I'll be keeping tabs on you."

CHAPTER NINE

> *"A moral being is one who is capable of reflecting on his past actions and their motives—of approving of some and disapproving of others."*
>
> —Charles Darwin
>
> *The Descent of Man*, 1871

Angelo cranked the Xabago's wheel sharply to the right as they wound their way around the third hairpin turn in the last five minutes. The wheels spun and bounced on the rutted clay of the road. "We are not," he announced, "lost."

Jubilee was sulking in the passenger seat. "We are *very* lost, Angelo."

He laughed. "We *can't* be lost, *chica*, we don't know where we're going."

She crossed her arms over her chest. "We at least knew what *direction* we were going, and when Logan calls me back, we may know more." She slumped in her seat. "Assuming if, like I think, she was blowing smoke when she said we'd never find the place."

Monet came forward, an opened road atlas in her hand. She pointed at the map. "We don't know where we are, Espinosa. I believe that is the definition of 'lost.' "

An hour earlier, when Ev had spotted a pair of black trucks coming up behind them, they'd made a panic turn at the next exit and attempted to lose their pursuers by making a series of random turns onto back-roads. Actually, they'd never seen the trucks after they'd turned off, and everyone now agreed that it had probably been another false alarm.

He gave Monet an annoyed glance. "Give it a rest, M. You're the navigator. We've got to be on that map somewhere."

"I assure you," she said coldly, "that this road is not on this map."

He grinned. "Well, just pick one of those empty places, take one of your crayons, and draw one in. That's where we'll be."

"I don't *do* crayons."

He waved her away. "Yeah, whatever."

"Hey," called Ev, who was still on look-out duty, "Monet or I could fly up and see if we can spot a highway from the air."

Angelo snorted. "It was you, Mr. Eagle-Eye GI Joe, who got us in this fix in the first place."

"I just call them as I see them. I didn't tell you where to drive."

Paige emerged from the bathroom and came forward to flop into the recliner. "Will you all just shut up? If I want to listen to this kind of bickering, I can just go home to my brothers and sisters." She sighed. "It isn't even all that far from here."

"I'll let you out," cracked Angelo, "and you can walk it."

"Shut up, Angelo."

"I—"

"Shut up."

For once, everybody did. Jubilee stared out the window, Angelo focused on his driving, and Monet curled up on the couch with a calculus book. Paige had recently struggled through the same book herself, and she had the feeling that Monet was using it as light reading just to get her goat.

Well, it was working. Paige sulked in the recliner. Everyone was fighting, they didn't know where they were going, and Jono was alone in the back, on a guilt-trip for having trusted Espeth. The phone rang. Paige looked at it and sighed. The last thing she wanted to do was give Emma or Sean another song and dance about how much trouble they weren't in.

Jubilee leaned over the back of her seat. "It might be Wolvie!"

Paige put the phone to her ear. "Hello," she said flatly. Then her eyes went wide. "It's Espeth!" Then louder, "Jono, it's Espeth!"

Angelo hit the brakes just as Jono came running forward. He tripped over Ev, who was swinging down from the crow's nest, Ka-Zar-style, and overshot, almost landing in Angelo's lap. Angelo nearly climbed over the top of him to get close enough to listen in.

"Okay," said Paige into the phone, "talk. You definitely have everyone's attention."

Espeth looked out the window of Black's car and watched the "Welcome to South Carolina" sign flash by. She turned and nodded to Black, to let him know she'd reached them. She sighed. This was hard enough without his listening in, but it had to be done.

"Let me talk to Jono," she said.

There was a pause, then Paige came back on. "You know he talks telepathically. All he'd be able to do is listen."

Espeth wasn't sure that it was true that Jono couldn't use the telephone, but it made a good excuse for him not to talk to her. She couldn't really blame him. "Paige, tell him I'm sorry. I was just trying to do what was best for everybody."

"Yeah," she said coldly, "so you say. So, did you just call to play the sympathy card, or do you have something of use for us? We'd kind of like to know where our friends are being held."

"I'll tell you," she said, "but not on the phone. In person. We need to meet."

"Yeah," said Paige, "so you can lead us into another of Black's traps."

"No," she said, "so you can meet with Black. There've been some new developments, not good ones either. He wants to sit down with you and talk the situation out."

"Trap," said Paige, "trap."

"Just you six, and the two of us. That's all. Nobody else will even know."

It was quiet. She probably had muted the phone and was conferring with the others. "We don't believe you. Why should we?"

Black was looking at her out of the corner of his eye. "Hand me the phone," he said.

She gave it to him.

"This is Black. You have my personal assurance that this will be a meeting on neutral ground. You will not be harmed or detained. I know of a location on I-95 in South Carolina, just across the border. It's very busy, very public. There's a hotel there, and I've already reserved a suite for you. Espeth tells me that you've been living in difficult conditions the last few days. Surely a nap in a real bed seems attractive right now." A pause. "No, it isn't intended as a bribe, but whatever works. The situation for your friends is a good deal more complicated than it was only a day ago, as is my own. It is never the wish of a true Genogoth to see a mutant harmed. Please meet with me."

A much longer pause. He smiled slightly. "Espeth has the information on our meeting place. I'll put her on."

Angelo stared at the information that Paige had written down. *"Little Latveria?"* He shook his head in puzzlement. "They want us to drive to Europe?"

"Not the real Latveria," explained Paige, *"Little* Latveria. I've heard of it. Some kind of major tourist trap for people traveling from the northeast down to Florida. Should be lots of attractions, food, shops, a hotel, lots of people in and out all the time. The Genogoths wouldn't dare risk doing anything there. It's way too public." She saw the look on Angelo's face. "I thought we agreed. I told them we'd come."

He smirked. "What if we just don't show?"

Jubilee put her hand on the phone. "We could just wait until after Logan calls back. Maybe we don't need her at all."

Paige shook her head. "They have other information that we need, and even if we do know where we're going, there's no saying we'll get past the Genogoths without Espeth's help. Maybe we can negotiate some kind of truce with Black." She shrugged. "Even if it's an ambush, we'd at least know where we stand."

Monet was looking at the atlas, and had pinpointed the exit for Little Latveria. "An ambush, with a desperate fight against overwhelming odds. For ten minutes in a hot shower, I would gladly risk it." She smiled just the tiniest bit. "Dibs," she said.

"Little Latveria?" Leather stared at the e-mail on his tiny computer's screen. According to the message he'd just received from Visor, Black had reserved an entire suite at Little Latveria's Doomstad Hotel using one of his personal credit cards. He took another sip of bitter, diner coffee, waved away a waitress in a pink uniform who was trying to freshen his cup, and considered the implications.

He already knew that Black hadn't put Espeth on a plane, as he'd indicated. That meant that she was likely part of his plan. If they intended to hide out from him, there was no reason for them to need an entire suite, or for him to reserve the room in advance by credit card. That suggested the possibility that he was reserving it for *someone else*.

He pulled his phone out of his pocket and hit the speed-dialer. "Pull our people back to a circle ten miles around Little Latveria. Yes, *that* Little Latveria. Tell them to stay out of sight until I give the word. *No* helicopters. Warn them that they may see Black or Espeth, and possibly the Xavier mutants as well, but they are *not* to be seen or to make contact. Clear?" He listened to the phone for a moment. "I'll be in Little Latveria, of course, waiting to spring the trap once everyone is safely inside."

Sharpe reviewed the video and telemetry playback of the Hound mission for what must have been the tenth time that afternoon. From where he sat in the control room, he could see the three young mutants strapped into their monitoring chairs. The Hound armor had been removed, but each still wore a headband containing the mind control circuitry, the very circuitry that concerned Sharpe right now.

The door to the room slid open and Happersen stepped in. He smiled. "Reviewing yesterday's success I see. The mission couldn't have gone better could it? Not a glitch, and we have a new mutant subject to refine the process on." Then he saw the expression on Sharpe's face, and his own smile faded. "What's wrong? The mission was a great success."

Sharpe motioned him over. "Look at this." The console in front of them had three large screens showing the view from a camera mounted in each of the Hound's helmets. Below these, a smaller bank of screens showed the view from each of the cyberhounds, and several others located in the nose, sides, and tail of the helicopter. Below that, a row of intermediate-sized screens showed columns of numbers and banks of graphs. These last could be configured to examine in detail any of the telemetry data that had been transmitted from the Hound armors, the cyberhounds, or sensors in the helicopter.

At the moment, all the displays were frozen. Happersen scanned the video screens. This was the moment of capture, when the mutant target had been trapped and frozen in a lake.

Sharpe moved his finger over a touch-pad and the displays began to move.

Happersen saw the amphibious mutant struggling against the ice. Sharpe had turned up the audio track.

"Let me go," the mutant appeared agitated. "Mutants ain't real, they're only in the movies!"

As he did every time he saw that clip, Happersen chuckled. But Sharpe wasn't pleased. "Did you see it?"

He shook his head. "See what?"

Sharpe rewound the recording, then ran it forward slowly. He pointed at a graph showing three lines, one purple, one red, one blue. As the mutant spoke, the lines spiked slightly, especially the blue one. "That," said Sharpe, "is an emotional response. The mind control device should have completely shut down that part of their brains."

Happersen studied the spikes. "The control systems are cross-linked at the command buss level. It could have just been a transient power spike. The cold might have cause it. At worst it was a moment of involuntary empathy that the system immediately compensated for. I don't see it as a problem."

GENOGOTHS

"I can't take that chance. One of the problems with Project Homegrown is that we were too lax in the mental control of our subjects. This situation is worse. These three were well connected in the mutant community. They will almost definitely be used against mutants they know, even close friends. There can be no trace of sympathy, no shred of mercy left in them."

Happersen sighed. He pointed at a control. "We could turn up the EMP gain, but it's dangerous. We could be risking brain damage in the subjects."

Sharpe reached for the control without hesitation and pushed it up to near maximum. "Better that than losing control. These Hounds of ours, they have always been expendable."

According to the story, immigrant businessman Peitor "Bubba" Vukcevich ran a once-popular truck stop that had been bypassed by the freeway. The good news for him was that an exit had been built only half a mile away. The bad news is that people weren't inclined to get off the freeway and drive even that short distance. He had tried billboards, but with only limited success.

Then one morning, he picked up a copy of a Washington, D.C., paper left in his diner by a passing trucker. On the cover was a photo, taken by a stringer for the New York Daily Bugle, showing sometime Fantastic Four foe, Victor Von Doom. Doom was appearing at the United Nations for the first time in his role as the ruling Monarch of Latveria. Vukcevich had been struck by the fearsome armored figure draped in regal green robes, his gauntlet covered hand held high and outstretched, as though issuing a command that could not be refused.

Struck by inspiration, he immediately changed the name of his establishment, and showed the picture to the company who painted his billboards. Soon, the billboard closest to his exit was decorated with a huge cut-out of Doom in the same pose as the newspaper photograph. Next to it were the words,

"Doom COMMANDS you to Exit here for LITTLE LATVE-RIA."

The day the sign was completed, his business increased two hundred percent. Soon there were dozens of signs, all up and down I-95 and spanning three states. He hired local women to sew Latverian peasant garb for all his employees. He added Latverian folk dishes and "Doomburgers" to the menu. Within months, the business had turned around enough for him to break ground on a new hotel. It would be a half-scale replica of Von Doom's castle constructed from painted cinder-block rather than stone, for reasons of economy.

Gradually, he expanded, adding carnival rides, gift shops, more restaurants, fireworks stands, tee-shirt airbrushing, go-karts, and an assortment of other attractions. Business continued to grow. On the fifth anniversary of his original Doom billboard, he started his greatest project, a two-hundred foot tall statue of Doom himself, towering over the freeway and visible for miles in either direction. A spiral staircase climbed up through his leg and armored torso. For a small fee, visitors could climb to the top and gaze out through the holes in his fearsome mask. And even though there was nothing in partic-ular to see, other than the air conditioners on the roofs of the buildings below and the freeway stretching long and straight to the horizon in each direction, on some days, the lines were a hundred people long.

"Howdy y'all," said the man at the hotel desk, "all hail Doom." He leaned forward and whispered. "That's just part of the show, you know. We're all good Americans here."

"I'll bet you are," said Paige, examining the painted faux stone and Styrofoam simulated open-beam interior décor. "You have a reservation in the name of Black?"

He checked his computer, and his eyes widened just a lit-tle. "Yes, Ma'am. Four-room suite, all paid for up front." He looked at her. "You're on some kind of school trip, it says?"

She nodded. "We're headed for the Varsity Snipe Hunting

National Championship in Miami. Our coach was held up with car trouble, but he'll be along."

The man behind the desk looked concerned. "You're minors? We have a policy about checking in unaccompanied minors—"

She waved at the computer. "As you said, it's all paid for in advance, and our coach *will* be along."

He looked unimpressed.

"For your trouble and understanding, why don't you just put a hundred dollar tip for yourself on the bill. Just charge it to Coach Black's card. Heck, make it two hundred."

The man's mouth fell open. "Uh—sure. I got no problem with that."

She smiled as he handed her a key.

"Room 300," he said. "Elevators up the hall there, past the Doombot Arcade. Can't miss it. Nice rooms. Close to the Snack-O-Matic."

In the course of capturing their two subjects in Seattle, Sharpe's people had assembled a rather thick dossier on their habits and associations, particularly on a campus mutant organization called M.O.N.S.T.E.R., with which all three subjects had apparently been associated. Public reports were that the organization had shut down after a series of arsons and hate-group attacks. But not according to a report from the Shared Mutant Intelligence network, which distributed such information among government agencies. It had simply gone underground.

It was outside an enclave of M.O.N.S.T.E.R., a former frat-house in Seattle, where two of the subjects had been ambushed and captured, and where the two had been observed to spend much of their free time. The file also included information about other individuals who frequented the M.O.N.S.T.E.R. house. Most of them were confirmed human-normals associating with mutants for unknown reasons, some were unknowns, and several were confirmed mutants.

GENERATION X

It was this last list that Sharpe flipped through on his computer screen. He picked one with whom the subject "Three-dog-night" had been seen on a number of occasions, a college sophomore named Peter Darcy, a.k.a. "Fourhand." His obvious physical mutation was relatively minor as these things went. At the elbow each of his arms sprouted two forearms, each with a fully functional hand. Apparently the mutation extended to his brain and nervous system, allowing him to do separate, mechanically complex, tasks with each hand.

"He has a brilliant future as a watchmaker," Sharpe muttered. But even for their Hound program, designed to exploit limited mutant powers, Sharpe wasn't sure how they'd be able to use this one. He made a notation on the file, just for future reference: CULL. There was one purpose, however, for which this "Fourhand" would be useful.

Sharpe routed their surveillance photographs and recordings into the Foxhole's super-computers where they were processed and overlaid onto a virtual training target. He routed the target into a virtual training exercise for Three-dog-night, then stepped from his office, down the hall, and into the Hound control room.

Beyond the glass front wall, he could see the three Hounds, strapped into their chairs, virtual training visors over their eyes.

Happersen was already in the room. He seemed a little startled when Sharpe walked in. "I was just going over the bio-scans. There a few things I wanted you to look at."

Sharpe slid into a chair at the console next to Happersen. "Later. I want to run a training exercise on Three-dog-night."

"Now?"

"Now. You'll find a target matrix already programmed into the system. Set up the environmental parameters, something the subject would be familiar with." Sharpe hesitated. He wasn't overly familiar with Seattle. "The Space Needle, observation deck. Is that in the standard library?"

Happersen checked. "Yes, sir."

"Set it up." While Happersen worked, Sharpe slipped on a

headset with boom mike and patched in an audio channel. "Attention, Three-dog-night."

"Yes, control." The voice was flat and unemotional.

"Prepare for training scenario. Target is being displayed for you now." He sent pictures to the subject's training display. "Do you recognize the target?"

"No."

Good. The memory blocks were working, at least on a conscious level. While the subject still had his memories from before the activation of the mind control device, he could no longer access them. Of course, the real test was yet to come. "Three-dog-night, this is the situation. You are in pursuit of a dangerous mutant. Your teammates have been incapacitated and you are alone. The target has been cornered in the Space Needle. Apprehend. Use any force necessary. Capture dead or alive. Understood?"

"Apprehend," said the flat voice. "Dead or alive."

Sharpe turned to Happersen. "Are you ready?"

Happersen nodded. "I've set it to nighttime, after hours, no bystanders."

Sharpe nodded. "Good. Keep the scenario clean. All we care about is the target. Start program."

The door opened with a click, and the Gen X crew filed into the suite. Angelo stopped to take in the fierce looking boar's head mounted over the fake-stone fireplace with its plastic logs and electric flames. "Razorback," he muttered, "why did it have to be Razorback?"

Razorback was a little-known super hero based in Arkansas, and possibly the world's most obscure mutant hero. He'd come onto the kids' radar screen the previous summer when he'd intercepted an assassin's bullet intended for the President, and briefly become a media darling. It had annoyed them all that he'd become a celebrated hero precisely because he *wasn't* widely known as a mutant. All that was obvious was that he was an ex-football hero with a silly costume, some gadgets, and a customized semi-truck called "the Big Pig."

Thanks to Professor Xavier's files, they'd all known differently. Razorback had a minor mutation that allowed him to instinctively operate any vehicle.

"What they don't know won't hurt them," said Angelo, to nobody in particular. Other, better-known mutants like the X-Men had saved the world on a regular basis, and got only scorn and grief for their trouble. "From now on," he said, "I'm telling people I fell into a vat of experimental skin cream or sumthin."

Monet scooted past him. "Shower," she said. "Hot. Mine. Now." She vanished into the bathroom, slamming the door behind her. It locked with a loud *click*.

Paige walked in and stared mournfully at the door. "Why do I feel like none of us are getting in there for a *long* time?"

There was a whoop from the next room. "No prob," called Ev, "there are more where that came from!"

Jubilee did a flying leap onto the nearest bed, bounced into the air, did a somersault, then landed sprawled on her back.

Jono was inspecting the small, free-standing wet bar. He pulled a spigot and watched as a stream of brown fluid came out.

Ev came out of the other room and strolled over to watch. "RC Cola on tap," he said. "Figures."

Jono released the tap. "Not that it does me much bloody good," he said. "But I do like to smell a good root-beer every once in a while."

Angelo walked around the room, inspecting the array of framed photos and newspaper clippings. A framed page from a guest register signed by Buford T. Hollis, indicating that he'd stayed here shortly after making the headlines last summer. The centerpiece of the collection was a painting of the man himself, a hulking individual in a leaf-green jumpsuit, yellow gloves and boots, and a boar's head, not unlike the one in the other room, perched on his shoulders. The man's wide, smiling face could be seen projecting from where the boar's mouth would have been. He reached up and touched the painting. "Black velvet," he said. "At least we're consistent."

Jubilee was looking at a brochure. "A truck stop that honors Doctor Doom, Razorback, and has a water ride themed around Monster Island." She squinted at a picture. "They've got like, giant, talking monkey-pirates. That's class."

There was a knock at the door. Angelo threw the safety latch and opened the door enough to look out. "Well, well," he said, peering around to see if their guests had brought additional company. Satisfied, he closed the door, threw back the latch, and opened it wide. Espeth stood at the door, along with a creepy looking beatnik that Angelo hadn't seen before. He gestured them in dramatically. "So," he said, "the prodigal daughter comes crawling back."

The 1962 Volkswagen De Luxe microbus had twenty-one windows, which was Styx's lucky number, and though it looked relatively stock, the engine, suspension, and running gear were transplanted from a Porsche roadster. It would cruise comfortably at a hundred miles per hour on the freeway, and could do a hundred and twenty in a pinch.

None of which was nearly as impressive as what was hidden behind those twenty-one, deeply-tinted windows. Though the equipment that Styx had installed in Leather's command van was sophisticated, next to the gear in the Styx-wagon it looked like some kid's science project. With the exception of a few exotic long-wave frequencies used by the military and S.H.I.E.L.D. he could tap into virtually any electromagnetic communication. The sunroof had been replaced with a electronically-steerable, planar, satellite panel with a capacity of several gigabytes per second. A handy little black box installed in his multi-processor computer array quickly factored hundred digit primes. According to its supplier, it was of extraterrestrial origin, salvage from some race called the "Kree," and had resisted all efforts at duplication, but it allowed him to crack virtually any code, scramble, or encryption at will.

All of which suited Styx. He liked to *know* things. He liked to know *everything*, though knowledge occasionally came at a price. Sometimes just knowing things wasn't enough. Sometimes it begged him to act, and then it became a burden. This was one of those times.

As he pulled his van into the airport passenger pickup lane, he considered his options. For days, he had been monitoring the communications of his Genogoth superior, Leather. He knew what he was planning, what he said about Black. Styx had known Leather for several years now, and had met Black exactly once, a few days before. But he thought he was a good judge of character, and of course, Leather's communications weren't the only ones he'd been monitoring.

A tall man dressed in a cowboy hat, black jeans, and a rodeo shirt walked up to the passenger door. Despite the get-up, Styx's eyes were immediately drawn to the silver slide on his bolo-string tie, one in the shape of the crossed helix. He'd never met Smokey Ashe before either, but his exploits from his younger days were the stuff of Genogoth legend. He defined bravery, honor, and devotion to duty.

Ashe tossed his bag between the front seats, took off his hat, and climbed into the bus. He put the hat in his lap and closed the door. "Appreciate you giving me a lift, Styx."

Styx studied the man. Ordinarily, he'd have been full of questions about the jamming device he'd designed, and that Ashe had tended with the devotion of a lighthouse keeper. Why had it failed? How could it be fixed? Instead, he thought about Leather, Black, and the confrontation that was coming. Time to choose sides.

"Mr. Ashe, you've known Black for a long time, haven't you?"

He bobbed his head. "Since our Rover days. Know him like a brother."

"Well," said Styx, "you have about five minutes to convince me that he's worth saving."

The Hound designated as Three-dog-night scanned the darkened interior of the observation deck. The way that it curved around the core of the Space Needle made it impossible, even with the advanced optics and sensors built into his helmet, to take in all at once. It was as though a dog had chased a squirrel onto a tree trunk, and the squirrel managed to hide by always being behind the tree.

Three-dog-night might have felt annoyance, if he were even capable of that emotion any more. But that, as with may other parts of his thought processes, had been suppressed, shut down. He knew only the cold logic of the hunt. There was a target, a dangerous target, one he had to bring down at all costs.

Surrounding the edge of the enclosed deck was a sweep of large windows. Beyond that, a curved outside deck open to the elements, and beyond that, the glittering skyline of Seattle and its environs. Towering skyscrapers clustered to the south, several rising above the once mighty Needle. A few large, black spots interrupted the rolling diamond carpet that was the city, Lake Union to the east, the Ship Canal to the north, and to the west and northwest Puget Sound itself, a vast emptiness marked only by the lights of an occasional ferry boat or freighter.

Three-dog-night moved slowly, silently, the synthetic rubber treads on the bottom of his boots moving across the smooth floor without the slightest sound. He turned up the gain on his audio sensors. He could hear traffic moving on the streets, five-hundred and twenty feet below, the horns of ferry boats crossing the Sound, the roar of a float-plane lighting gently on the Lake Union. One by one he tuned out the sounds. Listening.

This would be much easier with the help of Bloodhound. But Bloodhound, he reminded himself, was down, a victim of the very mutant he sought out. All the more reason he had to move carefully, and when the opportunity presented itself, to take the target down *hard*.

A sound! Not a person, but a mechanical sound, automatic doors opening and closing. His mutant powers made him keenly sensitive to the temperature change of a sudden draft. Just ahead, someone had gone onto the outer deck.

He moved, not toward the sound, but away from it. Around the inner deck, a series of doors led to the outside. At each of these he hesitated, using his enhanced-mutant ability to freeze the door shut. Finally, after having traveled completely around the deck, he stepped through the one remaining door. This, he carefully froze shut from the outside.

An unseasonably warm breeze blew in from the Sound, and a gentle mist fell from the solid deck of clouds above. Again, Three-dog-night summoned his powers, but instead of focusing them, he let them spread out, chilling the molecules in the droplets, so that each one, as it touched a solid surface such as a deck or railing, turned instantly to ice.

He waited. The target was on the deck somewhere, even if it couldn't be seen, even if it wasn't moving. He waited. The decking at his feet was thick with ice crystals, the railings and supports beginning to glaze over. It was time.

Three-dog-night began to walk, quickly, steadily, around the observation deck. With each step, his power caused his foot to be frozen solidly into position, even as the ice under the other foot melted to allow it to move. It was only a matter of time now.

He heard a thud, a cry of pain, as someone fell. Around the curve of the deck he saw a man in a loose fitting peasant tunic struggling to regain his footing on the icy deck, his hands, *all four of them*, gripping the handle of one of the frozen doors.

The man looked up, his eyes wide and glittering with the reflected light of the city. His feet scrambled, like a cartoon character, but he found no purchase. He didn't look dangerous, but Three-dog-night knew different. Perhaps this was exactly how he had lured in the others.

He moved purposefully forward, grabbed the man by his arm and the leg of his pants, and hoisted the struggling figure over his head. He turned. The railing loomed immediately ahead.

The man struggled weakly. He looked up. The face. *The face*.

• • •

Sharpe leaned forward in his seat. "What's happening? Finish him." He snapped on the communications channel to the Hound. "Finish him," he shouted into the console mike.

The virtual Hound stood motionless on the screen. Sharpe punched up a biometric display and saw the blue line spiked and plateaued at a high level. He checked the controls.

"Happersen, did you turn this EMP gain back down?"

Happersen frowned. "I was concerned we'd damage the subject. I thought—"

"The subject!" He reached over and pushed the control up to full gain. "And *never* think."

The face. The face. The—

Three-dog-night blinked, for a moment disoriented. Then everything became clear. "Target acquired. Dispatching subject with extreme prejudice." With the incredible power his armor-boosted limbs now possessed, he threw the target through the safety fence. Wire and metal snapped, the target tumbled through the air and landed on one of the decorative spines that projected from the Space Needle like a crown of thorns.

The target slipped, held on with his fingers. One of the four hands slipped, then regained purchase. His legs and body swung as he tried to get enough momentum to swing a leg back up.

Three-dog-night pointed. Ice formed out of thin air, coating the spine, making tired fingers grow numb. One hand slipped. Then another. And another. Then the last.

The audio gain was still on maximum. He could hear the screams all the way down.

Then the impact.

"Target terminated."

Leather pulled into one of the vast parking lots that surrounded Little Latveria. As a Genogoth hiding from another Genogoth, he'd gone to some effort to disguise himself by trading in his van for a teal-colored, rental Neon, and his signature black leathers for blue-jeans and a tie-dyed tee-shirt. He cruised the parking lot, and soon found Black's Thunderbird parked near the entrance of the Doomstadt Hotel.

That, by itself, was not damning. The truly damning evidence came when he circled around the complex, driving between the legs of the enormous statue of Dr. Doom, to the RV parking lot. There, almost hidden between two larger and more luxurious coaches, was the garishly decorated RV belonging to the fugitive mutant teenagers. He paused to study the plastic dome on the roof, the steer horns over the grill, and the red "X's" spray painted on the nose and sides.

There could be no doubt. The mutants were here, Black had found them, and he had failed to call in the troops for the capture. He picked up his phone and dialed. "The target is confirmed. Black has gone traitor on us. Move in and surround the place. This time they're *not* getting away."

Espeth frowned at Angelo. "Don't make this any more difficult than it already is, Espinosa."

"Hey kids," shouted Angelo from the door, "we got company."

Jono and Ev were already there. Jubilee bounced off the bed and joined them. There was a muffled curse from the far bathroom. The door to the nearer one opened, and Monet emerged, dressed in the training uniform which she had been wearing under her street clothes, and combing her freshly washed hair.

Jubilee glanced at her. "That was quick," she said.

"Super-speed," replied Monet.

Another curse, and Paige emerged from the other room, her hair wet and matted. She gave Espeth the evil eye. "Your timing sucks," she said.

Angelo eyed the older man with Espeth. "So this is your bad hombre, Black, huh?"

He nodded. "I am Black."

"Yeah," said Ev, "and I am Donny Osmond."

Jono stepped between them. "Back off, mates. Let's hear what he has to say."

Black gestured at a stool in front of the bar. "Mind if I sit down?"

Angelo shrugged. "Yeah, I guess, but no RC Cola for you."

Black smiled slightly. "A sense of humor under fire. Espeth had told me about that. It's a characteristic I admire. I'm afraid I'm not much of a humorist myself."

Jubilee popped a bubble loudly. "You might try dressing in pastels sometime." She plucked a sheet of pink gum off the tip of her nose and shoved it back into her mouth. "Does wonders for your disposition."

Black seemed to take an extreme interest in the suite's décor as he scanned the various items on the walls. "He was one of ours, you know."

Angelo looked at the portrait on the wall. "Pigback?"

"*Razor*back," Paige corrected.

"Whatever."

"I prefer," said Black, "his given name of Buford T. Hollis. He's one of the *little* mutants."

Jubilee had walked up and was reading one of the clippings on the wall. "Says here he's six-foot-six, and that's without the pighead."

"By 'little,' " explained Black, "I mean the less powerful mutants, one without a large and visible power that would normally attract the likes of Xavier or Magneto, searching for soldiers in their respective armies."

"Hey," said Jubilee, "watch what you say about the Prof."

He looked at her. "It's true, child. Look at yourselves. Xavier seeks out the powerful mutants, the ones who are most capable of taking care of themselves, ignoring those with lesser abilities. People like your friends Chill or Dog Pound are passed over."

Paige crossed her arms across her chest indignantly. "The professor can't help every mutant individually, but he's tried to help, build up organizations, get the word out."

"Oh," said Black, "he's certainly 'gotten the word out.' Through the public antics of his X-Men, his X-Factor, and others, he's fanned the flames of hate. Not in the way that, say,

Magneto has with his terrorist activities, but it's a matter of degree, not kind. He has made life harder for all mutants, especially those without the power to care for themselves, those for which he will not take responsibility himself."

Angelo scowled, something his mutant skin made him exceptionally good at. There had to be some flaw in Black's argument. He looked at the portrait again. "You say old Pigback is one of your 'little' mutants, right?"

Black nodded. "His mutant abilities are minor and easily hidden. His rural upbringing made him an ideal vessel to safely pass on the so-called X-gene. We'd been watching him, without his knowledge of course, for years, even placed one of our people close to guard his safety. But then, despite our best efforts, he developed his obsession with becoming a so-called 'super-hero.' "

Angelo found himself, for the first time, developing some admiration for Razorback. "So, you're saying he should have just stayed down on the farm, slopped hogs all his life, married his high-school sweetheart, and made lots of little X-babies?"

"Not in so many words, but—"

"Looks to me," said Angelo, "like Mr. Razorback is a dude who can take care of himself, 'big' power or not. Seems like he's just trying to do what he thinks is right, that maybe his dreams are a little big for the old farm, you know?" He pointed an accusative finger at Black. "So who are you to decide what he's supposed to do with his life? Sounds to me, too, that you're just as guilty of picking and choosing as anyone."

Black looked uncomfortable. "I really didn't come here to debate my life's work. I came here because I care about your safety."

Paige tapped her foot. "Or our *genes'* safety.'

"Is there a difference?"

"You can't see it," said Ev, who was looking out the window, "we sure can't show it to you."

"I came to try and convince you that this mission is a fool's errand."

Angelo chuckled sourly. "Stop with that sweet talk."

"Your friends are lost to you. They're being controlled, used to hunt other mutants. We've already lost one of our charges to them. I don't want to lose you as well. At this point, I am willing to accept your vow that you will keep our existence secret, allow you to return to your school unmolested."

"My," said Paige, icily, "what a generous offer."

Black scowled. "It is much more magnanimous than you imagine. Historically, the Genogoths have maintained their secrecy at any cost. *Any* cost. I fear a dark time is coming, and I'm attempting to change with those times. The preservation of your genetic line is more important than anything, even our secrecy."

Espeth looked desperate. "He means it. Maybe—" She choked on her own words. "Maybe it would be better to leave them be. We'd only be making things worse, for you, for all mutants."

Jono had been listening to the arguments quietly, but finally he stepped forward. "Espeth, bloody *listen* to yourself. Black says they're being used to hunt other mutants, that they've already captured one. You think it will just stop there? You say they've already taken a mutant under your protection? You can't protect one, what makes you think you can protect *any* of them."

Paige nodded. "You know our buddy Recall. His 'little' power is to find things, people, near or far. We don't know what the limits of his power are. I don't think he knows himself. But if the bad-guys have harnessed that, then none of your 'little' mutants are safe, no matter how you hide them."

"I know those three," said Ev. "If they can turn the 'Mutant Musketeers' against other mutants, then they can turn any mutant against any mutant. This could be just the trickle that starts the avalanche. It could make the Sentinels look like nothing."

Jubilee popped another bubble. "What they said."

Black said nothing, his skin more ashen than usual.

Espeth hung her head, chewing her lip. She shook her head sadly. "They're right, Black. I'm sorry." She stepped away from him, and stood with the rest.

Ev paced back to the window. "Uh-oh," he said. "Black brought company."

Black jumped off the stool. "What?"

"The parking lot down there is crawling with Genogoths."

"I didn't authorize this," said Black. "It must be Leather."

"Likely story," said Angelo. Then he turned and nodded at Monet. "Good call on wearing the battle togs, by the way."

"You heard him," called Paige. "Wear 'em if you got 'em."

"You, little man," said Monet to Black, "are starting to annoy me."

CHAPTER TEN

"No doubt stags challenge each other to mortal combat by bellowing; but those with the more powerful voices, unless at the same time the stronger, better-armed, and more courageous, would not gain any advantage over their rivals."

—Charles Darwin

The Descent of Man, 1871

Sharpe removed the VR glasses and put them on the console. "Excellent simulation, Happersen. It almost redeems what happened earlier." He massaged the bridge of his nose. Virtual reality always made the back of his eyes itch. His mood turned somber. "Don't *ever* reverse my orders again. I may not have a uniform with stars on it any more, but don't let that confuse you as to our relative positions here. We're still soldiers, and these—" He pointed out through the glass at the two figures strapped into their chairs. "These subjects, they're not people, they're weapons. You don't waste time wondering if a bullet is going to get a headache. Understood?"

Happersen nodded, then, after a moment, "Yes *sir*!"

Sharpe seemed marginally satisfied. "Now, we run this simulation again with the others. Then we go through the dossiers and find people closer to them and run it again. By the time we're through, we'll have them pitching their own grandmothers off a building without even blinking."

"This," said Black, looking out the hotel window, "was not supposed to happen."

"Save it for your memoirs," said Monet, who was helping Ev pile furniture in front of the doors.

"There'll be people on the stairs and elevators," said Espeth. "They may be in the halls already."

"Well, duh," said Ev, as he walked by carrying a dresser. "Does it look like we're going out that way?"

Paige was leaning against the frame of the window, trying to see out without exposing herself. "There must be fifty of them that I can see," she said, "but at least they don't seem to be carrying guns."

"Of course not," said Black, indignantly.

She grunted. "Well, after one of your goons opened fire on Jono and I yesterday, I'm not going to take it for granted."

"What?" Black paced the length of the room. "That's not possible."

"Listen," said Paige, "if I hadn't been metaled up, I'd have a few holes for show-and-tell. I had some pretty impressive dents at the time though."

"This," said Black, "has gotten totally out of control. *This is not what we do.*"

"Tell that," said Jubilee, "to your buddies downstairs."

"What was it you were saying," said Espeth, "about living with the consequences of your actions?"

Black scowled, motionless in the swarm of activity going on around him. "We'll go out the window," said Paige, "punch our way through to the Xabago, then improvise."

"I can do like the amazing Spider-Boy," said Angelo, demonstrating by "thwipping" his fingers out a few yards and then snapping them back again.

"Good," replied Paige. "If M and Ev can take down Jubilee and Jono, I'll take care of myself."

"I am not," said Monet, "getting Jubilee cooties."

"Then take Jono," Paige snapped.

Espeth stepped forward. "What about me?"

"You're not coming with us," insisted Angelo.

She got in his face. "Face it, stretch, you need all the help you can get against that army." She grabbed him by the waist. "So I guess I'm with you."

Angelo groaned. "This is my worst nightmare."

"Mine too," she whispered in his ear.

"You sure you're okay?" Jubilee had jumped on Ev's back, like she was going for a pony ride. "Like, if you turn into metal or something, from this high up, you could crater really bad."

"If you do," said Monet, "I'm not digging you out."

"Shut up," said Paige, "and knock out the darned window."

"The 'Goths have been holding back on you guys so far. This won't be easy," Espeth warned.

Angelo socked his fist into his other palm. "That's okay, *chica*, 'cuz I think the homies and me are ready to cut loose too."

"Wait," said Black, trying to put himself in front of the window, "give me some time to work this out."

"Too late, obsidian dude." Monet pushed him aside and strong-armed the window. It shattered, and she kicked the frame clear of shards. She grabbed Jono by the hands. "Here we go," she said, and swooped out the window, Jono suspended under her.

Jono was no sooner clear of the window than he started firing psi-bolts down into the parking lots, sending the Genogoths scattering for cover.

Ev whooped and dived out the window with Jubilee on his back.

Angelo stepped up to the window, stretched out the skin of his arm, and wrapped it around the top of a nearby light standard. He glanced over at Paige, who was busy ripping off her skin to reveal something smooth, red, and shiny underneath. "Hang on," he said, "or not." Then he and Espeth jumped out and swung down into the parking lot, bowling over a group of 'Goths.

Paige stood in the window-frame and looked down. More Genoths were running from all directions. The opening that Espeth and Angelo had opened was closing. They continued to fight valiantly as the mob closed in.

Paige stepped off into space, did a half roll, and landed on her back. There was a loud thump, like a hand-ball hitting the wall, and then she *bounced* twenty feet back into the air.

"Woo-hoo," Angelo whooped as she arced over his head, adding to the confusion. "She's rubber!"

Paige bounced several more times before a group of Genogoths managed to grab her and pull her down. She socked the nearest 'Goth on the jaw, sending him sprawling.

She grinned and hauled off on another one. They seemed shocked, and fell back as she flailed at them. Her grin widened. She didn't know what they'd expected, but as anyone who's ever played dodge-ball knows, rubber can hurt, and her solid-rubber fists were a lot harder than any ball.

Paige looked around. She couldn't see Jubilee, but she could hear her fireworks exploding. There was an enormous moving pile of bodies that must have had either M or Ev under it. A group of 'Goths had managed to get the jump on Jono and were holding him face down in the gravel, but M (leaving, Ev, by elimination, as the bottom of the dogpile) was swooping down to the rescue.

Paige decked another 'Goth. One thing a house full of Kentuckian brothers had taught her, it was how to bare-knuckle fight. The mob parted long enough for her to see Angelo. He had grabbed up a couple handfuls of parking lot gravel, wrapped each fingertip around a substantial chunk, and was using his extended hands like flails or bolos to drive back the mob.

Paige stumbled over a fallen Genogoth. It seemed like they were winning, but she suddenly realized they were no closer to the Xabago. The Genogoths were holding them back by sheer numbers, and more kept appearing.

She caught a glimpse of Black, standing in their window, yelling something, but nobody could hear over the roar of combat.

Then Monet swooped down in front of her. "Bad news," she said. "Reinforcements coming."

"Show me," yelled Paige.

Monet grabbed her hands and lifted her above the crowd.

Paige looked at the road that connected the freeway interchange with Little Latveria. A line of black vehicles was starting to pull into the parking lot. She could see the beginning of it, but as she traced it over the overpass, down the ramp, and onto the freeway, she couldn't see the end. She muttered a curse, also learned from her brothers.

At the lead of the vehicles was a black Volkswagen bus

with some kind of speakers hastily lashed to the roof. Paige had just enough time to wonder what they were for, when the sound started. It was high, piercing, painfully loud. She grabbed her ears. So did everyone else, including the Genogoths.

The brawl came to an instant stop, as people grabbed their heads, doubled over with pain. Then the sound stopped.

The doors of the bus opened. An overweight hippie climbed out of the driver's side, and a tall cowboy in black from the others. They both pulled off big "mouse ear" headphones.

The cowboy pulled a microphone on a cord from inside the van. "This here's the cavalry," his drawling voice boomed from the speakers. "Now break it up, or we'll break it up for you."

CHAPTER ELEVEN

"When a tribe goes to war, the chief cannot order one party to go here and another there; but every man fights in the manner which best pleases himself."

—Charles Darwin
The Voyage of the Beagle, 1909

T hings change.

In short order, the Genogoths were running the hotel. The students of Xavier's school were again their guests, in a new suite, this one without the broken window and with most of the furniture out in the middle of the floor, where it belonged.

Black, Leather, the Genogoth cowboy named Smokey Ashe, and a bunch of the elder Genogoths disappeared into a rented ballroom for a mysterious pow-wow that was still going on hours later.

Before all this could happen, of course, there had to be a cover story. Black and Paige had immediately gone to the manager's office. Black had begun by waving wads of cash around seasoned with intense apologies for their little deception.

"We're from Hollywood, baby. We didn't want, like, to draw too much attention, you know? But we're here to shoot an episode of *Barbie the Dire Wraith Killer*. You know it? Here," he waved his hand at Paige, "meet Barbie. Give the man an autograph, darling."

Ultimately his brush with "celebrity," the offer to rent every vacant room in the hotel and all the meeting space at top rates, to repair the damage done by their over-enthusiastic stunt men, and to provide a generous gratuity in exchange for keeping their visit quiet, had combined to win the manager over.

Everyone seemed to be happy, except for Paige, who back at the suite complained, "Why did *I* have to be Barbie?"

"You've got to admit," said Angelo, grinning, "that the resemblance is uncanny. If the light isn't too good. And if you squint. And if you close one eye. And if you gouge the other eye out with a stick—"

Then, the hitting began. The cost of several feather pillows and a large tip for housekeeping were abruptly added to Black's bill.

Hours passed, allowing time for long-hot-showers, naps, and small doses of gratuitous television viewing. A knock came at the door. It was Black and Espeth.

Jubilee ushered them in. Everyone gathered around to find out what was up.

"It's done," announced Black, "I am again firmly in control of the Genogoths."

"What happened to the trouble guy," asked Paige, "Leather or whatever?"

"He," said Black, "and some of his followers, are being sent to a place where they can reconnect with the simple things and consider their errors and their true mission as Genogoths."

Monet looked at him. "Jimmy Hoffa was one of you, wasn't he?"

Jubilee shook her head in puzzlement. "Jimmy *Whofa*?"

"What," complained Angelo, "no hot irons? No guillotines? No iron maidens? No being drawn-and-quartered by four black Clydesdales? Man, you guys are a major disappointment."

"We're civilized, Mr. Epsinosa. We hold ourselves to higher standards, and I admit—mistakes have been made."

Angelo made a buzzing noise. "I'll take 'Understatements' for a thousand, Alex."

"I acknowledge," he continued, "that this situation has spiraled out of control, and that this was in part our fault. I also acknowledge that our long policy of passive protection of mutants may be inappropriate in this case. Clearly Sharpe's hound program represents a special danger to the mutants we seek to protect, and something must be done."

"Then," said Paige, hopefully, "you agree that Chill, Recall and Pound have to be rescued."

Black nodded grudgingly. "And this program has to be stopped if that's even possible at this point. It isn't going to be easy, but we're prepared to put every resource at our disposal on the effort."

"Sweet," said Ev, "when do we get started?"

"I've put out the call, and every available Genogoth is already converging on the area. Rovers are scouting for a staging area near Sharpe's base and gathering intelligence on how we can approach it. Unfortunately, I can't spare anyone to escort you back to Massachusetts, but I trust you can find your own way."

Ev waved his hand. "Whoa, whoa, whoa! Can't do that, Blackjack. Uh-uh."

"Absolutely not," said Paige.

Jono stepped forward. "We didn't fight our way across six states and turn the Xabago into a bloody pretzel just so we could turn around and drive home before the action starts."

"I'm afraid," said Black, "that isn't open to discussion. This situation has placed too many mutants, including yourselves, at risk already. It's intolerable. You will return home and we will see this matter through."

"Look, Black," Jono loomed over him, "we're people, not your bleeding gene-banks-on-the-hoof. You don't own us, and you don't tell us what to do. We're going, and we don't need your permission."

Black didn't seem intimidated. "Need I remind you that you still don't know the location of the hidden installation?"

Jono glanced at Espeth.

She looked pained. "Look," she said, "I advocated your side of things to the Junta, and I got them to agree to the rescue. That's what you wanted, what we wanted, isn't it? They'd never have changed their minds without what you've done." Her eyes were almost desperate. "I'll get them out, I swear it."

Jono nodded. "Jubilee?"

Jubilee stepped forward, a big grin on her face. "Sorry, Blackhead, but I just got a phone call I've been waiting on. We've got, like, resources of our own, you know? So, nyah!"

"To be more exact," said Paige, "we have a list of abandoned government installations that our buddy Sharpe was reportedly checking out before this whole project went down. Three of them are in North Carolina. Shouldn't take us long to check 'em out. Heck, one-third chance we'll be right the first time."

Angelo tried to look confused. "But, how will we ever know which one? Oh!" He brightened. "That's right! It'll be the one swarming with Genogoths!"

Black was fuming. "Very well, it appears there's nothing I can do to stop you from joining our effort. But we'll do this our way, and you'll join our operation. Agreed?"

Jono crossed his arms in front of him. "Fair enough. No sense tripping over each other's feet."

"And you," he glared at Espeth, "are responsible for these—people. Now, if you'll excuse me, I have an assault to plan." He let himself out of the room.

Espeth grinned weakly. "Well," she said, "here we are, together again."

Sharpe was annoyed as he walked into the office of Sarah Namik, the Foxhole's security officer. He didn't bother to sit down, standing in the open doorway of the tiny, rock-walled space. "I don't like being summoned by my subordinates, Namik, especially without explanation. We're in the middle of a very intense series of capture simulations with the Hounds, and we're evaluating the new subject for conversion as well. I'm a busy man. If you have information of importance, you can bring it to me."

She glanced up from the trio of computer display panels on her desk. "I'm a busy woman, too, Sharpe. Collecting data is my job, and the data all comes *here*, not to wherever you happen to be. Now, do you want to know what I've found, or not?"

He frowned, but grudgingly nodded.

"One of my jobs is to monitor news and intelligence

sources from around the region looking for possible mutant activity or potential threats to the installation. I may have found both."

"What? Where?"

"Fortunately, some distance away, a tourist Mecca called 'Little Latveria,' near the South Carolina border. Official reports are that there was disturbance there yesterday caused by a crew shooting a television show. Stunt people, pyrotechnics, and monster costumes were supposedly involved."

Sharpe's eyes widened. "Mutants?"

"I have an eyewitness report of a woman jumping out of a window onto asphalt and bouncing thirty feet into the air. That's quite a little 'stunt.' So, just to be sure, I sent out a helicopter to fly over the area with mutant detection equipment."

"And found—?"

"Nothing. However, there are indications that some sort of jamming device, like the one at Muddy Gap, may have been in use. It's unfortunate that the jammer there self-destructed before we could examine it. We might be able to develop a counter-measure." She leaned back in her chair. "The implications are alarming though. We may have multiple mutants operating in the region under some kind of detection cloak. Also, a large number of strangely dressed individuals were seen there as well. I have no reason to believe that they were mutants, but somebody has been setting up these jamming devices to protect mutants."

Sharpe nodded. "Somebody organized, with the technical resources to pull something like this off. Somebody whose agenda would put them into direct conflict with our own. In one of our monitoring tapes, the subjects mentioned the possibility of rescue. We dismissed it, but—"

"I want to up the alert level, send out regular armed patrols."

Sharpe shook his head. "That will only make us more visible. It's time to run silent, run deep. No aircraft are to launch without my authorization. All personnel are confined to base until further notice. No outside patrols or maintenance crews. We have the best automated defenses money can buy and we're burrowed into solid rock." He chuckled. "If they can find us," he said, "let them come."

After a welcome, overnight stay in the Doomstad hotel, Generation X loaded up the Xabago and, with Espeth aboard, limped their way to the Genogoths' staging area, an abandoned state maintenance yard somewhere west of Greenville.

By the time they pulled in, it was late afternoon, and the Genogoths were already well settled. The crushed-stone yards were full of vehicles ranging in size from Volkswagen Beetles to semi-trucks, tents were set up, and camp fires were burning.

A remarkable metamorphosis had taken place as well. Now it was rare to see the leathers, nose rings, and black turtlenecks they'd come to expect from the Genogoths. Black was still the color of the day, but now it was commando black, dark fatigues, combat boots, and web belts with hunting knives. The mood in the camp was efficient and businesslike.

They all piled out of their battered motorhome and took a stroll around the compound.

"These people," said Paige, clearly impressed, "are loaded for bear."

Ev nodded toward the main gate, where another caravan of vehicles were pulling in. "I thought there were lots of them at Little Latveria. They just keep coming."

"Black is bringing in everyone he can," explained Espeth. "We have people coming from back home in Washington, California, Mexico, Canada, even a few from Europe and South America. Whoever could get here quick."

Angelo shook his head. "All these people, humans, out to protect mutants. I should be getting all Hallmark-warm-and-fuzzy-chick-flick-weepy. Instead, it just makes my skin crawl, and that's saying a lot in my case."

"Don't be so quick to judge," said Jono. "They mean well, even if we don't agree with everything they stand for. Look at 'em. These blokes look ready to lay it all on the line for our buds."

"They are," said Espeth. "They're ready to die for the cause if need be."

"Let's hope that won't be necessary," said Paige. "I'd hate to be beholdein."

Near the center of the compound they came upon Leather's confiscated van, now being used as a command post, and parked next to it, the Volkswagen van that had led the rescue charge at Little Latveria. Unlike most of the other Genogoths, its driver still wore his traditional garb. He sat at a folding table, staring through a magnifier at some tiny electronic device. He looked up as they approached and nodded.

"Guys," said Espeth, "this is Styx. He's cool."

"Cool," said Styx, "definitely cool. It's a groove since we didn't get introduced."

Jono reached out and gave him a shake. "Thanks for coming to the rescue, yesterday. It was turning ugly."

"My pleasure," he said. He glanced over at Ev, who reached out to touch the support post in the middle of the bus's windshield.

Ev grinned at him. "Phat Type 2, split-window, dude." He glanced around at the little row of oblong portholes high on the sides. "Twenty-one windows. *Definitely* phat."

"Ah," said Styx, "a connoisseur. Another day, I'd give you a walk-around and show you what's under the deck. No time right now though. Bummer. Glad you guys came by though. Saves me looking for you." He picked up something about the size and shape of an aspirin pill, made of flesh-colored plastic. "Need to give each one of you guys one of these."

Jubilee bent closer to examine it, puzzled.

"You put it in your ear," he demonstrated. "It's a radical little radio-com I designed. Wear it, and you're plugged-in, tuned-in, turned-on, and freaked out." He handed each of them one. "Espeth will show you how to use them," he said. "Then it's official. Welcome to the Genogoth army!"

• • •

Sharpe lowered the VR glasses for a check. They lacked good intelligence on the interior of the Pacific University M.O.N.S.T.E.R. house, so the entire simulation was set outside. Still, it seemed effective enough. Mutants, dozens of them, scrambled around in terror as the three armored figures and their pack of cyberhounds circled, containing them like a flock of sheep.

One by one they were taken down, lassoed or netted by the new capture-weapons in the Hounds' gauntlets. Immobilized, tagged, and put aside for pick-up. It was a model of efficiency, and it was going off without a hitch.

"Bloodhound," Sharpe said into his headset mike, "torch the building."

The Hound in red broke from the format and marched closer to the front of the house. He held up his right arm, and there was a whir and a click as the small rotary grenade launcher on his wrist locked in an incendiary round. He aimed at a big window to the right of the front door. There was a muffled *whoof*, the clattering of shattered glass, and then an explosion of flames behind the curtains. Bloodhound turned back to the job of rounding up mutants. As the flames spread, rapidly enveloping the building, he never looked back.

Sharpe removed the glasses and set them on the console. He'd seen enough. He looked over at Happersen and grinned. "Life is good."

Generation X had changed into their fighting togs before accompanying Espeth on the scouting mission. She had scowled her disapproval when she'd first seen them. "I really should scare you up something black," she said. "The dark red tights are okay, but all that yellow sticks out in the moonlight like a beacon."

Angelo had dismissed her concerns. "Get over it, chica. You said yourself, Black doesn't want us going anywhere near the place, just close enough to take a look."

They all piled into a borrowed black (of course) Humvee and headed into the low, tree-covered, mountains. Their destination was not the base, but a nearby peak where they could get a look at it, and where other Genogoth patrols were already searching for a place to install a command post.

They waited for moonrise, then used its light, with some help from a night-vision scope, to make it up logging roads to the top. It was something of a disappointment. "It just looks like another mountain," Angelo muttered. "I wouldn't know there was anything there, if you hadn't told me." His eyes narrowed suspiciously. "This isn't some wacko scheme to get us out of the way while Black hits the real base, is it?"

Espeth frowned. "Angelo, no! Here." She handed him the night-vision binoculars. She pointed him down the slope. "See that? That's the only direct access road. It winds up to a fortified tunnel entrance about five hundred feet below the summit. You can just see the top of the portal, that big concrete thing. The entrance road will be monitored, so no way in there. We'll take logging roads in from other directions, then come in overland on foot."

Angelo lowered the binoculars. "Where's the rest of it?"

"Underground, mostly, dug into the rock. There are some air shafts scattered around the upper slopes, what look like defensive installations of some kind, and a big camouflaged door that may be where they keep their helicopters and maybe other aircraft. We're hoping there are some weak spots up there that we can exploit."

Angelo looked at her, incredulously. "Hope? You don't know how you're going to get in?"

Espeth looked doubtful. "I know it looks like a hard egg," she said, "but tomorrow night we have to find a way to crack it."

CHAPTER TWELVE

"As the species of the same genus usually have, though by no means invariably, much similarity in habits and constitution, and always in structure, the struggle will generally be more severe between them, if they come into competition with each other, than between the species of distinct genera."

—Charles Darwin

On the Origin of the Species, 1859

The first movements of the attack started before dawn, as one by one the vehicles began to pack up and roll out of the staging area and move to forward positions closer to the Hound base. The movements would be spread out through the day, and the vehicles would take different routes, so as to avoid attracting the attention that a convoy would.

The Xabago left about noon. They might have departed earlier, except that Jono had trouble getting it started, and several hours of tinkering and cursing under the hood were necessary to get it operational.

Jono listened sadly to the motor once they finally got it cranked. "I tell you, this banger has about had it. It's gone all duff on us."

"Translation," cracked Angelo, "we'll be lucky to make it to Smash Mountain, much less back here, much less back to the school."

"Well," said Paige, "if it breaks down there, at least it'll make it harder for Black to get rid of us."

Jubilee grinned. "We could always have Monet push us home."

Monet looked at her askance. "If any biological spare parts could be of use, I'd be glad to donate Jubilee's."

Angelo shook his head sadly. "It's past that. I hope Leather-guy left his gun. We may have to shoot this thing."

Namik leaned forward on her desk and turned one of her desk screens around to show Sharpe. It was a complex line graph, the meaning of which wasn't obvious to "Him." "The submarine metaphors you used earlier," she explained, "are entirely appropriate. The automated detection network installed in the woods around the mountain is quite good, but I've never been one to leave well-enough alone, and God knows there isn't much else to do here. I've done some reading about submarines and passive sonar, and it gave me an idea. A few months ago, I had directional microphones installed on some of our exterior fixtures directed into the lowlands at the base of the mountain. It was cheap, didn't involve putting hardware outside the inner perimeter, and I could bootleg capacity on some of the research computers to automate the monitoring."

"You're saying," said Sharpe, "that you can *hear* someone out there?"

She shook her head. "Not exactly. I'm fairly certain that we have people moving around down there on foot. There have to be vehicles out there somewhere, but they're keeping them at a distance. So far, we haven't definitively heard anyone."

Sharpe frowned, "But you said—"

"Let me explain. After a few weeks of recording data on the mikes, I was able to develop certain patterns in the natural sounds. When disturbed, some animals flee, make loud sounds, or both. Others become very quiet and try to hide. The passage of a human through the forest, even one moving very quietly, leaves a 'fingerprint' in the natural sounds." She tapped a fingernail on the screen displaying the graph. "I was able to verify this by monitoring the movement of our own patrols and technicians, as well as the occasional hiker or hunter who strayed into our area." She pursed her lips and took a deep breath. "There is a sizable force, on foot, surrounding the Foxhole. I think we can safely assume they're hostile. If I could send out a helicopter or an ATV patrol, I could verify it."

A complex wave of emotion crossed Sharpe's face. He seemed almost pleased. "They've come," he said. "I knew they would. They always come. Last time they caught me unawares, unprepared. Thanks to your excellent work, Namik, that won't happen this time. Last time it cost me, dearly." The corners of his mouth curled up into a slow smile. "But this time I'm ready. This time, they'll pay." He looked back at her. "No, my orders stand. We don't provoke them, we don't show our hand. Nothing short of an armored assault could dig us out of these tunnels. Let them come, and once they're here, this whole mountain will blow up in their faces."

Sharpe turned and marched off down the hall.

Namik returned her screen to its regular position. She would continue to follow Sharpe's orders, running drills on the security personnel, verifying that all the automatic defenses were in full readiness, and waiting for the attack that now seemed inevitable.

But she would also have another agenda, one that served other masters, the men and women who had assigned Sharpe and the survivors of Project Homegrown to this isolated outpost. Sharpe's mental stability had been in question for some time. Namik had been sent here as insurance, a plant to collect what data could be salvaged if the worst happened, and most importantly, to maintain full deniability. If necessary, Sharpe's Hounds, this installation, and everyone in it, would be destroyed, and every trace of official sanction erased. Sharpe would be yet another madman in a hidden lair, working toward some ill-defined diabolical goals. Nobody would suspect a rogue government agency. It had happened often enough before.

The mechanisms were already in place, as fundamental to the construction of Foxhole as the air-conditioning or the plumbing. Namik had only to set them in motion.

Perhaps soon.

As the Xabago approached the area of the hidden installation, the radio earpieces they wore came to life. Espeth told them that the units were low power, short range, scrambled, and operated on frequencies adjacent to those used by common consumer-electronic devices. Even if someone did pick up the signals, they'd probably be mistaken for the garbled transmissions from someone's malfunctioning cordless phone.

The Genogoths were nothing if not organized. A dispatcher routed them to a roadside parking area just off the main highway and offered to send a vehicle to shuttle them into the forward staging area. They declined, and asked for directions to Black's command post. Then, in three trips, Monet and Ev ferried them in by air.

The command post was set up in a rocky notch facing out on the installation. Rope handrails, and camouflage netting had been placed over the exposed end of the notch during the night, providing a natural, and invisible, location to look directly down on the site. Lookouts with binoculars and spotter scopes were already stationed there.

Ten yards or so back from this was the command center, a cluster of folding tables and free-standing equipment. Styx, Smokey Ashe, and several other Genogoths they didn't recognize, were operating communications equipment, consulting computers, or checking maps.

Black was there, leaning over a table on which he had spread a large topological map of the area. Jono, Espeth, and Paige went over to talk with him.

"I wish these maps were trustworthy," he said to himself as much as them. "This has been a top-secret installation since at least the mid-60s, and I wouldn't be surprised if the U.S. Geological Survey maps have been doctored. Most of the available satellite photos conveniently have gaps in this area. We don't even know how much of the terrain we see out there is natural. It looks pristine from a distance, but—"

"So," interrupted Jono, "what would you like us to do? Monet and Ev could fly down to scout for you, or maybe even get high enough to shoot some aerial photos for you."

Black looked at him and raised an eyebrow. "What I'd like for you to do is stay here while my people make the assault on this 'Houndbase.' After the situation is contained, perhaps we can bring you in to help mop things up."

Paige's mouth fell open. "What? You said we'd be part of your operation."

"You are. You and your friends are part of the reserve force. But I'm not about to put mutants in jeopardy on the front lines of such a potentially dangerous operation."

"Bloody hell!" Jono glared at him. "We told you, Black, that we aren't your bleeding livestock to push around."

"Young man," he said, careful to keep his voice level. "This is a large and carefully coordinated operation. Even if you were not mutants, I wouldn't trust its success to a handful of untrained children."

That was too much for Jono, who lunged forward. Only Paige's intervention prevented a more personal confrontation. She stood in front of him, holding his shoulders, and gently pushed him back. "Listen, Jono, maybe he's right. Not about us, but about what we should be doing here. We don't know these guys, and they don't know us. We'd just end up getting in each other's way."

His brow wrinkled as he considered her words, but he didn't say anything.

"In any case," she continued, "if they don't want us there, then the worst thing we can do for our friends is to bull our way into the operation."

"Espeth," Black said. "Your situation is different on several counts, and it would seem that you have some need to redeem yourself among the Genogoths." He pointed at the map. "We could use you in the first wave up the near flank."

She grinned and nodded. "I'm so there." Then she turned to Jono, her expression apologetic. "Sorry, Jono, I know you and your 'mates' would like to be there too. But I'm doing this for our friends. I'll be fighting for all of you."

"Yeah," he said, "whatever."

After Espeth departed for the front lines, the Generation Xers gathered on a rock outcropping overlooking the command area. The overall mood had the character of a wake.

"I am *so* bummed out," said Jubilee. "I don't like missing out on the fun."

"Doesn't look like fun," said Jono, who perched on a rock facing away from the others, his knees drawn up in front of him. "It looks like war to me. These blokes look good, but they still aren't carrying guns. I've got a bad feeling about it."

Paige looked at him. "But—?"

"But, I'd rather be down there too. And I'm worried about Espeth. She's like on to try n' prove something, do something bloody stupid. Black is like, 'hey, we need some cannon-fodder,' and she's right at the front of the queue with her hand up."

Paige's face was a mask, and she became very quiet.

"Hey, Jono, don't sweat it," said Jubilee. "She's a survivor. I mean, none of *us* have killed her yet, and what are the odds of that?"

"Yeah." Angelo laughed. "Nobody survives the 'wrath of Monet.' "

Monet sat off to one side, inspecting her nails. "I like her. She's interesting. It's the rest of you that bore me to tears. I would like to break something right now though. That, or go back to the hotel. I never did get to try the Jacuzzi-tub."

"Uh-huh," said Angelo dryly. "Thanks for sharing."

Styx and Smokey Ashe wandered over. Smokey tipped his hat to the girls. "Hear tell that Black told you young'uns to hold back with the reserves. Just came to express my sympathies."

"What's it to you?" Jubilee snapped.

"Black's made me the new field commander for this little rodeo. Puts me a little closer to the action than you when the excitement starts, but me, I'd just as soon be the first one up the hill. Heard you got some friends in there. Well, I got me one too. Feller name of Catfish. Hope you can meet him when this is all over."

Jubilee's mouth contracted to a tight pucker, and she stared seriously down at her feet. "Didn't know," she said.

"I know it's hard for you young'uns, that you're riled at Black, but it'd be a great favor to me, my buddy Catfish, and to your three friends, if you'd do what he says and stay here. I'd feel a right bit better knowing you were watching our backs when we go up that hill."

They all reluctantly agreed.

Smokey tipped his hat again. "I got to get down with the

troops. Sun will be down soon, and we hit 'em when the moon comes up."

He turned and left. Styx grinned, as though he'd suddenly materialized on the spot. "Listen," he said, "I get the feeling that, sooner or later, you dudes are going to be going down there. I want you to be on the lookout for any of this stuff." He pulled out a handful of six-inch sections of cable, in various sizes and colors and fanned them out for inspection. "You see any, call me in a hurry."

Ev inspected it closely. "What is it? Are we going to steal their cable TV?"

Styx grinned. "Close. This is—"

"Optical fiber," said Monet, before he could finish. "Low-loss, full-spectrum, ultra-wide data-bandwidth, mil-spec/S.H.I.E.L.D.-spec." Everyone looked at her and she shrugged. "Sometimes I read *Aviation Week* at the library. It's more interesting than *Vibe*."

"So," continued Ev, "what do you want with this stuff?"

"I'm a hacker," he said, "but every wire coming out of this place is shut down tight. Find me a wire *into* the place, and you never know what might happen."

Smokey Ashe lay on his belly watching the slow movements of the heavily camouflaged Genogoth commandos on the hillside above. They climbed carefully over where the tree-covered mountainside was broken by open rock. He waited until they had moved out of sight over the next rise before moving forward a few yards himself.

Something with too many legs had slipped inside his shirt and was now crawling across his bare back. He ignored it. In his ear, he could hear whispered radio traffic as the advance troops coordinated their work. Occasionally he would whisper a command or bit of encouragement, but mostly, they knew their jobs. Good thing, he thought, given that he hadn't commanded a major field operation in nearly two decades. He hoped Black's confidence in him wasn't misplaced.

The widely distributed force moved up the slope an inch at

a time. A massive frontal assault on an installation like this would never work. Even a direct hit with a nuke might not take out the lower levels.

Instead, they had mapped out the location of the ventilator shafts, and fed down hoses connected to nausea-gas bombs. As a nuclear-hardened installation, the ventilators would be designed to slam shut at the slightest sign of contamination, but the crush-proof hoses ran all the way to the bottom of the shaft, and would block any shutters or louvers slightly open, allowing a passage for the compressed gas.

If the Genogoths couldn't open the Hound base's doors from the outside, the natural thing to do was to get occupants to unlock them from the inside. Most of his people were stationed around the big hangar door. As the largest, highest, and best hidden opening in the installation, it was the logical door to open in order to expel the noxious gas. The timers on the bombs were set to go off at four A.M. The anti-mutant forces inside were in for a literal rude awakening.

Then he heard Espeth's whispered voice in his ear. "Smokey, I just found some kind of *seam* in this rock outcropping my group is just passing. It seems artificial, I think we may have missed some—" Then a moment of silence. Suddenly her voice was loud, even yelling. "Darwin's name!"

Then things got worse.

"It's quite clever," said Namik to Sharpe. "Pressure-forced gas released deep in the system, bypassing all our safety systems. It might have worked too, if I hadn't had enough warning to shut down the ventilators well before they got there. They have their hoses at what they think are the bottoms of the shafts. Actually they're stopped at the closure of the number one safety louvers. We're on internal oxygen now."

Sharpe nodded. "Which gives us about a week before we have to worry about that particular problem. I don't think we'll need near that long."

Namik's hand hovered over a switch on her defensive panel. It was labeled AUTOMATED DEFENSE TURRET MASTER-

SAFETY, and below that there were three switch positions, STANDBY, AUTO, and ACTIVE. The switch was set at STANDBY.

Sharpe watched the screen. Their camouflage was good. Even with the infrared cameras, he could barely see the figures crawling up the mountain. But he *could* see them. And if he could see them, so could the turrets.

Namik looked at him. "Now?"

He nodded. "Do it."

She pushed the switch under her hand to ACTIVE.

Espeth lay stretched out on a rock shelf, her fingers forced into the narrow gap at the base of the rock outcropping, trying to determine how deep it was, and if it was definitely as artificial as it seemed. It would be an embarrassment if it just turned out to be some natural cleft.

A jagged rock edge cut into her stomach. She was glad she'd left the belly ring back at camp. If the piercing closed up, it would be the least of her problems. She tasted chalky rock dust on her lips and some of it stung her left eye. She pushed her fingers deeper.

Suddenly the rock under her body began to vibrate, and the cleft she'd been probing parted with a snap and a high-pitched whine. Her hands slipped into empty space, then touched smooth, oiled, *moving* metal.

She said something loud and unintended, she didn't know what. Then rolled back out of the way. She could see the whole outcropping rising up in the moonlight, like a sprouting mushroom, and under it something large and moving, something that rotated toward her. She saw the twin gun barrels, black against the sky just before the flash blinded her.

Black stood in the lookout at the end of the notch. Even with the night vision scope there wasn't much to see. That should change once the gas grenades went off.

He heard someone walk up beside him. It was the English lad, Starsmore. "I trust your friends are getting some rest?"

"Most of 'em," he said, his odd telepathic voice in Black's

mind. "I couldn't sleep though, not with Espeth down there. Not even if this bloody operation is—Well, I've watched more exciting paint dry. Plus, I figured you'd like to know we were being good little *muties* and staying out of trouble."

Black sighed. "It's not like that. I wish I could make you understand."

They both heard Espeth's cry of alarm in their ear-set radios. Then the muzzle flashes started, in a belt around the mountain, about half-way up the slope, and behind most of the Genogoth forces, followed by dancing lines of tracer bullets, and the rattling roar of machine guns.

"Bloody hell!" Jono stared out into the night, trying to figure out what was happening.

He could hear the frantic calls on the radio, cries of the wounded, and requests for reinforcements. The Genogoths were pinned down and on the verge of being eaten alive. "Be careful," he muttered to himself, "what you bleeding ask for."

Espeth lay on her back, colored balls and streaks like one of Jubilee's light shows still clouding her vision. She could see the gun turret above her transversing rapidly and firing in response to any movement or sound. She lay, almost literally, in its shadow, too close for the guns to tilt down and lock on her, a tiny umbrella of safety in a sea of hellish fire. She was fine, so long as she didn't rise from the ground or move more than a few yards from her current position. Violate either of those two conditions however, and the guns would cut her in half in a millisecond.

Jono moved through the group, his carefully focused telepathic voice rousing his fellow Generation Xers without alerting anyone else in the area. Several of them, including Paige and Monet, hadn't been as asleep as he'd thought.

He explained, once they were all up, "The whole lot of them got ambushed by some kind of machine-gun turrets. There are wounded. Espeth—Well, she was the first one to sound the alarm. I don't know what happened to her."

Jubilee rubbed her eyes. "Did old Blackhead sign off on this?"

"What he don't bloody know," said Jono, "won't hurt him. Why give him a chance to say 'no'?"

"Good point," said Jubilee.

"Do I get to break something now?" asked Monet.

"Ooooh, yeah," said Angelo, "I think you do."

Paige was pacing, in furious thought. "From what you've said, they're pinned down up there. We need to punch a hole in those defenses so they have a line of retreat."

Jono stepped forward. "I can blast them from a distance."

Paige frowned. "That makes sense, but using your power and keeping your head down is an oxymoron. Don't get anything *else* blown off."

"Point taken, luv."

"I can fly him up," said Monet.

Paige nodded. "Ev can take one more up. I could do something bullet-proof."

Jono's eyes narrowed. "These are some pretty big bullets."

"I'll go," said Jubilee.

Angelo looked incredulous. "What? You'll get killed."

"No more than Jono will! This is just like a walk through the old Danger Room for me. I can handle it. And I'll keep those turrets busy while the fly-guys shuttle the rest of you in."

Paige studied Jubilee's eyes for any sign of doubt. "Take her, Ev. Just don't get shot on the way up, even if it means she has to climb the last bit herself."

"I can handle it," said Jubilee, confidently.

"I hope so," said Paige.

Smokey wiped a streak of blood off his face. A near-miss had shattered a rock near his head, showering him with sharp fragments. He was grateful none of them had hit him in the eye. Unlike most of his troops, he was below the line of fire. If he was careful, he might be able to retreat down the slope. If he wanted to.

He cleared his throat and spit. He could see the flashes from turrets on either side of him. Ahead, a split between some rocks seemed to offer cover. He started to climb.

More flashes. He threw himself down before realizing that these were not tracers or muzzle flashes, but dancing ribbons and spheres of colored lights that swarmed up the hillside like a flock of fairies. The turrets all turned, locking on the rapidly moving lights, firing again and again. The bullets passed through the lights harmlessly.

He was still puzzling it out when something large and dark whooshed over his head, like an enormous owl swooping down on a field mouse. Then it was gone, and he was left to wonder if this was a good time to start being superstitious.

Monet dropped Jono off just below a ridge line, then turned back to go pick up Paige. Jono could see the flashes of the turrets just above him. He climbed up the rocks, loose pebbles slipping under his boots as he climbed. Near the top, he paused, popped his head up for a quick peek, then back down again.

A moment later, a line of bullets ricocheted off the rocks just above him. He would have whistled if he'd been so equipped. He'd just caught a glimpse of the turret, a metal tower mounted with twin machine guns, a fake boulder sitting on top like a party hat, and it had still had time to lock on and take a shot at him.

He was guessing, *guessing*, that a full-force TK blast would disable the turret. Trouble was, he'd have only one chance at it, and he'd have to be fast. There'd be no time to duck if he missed, or if he didn't have enough juice. "Don't think," he coached himself, "just do it. Use the bloody force, Luke."

Jono tugged down the wrappings over his face and chest. Flickering orange light from the energy that filled his body danced on the rock face. "Great," he said, "I'm a blinking illuminated target. Oh, well."

He braced his feet so he could pop-up like a Jack-in-the-box, silently counted to three, and then jumped.

Loud things happened.

GENOGOTHS

• • •

Jubilee moved up the slope gesturing like a puppeteer operating marionettes. In fact, what she was doing wasn't much different. The plasma constructs she controlled drew the fire from the nearby turrets. Every time a gun would swing toward her, she would draw it away with one of her little targets.

It was good for a laugh, but it was getting old, and she was getting tired of concentrating so hard. Keeping this many objects under such control was taking a lot out of her.

Not to say that she was otherwise straining her abilities. Fact was, Jubilee's powers scared her. A lot. She'd once blown up an entire house, and since then she'd usually kept her plasma projections at the level of fireworks. But there were times when you just had to cut loose.

She crossed her arms over her head, left hand pointed right, right hand pointed left. She bit her lip until she tasted blood. It wasn't the bullets that scared her.

A blast of plasma shot from each hand like a rocket, and they lanced toward the two nearest turrets.

Then the world seemed to explode.

Espeth climbed as far under the turret as she could. She knew that, if it retracted right now, she'd be squashed like an insect, but she had to find a weakness, some way of disabling the turret. It was dark down there, the turret and rock shell above blocking most of the moonlight. She tried to puzzle things out by the light of the strobe-like flashes, by touch without getting her fingers caught in the constantly moving mechanism.

Then she heard a shout. She rolled over in time to see someone running across the open ground toward her, saw the turret spin above her head, was deafened by the report as the running figure was cut down, fell and lay still.

Espeth's mouth was open in an unvoiced scream. *Who?*

The turret swung away, tracking for another target.

And the figure was up and sprinting toward her. The guns

came round again. The figure ducked, the guns passing over his—no—*her* head.

She ducked, rolled into the recess under the turret next to Espeth. Espeth reached out to touch a hand, shockingly cold and metallic.

"Well, Espeth, darlin'," said Paige, "fancy meeting you here."

Smokey ducked behind a tree. Ahead of him he could see an open space, and in the middle of it, what looked like a girl, doing what almost looked like some kind of dance. It took a moment to register. *Those mutant kids. Did Black actually send them in?*

Then the girl swung her arms and some instinct told him to cover his eyes. For a split second he saw the bones in his fingers, black outlines in red. When he uncovered his face, the two closest turrets were smoking ruins. He'd lost sight of the girl though. Then, to his right, another explosion, orange, not as bright, but with a force that he felt deep in his chest. Another turret fell silent.

No time to look for the girl now. "All forces," he said to the radio, "we got breaks in the defenses on the west and northwest quadrants of the mountain. Fall back and regroup outside the fire zone. I repeat, fall back and regroup!"

Sharpe watched the red lights appear on the defense console. Namik gave him a look of concern.

Sharpe shook his head. "They're just the outer defenses. They're no closer to getting inside than they were two hours ago."

"Do you want me to send out the defense drones?"

"Save them," he smiled slightly, "there are mutants out there. This is just the opportunity I've been looking for to play my aces in the hole."

Ev didn't have as much confidence in his synched invulnerability as Monet did in hers, but he found that if he flew fast, low, and erratically enough, the turrets couldn't *quite* get a lock on him. The near misses were getting unnerving though, and it was a great relief to fly into the zone cleared by the two exploding turrets. Around him, Genogoth commandos were scurrying down the mountain.

One, a muscular woman with close-cropped hair stopped and put a hand on his shoulder. "Get yourself to safety. *Please.*"

He shrugged her hand off and proceeded to climb up the slope. Those were Jubilee's plasma balls. She had to be around here *somewhere*.

Something moved in a clump of bushes to his right. "Ev," a voice said weakly. "Synch?"

"Jubilee?" He followed the voice. She was curled on her side in the bushes. He reached to help her up, and she threw her arms around him. She was trembling.

"I think I did good, Ev."

He nodded. "You did good." He realized that he was supporting most of her weight.

"Could you take me out of here, Ev? Someplace where I can blow-chunks in peace?"

Paige hammered on the turret's mechanisms with her metal fists, but other than making a sound like an anvil concert, it didn't seem to be doing any good. "I could pound on this thing a week before doing any damage," she grumbled.

Espeth pointed over at the next turret. "Notice how that one has a clear shot of us, but hasn't taken it? I think they're programmed not to shoot each other."

Paige squinted up at the moving gun barrels. "I wonder how much force it would take to redirect the aim?" She reached up and grabbed the barrels as they swung by. The barrels were nearly red hot, but she barely noticed it through her metal skin. She felt the guns elevate to avoid pointing at the next turret, tried to pull them down. They resisted, moved a little, then lifted her weight off the ground. She grunted and dropped free.

She looked at Espeth. "How much do you weigh?"

"*What?*"

"Never mind. Let's just hope it's enough. Grab around my waist, and hold on for all you're worth."

The gun swung back in the other direction, tracers shooting out. Espeth grabbed her. Paige grabbed the guns. Felt them resist. Felt her body lifting. Something inside the mechanism slipped. She dropped. The next turret was blasted full of holes, something inside caused a small explosion, and the guns fell dead.

Paige kicked her feet in delight. "Whoo-hoo!" She rolled. There was another turret to the north. "Crawl over this way," she said to Espeth, "we'll do it again."

"A couple yards of extra skin," complained Angelo, as he ducked behind a boulder. "More area to put holes in is what it is."

Then there was a sound like a mallet striking metal. The whir of the turret's mechanism became labored, then turned into a screech. Something snapped, and the shooting stopped.

Angelo cautiously poked his head over the rock. Monet stood in front of the turret, one of the two twisted gun barrels still in her hand. She let go of it, and the barrels swung down to the limit of their travel with a clang. She spun and did a spinning side-kick, smashing a panel above the barrels that seemed to be the tracking system. "That was refreshing," she said. Then she squinted at him. "You make a good target, Angelo."

He scrambled up the slope. "Thanks a bunch, *chica*. Thanks a bunch." As he passed the disabled turret, a glint of something light-colored caught his eye. He turned back and peered inside the smashed sensor panel. "M, wait up. I got something here."

There was a crack in the panel, too small to get his hand into, but he was easily able to snake his extended skin through the opening. He fished around blindly for a minute. "Ah!" He pulled the skin back out slowly and produced a bit of blue cable with a connector and a fragment of circuit board still hanging from the end. He carefully pulled, and was able to extract several yards of slack cable before it stopped moving. He held up the end of the wire and grinned. "Get Styx on the horn. We got Satan's pay-per-view right here!"

Smokey looked up the slope as another turret went out. There was now a gaping hole in the defenses. There were wounded, but they were being pulled back for evacuation. Now that surprise was no longer an issue, the helicopters could be brought in to fly them to hospitals.

Around him, his troops were regrouping. There was an opportunity in front of them, and he was going to do what he could with it. But just in case. He spoke to his radio. "Black, this is Smokey. Listen, old son, principles are a good thing far as they'll take you, but those kids just saved us from havin' our heads handed to us in our hats. We lost our element o' surprise. We need some heavy firepower here, and we need it pronto."

Jono crouched behind the rocks, ready to do his trick again. *One, two, three, GO!* He jumped up, and a millisecond before he let loose with his blast, saw the two people crouched under the turret. He fought back the blast. It was like swallowing a mouthful of bile, when he'd still had a mouth.

The turret's guns swung around. He looked down the black center of the two barrels and saw death there.

Then the guns retracted. The turret began to lower back into the ground, and the two people underneath scrambled out just in time. Only when they were in the full moonlight did he recognize them. "Paige! Espeth!" He ran toward them as the turret settled into the ground, again looking like just another boulder.

"Hi, Jono." But Paige was distracted. She stared at the rock. "Why do I think this isn't a good thing?"

Then a wind kicked up around them. Espeth clutched at her exposed arms and shivered.

GENERATION X

It started to snow.

Something low and dark rushed by, so quickly that Jono couldn't quite focus on it, and then another. Glowing red eyes surveyed them from the shadows.

A movement up-slope caught his eye. Three figures were visible there, outlined against the sky. They wore some sort of armor, but the body types were eerily familiar.

"Oh, no," said Espeth.

"I don't think," said Jono, "that it's the Powerpuff Girls."

CHAPTER THIRTEEN

"The final aim of all love intrigues, be they comic or tragic, is really of more importance than all other ends in human life. What it all turns upon is nothing less than the composition of the next generation. . . . It is not the weal or woe of any one individual, but that of the human race to come, which is here at stake."

—"Schopenhauer and Darwinism"
Journal of Anthropology, Jan. 1871

"**T**argets acquired," said the voice of Bloodhound, "two mutants, one human noncombatant."

Sharpe grimaced. The training protocols had made the assumption that the Hounds would be collecting mutants from among innocent humans. He should have known that in a true war, nobody is an innocent bystander. He activated his headset mike. "Override authority Sharpe, Omega-zero. All humans not identified as Foxhole personnel are assumed to be hostile. Collection of humans is unnecessary. Eliminate threat only."

He turned off the mike and reviewed what he'd said. The Hounds weren't robots. Verbal commands had to be carefully phrased and unambiguous.

There were three of them on the screen, and it was obvious which two were the mutants. One, a female, seemed to have a body made of living metal. The other, a male, had some kind of energy coming from his lower face. *Or*—Sharpe squinted and leaned toward the screens connected to the helmet cameras. *Good Lord. Half his face was missing.* Sharpe had seen things like that before, fighting in the South American jungles, but those people had had the good grace to lie down and die.

He activated the mike again. "Dispatch targets, but not too quickly. Use this as a training opportunity. Prioritize capturing the male. I want to see what makes him tick."

The three armored figures stopped a dozen yards up-slope from Jono, Paige and Espeth. The closest of the three, in the purple, by the build had to be Dog Pound. Paige felt her stomach knot. Pound, despite his rather fearsome appearance, had to be one of the sweetest and most inoffensive guys she'd ever met. What had they done to him?

She stepped a little closer, careful not to make any threatening moves. "Pound, it's me, Paige? Remember? I don't want to hurt you, any of you. Please, fight whatever it is they're doing."

Pound just stood there. Then something smashed into the front of her body with a clang, throwing her back onto the ground, landing on top of her. The robot dog snapped at her throat viciously, the serration of its metal teeth rattling across her skin.

She struggled to throw the thing off, but something else grabbed her right wrist, then her left, then her legs. Teeth were sawing at her. She couldn't stay in this form forever, and if she changed back now, she'd be cut into pieces before she had time to scream.

Smokey Ashe followed the charge back up the slope, an open run rather than a slow crawl. The Xavier kids had opened at least a temporary hole in the defenses. Smokey didn't like charging into the unknown without a plan.

His people had demolition gear, but lacked heavy weapons. Still, Genogoths were nothing if not resourceful, and it was too good an opportunity to pass up. In a few hours, the turrets might be repaired or replaced with something else, and in less time the sun would be up, losing what advantage the little remaining darkness might offer.

He stopped for a moment to catch his breath. He wasn't as young as he used to be. Then, ahead of him, he heard a cry of alarm, and another one. He didn't see any defenses, didn't hear any shots or explosions, but suddenly he saw people in front of him going down.

He dropped into a crouch, alert for danger, but the only unusual sound was a wet, greasy, crackling noise. Then he looked down. The ground under his feet was *boiling*. Or rather something was boiling *out* of it. Earthworms, grubs, larvae, maggots, soft slimy things by the thousands, the *millions*.

Slippery things. Suddenly he was falling, sliding down the steep mountainside. He tried to stop himself, and got only handfuls of slime for his trouble. He rolled, got half his face coated with slime and squirming things, saw that others were sliding down the mountain with him, until the odd tree or rock painfully stopped their progress.

He rolled again, trying to steer himself away from one of those sudden stops, and saw that this wouldn't be a problem. He sailed over the ledge and saw the ground thirty feet below. Then he hit leaves, branches slowing his fall. He grabbed, slipped, grabbed again, twisted, fell, and landed solidly on the lower branch of a tree. He clenched his eyes tightly shut and wrapped his arms and legs around it, feeling the blessed loss of motion.

With luck, some of his ribs were still intact. With luck, there was some part of him unbruised, unscratched. With luck he'd have the taste of worm guts out of his mouth in a week or so. Then Smokey opened his eyes and knew that any luck he had at the moment was bad.

The hawk sat on the limb only a yard from him. It contemplated him only a moment before trying to sink its talons in his face.

Angelo sprinted as fast as he could while holding his arms in front of him. The skin on his fingers shot out, wrapped around a low tree limb, and allowed him to swing up to safety just as the wild pigs squealed by underneath. He pulled himself tightly to the limb and listened to the earphone radio, not believing what he was hearing. He scrambled up onto the limb just as Monet came down to hover just out of the circling pig's reach. "Did you see that? He asked her. "A flock of pigs just tried to kill me!"

"The correct collective noun for pigs is a 'litter,' not a flock. However these are wild pigs, and the proper collective for boars is a 'drift,' so I just don't know which one applies."

"Yeah, whatever. All I know is, hornet attacks, worms, coyotes, skunks, birds, either it's sweeps week on FOX, or this is our buddy Dog Pound's doing. He's got that whole 'animal telepathy' thing going."

Monet shook her head. "He's never claimed any special ability to control animals, even one, much less something on this scale."

Angelo looked down. "Hey, where'd the pigs go?"

Something snorted, something big.

A black paw the size of a dessert plate hit Monet in the stomach and slammed her to the ground.

Anglo yelped and climbed higher in the tree, as six-hundred pounds of angry black bear perched on M's back.

As the snow fell around her and the cybernetic wolf pack tore at her, Paige reflected that it was all turning into some dreary Russian novel. At least for the moment, she was safe, if immobilized. If what she was hearing in her radio was any indication though, Pound's influence extended far beyond the robot canines. He seemed to have an entire mountain packed with wildlife at his disposal.

She was more concerned about Jono, who was circling, trying to get a clear shot at the robots with one of his bio-blasts, and not watching his own back.

As for Espeth, she was trying to appeal to the tall figure in blue armor that had to be Chill, and therefore the source of their sudden cold snap. Which was crazy. A few months ago, making a Sno-Kone would have been a taxing demonstration of Chill's cold powers. How was he doing this? How was Pound commanding a forest full of animals? It didn't make sense.

"Listen to me," Espeth said, "it's me, Chill. Me. You've got to snap out of it. You've got to stop this before somebody gets hurt. Before somebody *hurts* you."

So intent was Espeth on Chill, that she didn't see the smallest of the three, Recall obviously, step up behind her. He put out his armored hand and pressed his fingers, almost gently, into her neck. She gasped, her eyes rolled back in her head, and she fell like a marionette with the strings cut.

Paige shoved a snarling robot out of the way to see what was happening. Obviously Recall's location powers now

GENOGOTHS

extended to finding vulnerable spots, pressure points or nerves that could be disrupted with a touch.

Jono shouted and ran towards Espeth. Chill turned, lifted his arms, and a shimmering beam of what seemed to be pure cold shot out. Jono cried out, stumbled, and fell to the ground like a sack of potatoes, the energy in his chest dimming like the coals of a dying fire.

Chill and Recall, no the two *Hounds*, grabbed his hands and feet and began to carry him away. There seemed to be nothing of their friends left in these armored terrors, and the very idea gave Paige shivers. *What if they were beyond help?*

Pound turned and left as well, leaving his robots pack to finish things. Paige kicked at one of the cyber-hounds in anger, pushing it away, if only for a moment.

Then there was a whoosh, and one of the hounds went flying away into the distance. Paige looked up and saw Monet reaching down to grab another one of the things and toss it away. The hounds had barely taken notice of her, but her uniform was already in tatters.

"Wait!" Ev trotted into view. "If Pound commands these things, I should be able to synch into his power and try to override that." He seemed to concentrate, then the visible, multi-colored aura that often surrounded him when he was using his powers flared. "Weird—aura," he gasped. His eyes went wide, and he tumbled flat on his face.

"Oh," said Monet, tossing another robot, *"that* was useful." The robots seemed to return as fast as she could toss them away.

"Never mind them," said Paige, "just pull me out of the pile here."

"Without you as a chew toy," said Monet, "they might go after Espeth, or Ev." She sighed. "Do I have to do *everything* here?"

"No," groaned Ev, rolling over, "you don't." He clutched at the skin on his face and husked into something like living granite. He waded into the hounds, and with his help, Paige managed to get to her feet. "I would have synched with M

219

again, but getting her synch is more work, and I'm not at my best."

The robot dogs suddenly broke off their attack and sprinted off in the direction the three Hounds had gone.

Paige waved after them. "Follow them, Monet!"

She flew after them.

Ev gritted his teeth. "I'm going to try this," he said. His aura flared momentarily and he rose into the air and flew off jerkily after M.

Espeth was sitting up and rubbing her neck. She looked at Paige mournfully. "We lost Jono, didn't we?"

Paige nodded.

"Lot of use we were. Especially me."

"They're mutants," said Paige, "Pretty heavy-duty ones too, somehow. They caught us all off guard. You had nothing to fight back with. You're just—" She stopped herself.

Espeth smiled weakly. "Just human. It isn't a dirty word." The smile faded. "Sometimes human just isn't enough when the people you care about are in danger."

"I'm worried about Jono too."

Espeth looked confused. "Well—of course I'm worried about Jono. Chill seems to have really hit him hard, and I feel like it's my fault. But—you think I have something going on with Jono!"

"Don't you?" asked Paige.

"Paige, Jono is a great guy, but—the reason I turned my back on the Genogoths, everything I believe in." She licked her lips. Her eyes were moist, and she looked away. "I'm in love with Chill."

Paige just sat there, unsure what to say.

Monet and Ev returned a few minutes later, frowns on their face.

"The robots didn't use a door," said Ev. "Their legs folded up and they slid down something like a pipe. Too small to follow, and we have a feeling that it would lead to a trap anyway."

"We don't know how the Hounds got back in the mountain

with Jono. There must be a hidden door there somewhere, but we couldn't find it, and the Genogoths are pulling back."

"We can't just leave Jono in there," insisted Paige. Espeth agreed.

Ev shook his head. "Unless you know a way to drill through ten meters of solid rock, it isn't happening right now. We need to pull back and get a new plan."

They heard a roar, then again, closer. Monet lifted off a few meters for a look-see. She groaned. "More black bears," she said. "I've had enough fun with those for one day."

Paige frowned. "Then I guess we have to leave. Where are Jubilee and Angelo?"

"Jubes wiped herself out zapping those turrets, I took her down to the base of the mountain, and Angelo—" He looked puzzled.

Monet blinked, suddenly looked concerned. "I forgot about him. Can bears climb trees?"

CHAPTER FOURTEEN

"In regard to the wildness of birds towards man—many individuals—both at the Galapagos and at the Falklands, have been pursued and injured by man, yet have not learned a salutary dread of him. We may infer from these facts, what havoc the introduction of any new beast of prey must cause in a country, before the instincts of the indigenous inhabitants have become adapted to the stranger's craft or power."

—Charles Darwin

The Voyage of the Beagle, 1909

Smokey Ashe was a mass of bruises and scratches. He sported nasty cuts on the forehead, right and left cheek, the latter apparently received in an altercation with a hawk. He paced the length of the little notch that served as the Genogoth command post. "We need weapons, Black. I hate to say it, but we do. This isn't an 'operation' or even an 'assault' any more, it's a war, pure and tee. Call it what it is. We've always worried that the Dark Times would come. Well, could be they start here, unless we stop 'em. Now."

Black nodded grimly. Clearly he respected this man Ashe. "I'd hoped we'd never be opening the caches, not in my lifetime, but it seems like there's no choice."

Paige and Espeth sat on a rock outcropping high on the side of the notch, watching and listening. Ev and Jubilee had both been left exhausted by the battle, and were napping up among the trees. Monet was standing lookout at the end of the notch. She tried to act unconcerned, but her eyes never left the Hound mountain.

Paige considered what she'd just seen, and leaned over to Espeth. "What's he talking about, this 'cache' business?"

Espeth looked uncomfortable, as though some dark family secret had been brought out of the closet. "The Genogoth way is one of peace where possible, but we don't assume it will *always* be possible. For a long time the Genogoths have believed that the world might one day slip over the brink into an apocalyptic age, where violence would rule, and only by fighting to the last man would we have any hope of preserving any of what we seek to protect. For generations, the Genogoths have been hoarding weapons of destruction, hidden in secret enclaves around the world."

"So," asked Paige, "why so glum? They'll bring in the big

guns, break our guys out, end of story." She looked at Espeth expectantly. "Right?"

Espeth's head sagged. "These aren't pop-guns, Paige, they aren't half-way measures, they're weapons of last resort, advanced technology, powerful and ugly." She looked up to make sure Sharpe and Smokey weren't paying attention to the two of them. "At the same time, I get the feeling that our three enslaved friends are still figuring out their new powers, and that we've only seen the beginning of what they can ultimately do. I also believe that the Hound mountain hasn't played all its defensive cards yet either." She rubbed her forearm nervously. "Somebody is going to die, and our friends will be right in the crossfire."

Paige picked at a rock in the tread of her boot. "Hank McCoy once said to me, 'when you don't like the answers you're getting, ask another question.' Actually, when Hank said it, he used much bigger words, but that was the gist. Anyway, I'm thinking, what do we want here? We want our friends back, and that other captive mutant, Catfish, too. We didn't come here to shut this place down, and the Genogoths had to be dragged here kicking and screaming. So why are we building up for a war now?"

"I give up," said Espeth, "why?"

Paige made an unpleasant little sound. "I was hoping you'd know. I was just thinking out loud. You know, if that was all we really wanted, we had the three of them right in front of us today. They could have walked away with us and this all would have been over."

"First, they didn't even seem to know us, and second, it would only be over until the Hound Program went out hunting more mutants to replace our guys."

"Mutants we don't know, hopefully, and that makes it okay." She growled. "Of *course* it doesn't make it okay. I know that. But where does your responsibility end? At the end of your nose, or the edge of the world." She sighed. "If I ever want to be an X-Man for real, I guess I know the answer. But I also know that, if we could have walked Chill, Recall and

Pound out of there today, at least *they'd* be safe while whatever else went down."

Paige sat up suddenly. "The question," she said, "is not how to get from A to B, it's how to get from A to C, C being a way point on the path to B." She slid off her perch and looked around to see if anyone was paying attention to them. "Listen, I'm going for a walk. Anybody asks, cover for me."

"Walk?" Espeth stared at her. "Where to?"

"To C," she said, as she climbed up the side of the notch and disappeared over the top.

Espeth looked down at Black and Smokey, planning their big assault, their shooting war. Maybe they were answering the wrong questions too. She took a deep breath and let it out slowly. She'd made her choice. She turned and climbed up the loose stone of the slope after Paige.

Not for the first time Jono yanked at the shackle holding his wrist. His life already had enough strictures on it, he certainly didn't like being chained down.

The room had no visible walls, something that Jono suspected had been done for psychological effect. The chair sat in a shaft of harsh light that kept him from resolving the walls and ceiling that he knew had to be there. The light source was perhaps six or seven meters above him, but he couldn't tell if it was at ceiling height, or suspended from a cave roof fifty meters up.

He wondered if Pound, Recall, and Chill were nearby, perhaps standing guard. On the other hand, his captors may have considered it unnecessary. He wasn't going anywhere, and the chair itself seemed to have some kind of damper field that kept his mutant powers in check. Not completely, fortunately, there was enough of the psyonic energy that powered his body to allow him to move and think, but he doubted he could come up with enough of a bio-blast to knock over a house of cards.

There were eyes out there in the darkness, watching him. He was sure of it. And that was the most frustrating aspect of his situation. The power damper had also knocked out his telepathic "speech." He could see them, but he couldn't say anything, couldn't protest, call for help, or yell useless but satisfying insults at his captors. He could only stare into the darkness and wonder who was there.

"These readings," said Happersen, "are just amazing. In some ways, he's the ultimate expression of the X-gene, power personified. He doesn't *have* power, he *is* power. On the other hand, if I turned up the restraining field just a little more, I think he'd just go out like a light-bulb. I'm not even sure if there'd be anything left of him afterwards."

Sharpe paced the control room. "That could be an interesting experiment. I'll take it under advisement."

Happersen blinked in surprise. "I wasn't seriously proposing—"

Bouille looked up from her console. "I'd assumed that you'd want us to start prepping him for the hound conversion process. To be honest, I don't know how much more powerful we could make him, but there are control issues."

"We don't want his kind as hounds," said Sharpe firmly.

Happersen looked puzzled. "His kind?"

"The powerful ones. If Project Homegrown taught me anything, it's not to trust any one method of control. He has power, he doesn't need us to give it to him, and that's just too dangerous. Power I give, I can also take away, and that's where true control lies. Our operational Hounds, the new subject—the amphibian, take away their power, and they're *nothing*."

Happersen looked up at the restrained mutant sitting out in the examining room. "What do we do with him, then? I mean, we can study him for a while, but after that, he's going to be very dangerous to keep around."

"Can I have him for dissection?" asked Bouille.

Happersen looked up and frowned at her. "Not vivisection?"

"I'm not sure I'd call it that," she said with a straight

face. "I don't know if you could call his condition exactly 'living.' "

Paige followed a game trail through the underbrush, jogging briskly. As she ran, the limbs and vines snagged at her, ripping away pieces, revealing something bright and silvery underneath. The mountain looked so different in the gray overcast of day. It reminded her of her home in the mountains of Kentucky. On another day, another time, she would have been happy, enjoying the fresh air, the simple beauty of the woods and hills.

This was not that day. This was business, and she wasn't sure if she was coming back.

"Paige," Espeth's voice called behind her.

Paige moaned quietly, her concentration broken. She'd have to start psyching herself up all over again. She trotted to a stop and turned to wait for Espeth.

Espeth appeared up the trail and slowed as she saw Paige. She trotted the rest of the way slowly. When she stopped, she bent over and propped her hands on her knees catching her breath. Espeth was in good shape, but clearly she wasn't a serious jogger like Paige.

Paige shook her head. "I don't remember inviting company."

Espeth lifted her head and raised a hand to brush leaves and twigs out of her Mohawk. "I don't remember saying that I'd cover for you either. Where do you think you're going?"

Paige gestured at the mountain.

"Why? You think your five friends and a couple hundred Genogoths commandos were just cramping your style last time?"

"You said yourself that people were going to get killed if we let the big confrontation happen. And the guys *could* walk out of there, if only they would."

Espeth stood and gave her an annoyed look. "You think you can just go up there and *talk* to them, Paige? I tried that with

Chill." She bit her lip. "It was like he didn't even know me."

"I don't believe he did. They aren't controlled like robots. They still think, they just don't remember."

"Paige—look, I told you my secrets. I've got feelings for Chill, and he has feelings for me too." She looked away. "Things were just starting to come out into the open when the three of them were abducted, but I'm sure that if Chill would remember *anyone*, it would be me."

Paige smiled slightly and picked away bits of skin from her arm. "You've got it bad, girl. Which is why you're going at it all wrong. Chill isn't the one to go after. He's the determined one, the confident one, the leader, yeah, but this isn't a 'movie of the week.' Love doesn't always conquer all, not out here in the real world."

"What then?"

"Recall is the key. He's talked to us about the memory tricks he can do with his powers. The human brain is an incredible storage device, but figuring out where that information is filed, that's where most of us fall down. How many times have you had a name or number 'on the tip of your tongue'? Recall never has that problem."

She frowned. "So why doesn't he just shake off whatever they've done to him?"

Paige sighed. This is where the logic gets weak. "Recall's powers work consciously. He has to *remember* to try and remember. Once somebody gets him past that block, causes him to make that first effort, it should be like fluid through a siphon hose. It should all come out in a rush."

"Are you sure?"

Paige shrugged and pulled off a big hunk of skin from her thigh, revealing the silvery metal underneath. "I don't know, but I'm about to go up on that mountain, make a big, shiny target of myself, and find out."

Sharpe picked up the control-room phone. "Yes."

"It's Namik. We have intruders approaching the outer perimeter."

Sharpe frowned. "Another attack? Why didn't we have more warning?"

"There are only two of them," she said, "and making no particular effort to disguise their approach. They made so much noise, that when the computers alerted me, I thought it was just a deer or a bear wandering through."

Sharpe frowned. It didn't make sense. "Could it just be hikers?"

"They've passed some of the security cameras. One of them is an obvious mutant."

He turned to Happersen. "Get the Hounds ready for a run. I have two intruders on the exterior I want captured and brought in for questioning. Since our latest captive can't seem to talk, let's get some prisoners who can tell us what's really going on out there."

He put the phone back to his ear. "Are they headed for the defensive turrets?"

"No," she said, "they're making a bee-line for the hole in the perimeter from last-night's battle."

"Well," he said, "pop the turrets up, maybe give them a little scare. If it's a trick, maybe they'll show their hand. But don't activate the guns unless there's an obvious threat. Otherwise, let the Hounds handle it."

Paige peered over the rise at the distant turret. Though it seemed to be active, they were in no danger where they were. "I think," she said, "that this is just their little way of letting us know that they know we're here. So far, so good."

Espeth crouched among the rocks and bushes next to her. "Explain to me again how this is going to work. You think you can free Recall, but what about the others? What about Jono, and the Catfish guy?"

Paige shushed. "One step at a time."

Espeth parted the bushes for a better look uphill. "Well, so far your plan is working just fine. *Here they come!*"

"You lead them off down slope. I'm going to see if I can do something to single out Recall."

"How?" she asked as Paige slipped into the bushes.

"I'm going to do the one thing Recall won't be able to resist. I'm going to hide."

Jubilee grabbed the note out of Ev's hand. "She did what?"

Ev shrugged. "Went to get captured, it sounds like, and nobody has seen Espeth since this morning either."

Jubilee shook the note. "Where was it?"

"Inside my boot. I took them off when I was sleeping, and when I got up—well, I didn't notice it was in there at first. My bad."

Jubilee stared at the note in sudden realization. "Is that why it's all damp?" She jerked it out to arm's length. "Eeeeew!"

Angelo and Monet returned. "We told Smokey Ashe," said Angelo. "He's rounding up their people to go in for a rescue. The 'big guns' haven't arrived yet. I don't know if that's a good thing, or a bad thing."

Ev looked off at the distant mountain. "It's not going to be fast enough anyway. We just have to consider them backup." The aura flared around his body. "Recall's not the only one who can track a mutant at a distance. I can trace the synch with Paige's aura, and lead us right to her."

"What are we waiting for," demanded Angelo, "the next bus?"

Espeth ran as fast as she could down the slope, and that was dangerously fast. She wasn't sure she could stop, and she was in constant danger of striking some obstacle that she couldn't steer around. Still, when she caught occasional sight of the cyber-hounds, they were just trotting. *They're toying with me.*

She didn't know if she should be relieved or insulted. It didn't matter though. The object was to put some distance between herself and Paige, to give her some time with Recall, and at this rate, she might be running all day.

A cyber-hound popped out of the brush and nipped at her. It missed, but she was startled and distracted for a moment.

Then she hit the ice.

It was a solid sheet, forming a slide down the slope. Her feet went out from under her and she landed painfully on a hip. She was a runaway toboggan. It seemed she would keep sliding forever, when she hit the net.

She jerked to an abrupt halt, the net tightening around her until she was curled in a ball. She looked up at the tall figure in blue standing over her. Her chest ached. *My knight in shining armor has finally come. Why aren't I happier?* She reached her hand up toward him as much as the net would allow, wanting to touch him, wishing for some tiny reaction.

But of course there was none.

"Hi, honey," she said weakly, "I'm home."

Paige had spotted the little cave on the way up. Actually, it was little more than a hollow eroded under a rock outcropping, not a real cave, but it was just big enough to climb into and crouch in the semi-darkness. Something moved under her, and she reached down and pulled out a timber rattler.

She shuddered, but of course, the snake couldn't hurt her in her present form. She tossed it out before it could break its fangs on her chrome steel skin.

She sat there what seemed like a long time, her knees pulled to her chest. She'd never liked playing hide-and-seek as a child either. The waiting made her crazy.

She heard a rock shift outside the cave. She looked up in time to see a flash of red through the entrance opening. She wanted to call his name, but she was supposed to be hiding.

But he knew where she was, of course. He pointed his arm at her. A line shot out of his gauntlet, exploded into a hydra of individual lines that opened like a flower, each tipped with a sticky weight.

It was over in a blink, the lines whipping around her, sticking to her like instant epoxy. She instantly regretted her position. Not only were her arms pinned, but her legs as well. *Trussed up like a turkey.*

Then she was yanked roughly out of her hiding place. She gasped as she landed on the rocks outside, hitting hard enough to feel it through her metal hide. Recall lifted his wrist again. A net fired out, wrapping tightly around her, leaving her not the slightest possibility of escape.

"Recall," she said. "People call you Recall. You live in Chicago. Your father owns a cold-storage warehouse. You have a radio-show with a pain-in-the-butt named Walt Norman. You have to try to remember. You have to *want* to remember. You're *Recall*. You have the power. You can find anything, remember anything, if you'll just try."

She looked for him to relent in his attack, to show some slight hesitation, but it didn't happen. As Recall grabbed the net and with one hand yanked her roughly off the ground, she realized that he simply didn't see any reason to try.

CHAPTER FIFTEEN

"We voluntarily close our eyes when we do not wish to see any object, and we are apt to close them, when we reject a proposition, as if we could not or would not see it; or when we think about something horrible. We raise our eyebrows when we wish to see quickly all round us, and we often do the same, when we earnestly desire to remember something; acting as if we endeavored to see it."

—Charles Darwin

The Expression of Emotion in Man and Animals, 1899

Paige was being toted up the mountainside like a ten-pound sack of potatoes, and she didn't like it a bit. It was a cliché that she'd heard before, "you can't change somebody, they have to want to change themselves." She'd never been sure she believed it, much less imagined that it would have such important real-world implications.

She tried to take a deep breath, something that was difficult to do balled up inside the net and the sticky bolo lines that Recall—*the Hound*—had zapped her with. *Ask another question.* Not how to reach Recall, how to reach the Hound. "You'll never get near any of the other mutants without the secret code word. Ha! It's my name, and you've forgotten it!"

"Identify: Paige Guthrie," said the Hound. And there, in mid-stride, the voice changed. "Paige! It's you!"

The alarm horn broke the relative calm of the control room. Sharpe jumped from his chair and ran to lean over Happersen's shoulder. "What's happening?" But he could already see, the emotional indicators spiking like shark's teeth ripping apart his plans.

"We're losing control of Bloodhound," said Happersen. "I can't stop it."

"The EMP gain, we didn't max it on Bloodhound because he didn't seem to require it. Go!"

Happersen hesitated.

Sharpe shoved him aside and maxed the slider himself.

At first Recall couldn't remember what had happened to him in the last few days, then abruptly he did, in every horrific detail, especially the capture of Catfish Quincy. He looked at Paige in shock and surprise. If she'd had one eye and a wart on her nose, she still would have been the most beautiful thing he'd ever seen. "You came for us! How did you know?"

She struggled against the net, and suddenly he was aware that he'd been the one who put her there. He reached down and with amazing ease ripped it open. Then he, more carefully, snapped the bolo lines. "I'm sorry, Paige. I didn't know what I was—"

Suddenly someone slipped an ice-pick into his skull. He screamed, fell back in agony, never even feeling himself hit the ground. He was a man drowning in his own head, falling down into the empty mental pit from which he had only moments before been plucked. Memories faded. He pulled them back. Others went. Faster, till memories were forming and bursting in his head like bubbles in boiling water.

Paige shook off the remains of the net and crawled to Recall's side. He was tearing at his helmet. She tried to get it off, but it was locked in place by some fastener or release she couldn't see.

"Stop it," she yelled at his invisible masters, "you're killing him!"

Namik watched from the back of the control room with bemused detachment. This is where Sharpe's mistakes became apparent. This is where the information her superiors wanted would be gained.

"He's resisting somehow, pulling things back as fast as we can block them. This never happened in the lab!"

Sharpe stood and stared at the screen. "That's his power doing this, you idiot! We're amplifying it! Shut down the amplifier, now!"

Happersen stabbed at some buttons on his console. "It isn't working. Some kind of power feedback loop has fused the circuit closed." He shook his head, frustrated. "He's going to burn himself out anyway. We've lost him."

Namik slipped from the room and walked down the hall to her office. She didn't need to know how it ended. It would all be in the data files she was about to pilfer from the Foxhole's computers, using the back door she'd hacked using her sound analysis program as a cover. Time to reveal her little Trojan horse's real purpose.

As Recall/Bloodhound felt his/their mind melting like wax, there was one crystal of pure purpose, to find things. He/they latched onto that, focused it on one simple purpose, to find the hidden latch that would release the armor's helmet. *There*. He had only to guide his/their hand what seemed a thousand or so miles, and press it just so.

Paige was pulling frantically at the helmet when there was a loud *hiss* and it fell free in her hands. She pulled it off as gently as she could and threw it away with more disgust than she'd reserved for the rattler earlier.

Recall looked stunned, dazed, his eyes dilated and fixed on infinity. Had she been too late? Had she killed him?

Something in the armor's yoke popped, sputtered, and smoked. Recall jerked, blinked. Again. His pupils narrowed and he looked at her. "Paige? I was trying so hard to remember your name, for just a moment there, if felt like I remembered everything, knew everything." He waved his hands expansively. "I mean *everything*. Weird."

She threw her arms around him. "You're back, you jerk, you nearly killed me!"

He laughed weakly. "Glad to be here, I guess."

The four remaining members of Generation X flew up the side of the mountain just in time to find Paige sitting next to Recall on the hillside. Paige waved frantically as she saw them.

They swept closer. Angelo was hanging under Monet, his hands clasped in hers. He shouted, "Welcome back, *amigo*!"

"Never mind us," shouted Paige. "Chill and Pound have Espeth."

"Where?" said Ev. "We didn't see them coming in."

Recall didn't hesitate. "A hundred and ten yards that way," he pointed.

"Giddy-up," said Jubilee, who was riding on Ev's back.

Ev banked into a turn and swept under the tree canopy in the direction she had indicated.

Monet and Angelo were right there with them. "Drop me," Angelo yelled, "just before we get there, maybe thirty feet out."

"Put you down?" asked Monet.

"Don't even slow down, just drop me!"

"It's your funeral," she said.

They came on the pair and their struggling captive just where Recall had predicted. On cue, Monet opened her hands, and Angelo fell. Then, the skin on his hands and feet snapped out, and Angelo was gliding, like a tree-frog Ev had once seen on a nature special. He wasn't gliding very well, mind you, but it seemed to be okay, since he used Dog Pound to break his fall.

Ev swept past the two Hounds, both to drop off Jubilee at a safe distance, and to provide a distraction for Monet, who slipped in behind him to attack Chill.

He put Jubes down a few yards away, and when he turned back, Monet was standing on the ground, squaring off hand-to-hand with Chill. Angelo had Pound all wrapped up in his skin so that he couldn't see, and the robot dogs circled them, seemingly unsure what to do. Monet rabbit-punched with enough force to knock over a small tree, but Chill ducked under it, reached out and put his hands against her side.

Monet just *stopped*. Frost formed all over her, and a breath escaped from her lips, instantly turning to fog, condensing snow out of the air. She fell to the ground, not like a statue, but more like a side of half-thawed beef. "That—hurt," she gasped.

Ev saw Chill turn towards him. Ordinarily he was a confident guy, but he was up against somebody who had stopped both Monet and Jono without breaking a sweat. "Hoo, boy," he heard himself say.

Sharpe pounded the console in frustration. They'd lost one of his hounds. *This shouldn't have happened!* But there was still one last fail-safe available to him.

• • •

Paige ran up the hill after Recall. The powered armor still gave him a speed advantage, even over her. "I should have had one of them fly me," he said, "I can get them back. I know it!"

Paige lifted her head. If Recall was right, and she had no doubt of it, they shouldn't be far ahead.

Then he suddenly fell to his knees, so abruptly that she nearly tripped over him. She ran back. "What's wrong?"

"They cut the power to my armor. Stuff is heavy."

"Can you get it off?"

"No time. Help me up the hill."

Chill was just about to do something nasty when a swarm of plasma fireworks swept around Ev and started exploding between the two of them. Ev jumped for cover, just as a beam of shimmering cold swept past him.

The cyber-hounds seemed to regain their composure, and one of them leaped toward Jubilee. Ev jumped in-between, the robot beast locking its jaws down on his arm. Fortunately, he was still synched with Monet, so he wasn't hurt. Then he saw a second one closing on them. It was going to get complicated.

He was so intent that he didn't see Chill until he was practically within touching distance. And if Chill touched him—

"Three-dog-night!" It was Recall's voice.

Ev turned to see him just down the slope, his weight sagged heavily against Paige.

"Listen to me," Recall continued. *"Circus peanuts!"*

Three-dog-night had an intense memory of sweet marshmallow and metallic artificial orange flavor. Like a jeweler's chisel striking the one flaw in a perfect diamond, something in his mind shattered. He remembered cellophane that crackled under his fingertips, green and stringy Easter grass, a splintery basket full of jelly beans, his mother's smiling face.

Chill gasped like a swimmer breaking the surface.

He was back!

• • •

"Three-dog-night is already maxed on EMP gain," yelled Happersen. "They're taking off his helmet. We've lost him for good."

Sharpe cursed under his breath. "Shut it down, the armor power, the amplifier. Just shut it down." He felt his lunch wash in like a breaker in the back of his throat. "We've got to activate the inner defenses. Launch the defense drones." He looked up. "Where's Namik?" He spun around. *"Where's Namik?"*

Namik sat at her desk, watching the progress indicator on her computer screen. In a few moments, all the data from Project Foxhole would be in her possession. Time for the final step.

She lifted a hidden panel on her desktop and pressed her palm against the panel there. It scanned her handprint, then a small display flashed INSERT KEY. She reached up and snapped the chain around her neck, carefully taking from it the decorative pewter sword that she always wore there. She inserted the blade of the sword into a slot in the panel. Tiny magnets aligned with sensors in the slot. TIMED DESTRUCT ACTIVATED, the display read. Below it, a timer began counting down the sequence.

She smiled as she stood up and prepared to leave. It wouldn't all happen at once, of course. First Sharpe would lose his precious Hounds. For good.

"Top Dog," yelled Recall, "Tabasco sauce!"

Red, so like candy, metallic green band around the top like Christmas wrap, the little bottle so tempting. Tiny hands grasping, his tongue licking the crusty scarlet lump on the top of the bottle. Searing agony, his own cries of fear and pain. Strong hands guiding him, his grandfather's brown eyes as he pressed the cold, quenching carton of milk against his lips—As though someone had pulled a loose piece of yarn on a knitted sweater, his memories began to unravel.

"Awk!" Pound thrashed, like someone waking from a nightmare.

Happersen looked up and made eye contact with Bouille. They both knew things were going horribly wrong. Namik was gone. Sharpe was gone. They'd lost the last Hound. He shut down the armor and amplifier controls with a sigh. "Shut down the cyber-hounds," he instructed Bouille.

Then his screen went blank. *All* his screens went blank.

He looked up at Bouille. Her eyes were wide. She punched frantically at her controls. "Yours too?"

He got up and ran from console to console. Everything was dead.

Then the disaster alarms sounded.

Sharpe held his service automatic to Namik's head with the cold efficiency of a trained killer. "What have you done?"

Despite the cold gun metal pressed against her skin, Namik laughed. "It can't be stopped, Sharpe. This whole place is going down like a house of cards. Your bosses don't care about you, and frankly, neither do I. Get out while you still can."

He lowered the gun and turned to the hidden panel in her desk. His fingers traced over it, trying to figure it out. She managed a single step away from the wall before he snapped the gun's aim back on her. "Turn it off," he said.

"I can't," she said coolly. "Shoot me if you want, but I'm the only one who can activate the security drones to cover our escape." His aim wavered slightly. "Your Hounds are gone, Sharpe. Dead. That was part of the plan. But you don't have to be."

Chill and Recall were already out of their now powerless armor, stripped down to the tights they wore underneath. With Angelo's help, the bottom half of his armor slipped off the still groggy Dog Pound's legs.

Recall bent down and picked up Pound's discarded helmet,

looking at it. "Alas, poor Top Dog, I knew him well." Then his eyes went wide and he threw the helmet down. "Get away from the armor," he yelled, "all of you!"

Angelo and Ev grabbed Pound, half-lifting, half dragging him away from his armor. Everyone else scrambled as well. Recall stopped eight or ten yards away and crouched warily. The others fell in behind him. Pound managed to get his feet under him, and he noticed for the first time that the cyberhounds were now trotting along behind like obedient pets.

Then the armor exploded. Every disarticulated bit of it was blown into powder. Pound choked, coughed. "That could have been *us!*"

Paige stared at Recall. "How did you know?"

He shrugged. "I said that for a minute there, it was like I knew everything that ever happened, and everything that ever *would* happen. I'm still getting little flashes of it." A strange expression crossed his face. "I wonder what 'cosmic awareness' means?"

There was a rumble, growing in intensity, as though a stampede were approaching. "It means," said Angelo, "that we're done for if we don't get moving." He pointed up-hill. Through the trees they could see a profusion of moving metal, man-sized, crab-like robots, blue arcs of electricity crackling between their shock-prod claws.

They turned down-slope only to find themselves looking into a line of charging Genogoths, extending as far as they could see in either direction.

And they were in the middle.

Sharpe charged down the corridor towards the control room, but he met Happersen, Bouille, and the other technicians halfway there.

"Everything's dead," said Happersen between gasping breaths, "some kind of virus wiped the entire system."

"I know," growled Sharpe, "Namik was a plant. There's a self-destruct timer running. Get everybody to the hangar bay for evacuation."

Happersen looked at him. "Where are you going?"

Sharpe looked at the spiral staircase at the end of the hall. "Up to the anti-aircraft missile battery. I had to let Namik go to cover our escape, but I'm hoping she might have missed a few loose ends. She's not getting away with *my* data."

Paige had read somewhere that when caught in the middle, it's best to pick a side.

That was the easy part. Generation X and the liberated Mutant Musketeers simply waited for the Genogoth charge, then joined in as it swept past them. It was a furious battle, close-up and hand-to-pincer. It smelled like blood and ozone, sweat and fear.

Paige had considered it a given that her teammates would give a good accounting of themselves in the fight, and they did, but what surprised her was the ferocity and resourcefulness of the Musketeers. They might have lost their megapower-enhancements, but they'd gained a new confidence and determination she'd never seen before.

Chill iced over sensors, shorted out shock-prods with condensed moisture, and formed slush under his feet to instantly slide himself away from danger. Though he'd lost his ability to command all animals, Pound still had the cyber-hounds, which now behaved more like loyal hunting dogs than vicious killers. And Recall—he'd picked up a riot baton from a fallen Genogoth and was dashing in among the robots, always seeming to find the one path between their flailing limbs, always striking the one place where his simple weapon could do the most damage.

But the robots came without number, and the Genogoth charge had stalled. Paige paused among the chaos, waited for Recall to pass near, and grabbed his arm. "Recall," she yelled over the din, "find us a way into this place."

He nodded and closed his eyes for a moment. He frowned and opened them again. "There isn't one."

"What?"

"Not now, not without a big can-opener of some kind.

Everything is sealed up tight from the inside. Unless you have a way to blow off the front door, we're out of luck." He closed his eyes again for a moment, then opened them, wide. "Paige, there are going to be lots of ways in real soon now, but it won't do us any good. This place is going to self-destruct! We've got to get Jono and Catfish out of there!"

Paige ducked under the arm of a damaged robot and buried her fist wrist deep in its optical sensor. It twitched and fell. "You just said," she hardly missed a beat, "there was no way in." She blinked. "No, you said unless we could think of a way to blow open the front door."

Paige activated the radio in her ear. "Black, this is Paige Guthrie. Answer me."

"I'm busy," he said.

She shoved aside another robot crab, and it staggered down the slope, only to have Monet and Ev tear it in half. "So am I. Listen, Black, pull your people back. The base is going to self-destruct."

"How do you know?"

She looked at Recall. "I just know, that's all. Pull them back. Listen, do you have explosives here, lots of them?"

"Yes," he said.

"We're going to blow the front gate. It's the only hope Jono and Catfish have."

"There are turrets," he said, "we have no way of setting the charges. In an hour there will be armor-piercing missiles here."

"Too late," she said. "Have them down on the main road, just beyond defensive range, ten minutes top."

Silence.

"Do it!"

"Ten minutes," said Black, the skepticism in his voice obvious as he broke the connection.

Paige signaled Monet over. "Go get the Xabago and drive it down to the main mountain road. I'll round up the team and meet you there in ten minutes."

Monet looked at her, puzzled. "We're leaving?"

"No," she said, "we're going to invite ourselves in."

GENOGOTHS

• • •

With a squadron of defense drones standing guard, the Foxhole's hangar doors opened just long enough for the helicopter to slip put. Namik didn't know how to fly the sleek black machine, but the automatic piloting system made it unnecessary. She simply punched the map coordinates of her rendezvous point into the system and pressed the "go" button. The computer would take care of the rest.

With computers on her mind, she pulled out the palmtop from her coat pocket. Though it looked like a store-bought model, it was actually an advanced technology prototype, with more than enough storage to house all of Project Foxhole's data. It wouldn't hurt to check it before she turned it over to her contact. She flipped up the screen and turned it on.

The screen glowed, then a cartoon skeleton danced onto the screen, followed by another, and another. They danced and chattered like monkeys in a zoo. They seemed to be laughing at her. Then the words "Styx it to you!" appeared on the screen and the computer froze.

She was still trying to figure out what had happened when an alarm buzzer sounded and a red light started flashing on the dash. The label under it read, RADAR LOCK. *What did that—?* Then, with horrible realization, she pressed her nose against the cold Plexiglas of the helicopter's side window. A black dot streaked up towards her from the distant Foxhole, climbing on a trail of smoke.

The computer slipped from her fingers, but the missile hit before it could reach the cabin floor.

Given that they were sitting among four-hundred pounds of plastic explosives, the distant detonation caused everyone to jump. Paige swore that she saw Styx's beard turn one shade grayer.

The Genogoths' demolition person staggered out of the Xabago. "What was that?" she asked. "It is unbecoming of a Genogoth to wet themselves."

Black stared at the sky of the mountain, where a spreading

cloud of smoke could be seen. "Surface-to-air missile," he said, "radar guided. Probably a surplus variant of the Soviet OSA-AK."

Monet walked by, carrying one last box of explosives. "You know a lot about missiles," she said, "do you read *Aviation Week* too?" She disappeared into the Xabago without waiting for an answer.

Angelo slid up next to Paige. "Let me get this straight," he said, "we're going to ram the Xabago into the gate at full speed and blow it wide open, right?"

"Right," she said. "The Xabago's on its last legs anyway."

He cleared his throat. "So, who's going to drive this thing?"

"Me," she said.

"Good," he said. "I thought this was all some elaborate way to get rid of me after I put salt in the sugar-bowl last month."

Paige glanced at him. "That was you?" She smiled slightly. "No, I'm just going to slip into something more indestructible—" She "husked" to reveal a dull, silver-gray metal. She tapped her fist experimentally against her stomach. "Does that look like adamantium to you? I'm not real sure of the molecular structure."

"You're asking me?"

"It'll have to do."

The demolition woman emerged from the Xabago again with a switch in her hand connected to the Xabago with a wire. "Radio's *off*, everybody. I don't want this to go off prematurely when I arm it." They all complied, and once she'd verified it, she flipped the switch to one side. She offered it to Paige. "Flip it the other way, and boom. Good luck."

Paige climbed past her and into the Xabago's driver's seat. Jubilee jumped up by the side window. "Come back safe, hick," she called.

Angelo stood at attention and saluted. "Xabago, we will miss ye."

Paige waved and turned the key, having flashbacks of what

always happened when you started a car in a mobster movie. The Xabago groaned once, twice, then nothing. She cursed and pounded the steering wheel. "Not now!"

The door opened and somebody climbed in next to her. It was Monet. "I'll push," she said, "you drive."

"You sure?" said Paige.

Monet scowled. "Don't test me," she said.

On his way to the hangar bay to meet the others, Sharpe found himself passing the holding cell where the two mutant prisoners had been left. He looked at them, the fish-man and the thing-without-a-face, the latter with an inhibitor collar locked around his neck. The fish man looked at him fearfully from the corner of the cell's single bunk, the other one stood, angry and defiant. He smiled. Small satisfaction, but it didn't matter, they'd both be as dead as Namik soon enough.

This one's for you, Havok.

Paige fought to keep them on the road as Monet accelerated them like a rocket-sled. Monet was down near the floor, pushing against the same solid spot she'd identified earlier in the trip. Paige could see the massive concrete portal and the two huge iron doors ahead. Hidden turrets on either side of the door had popped up and were firing at them, but they didn't seem programmed to expect such a fast-moving target on the narrow road. One shell passed cleanly through the rear quarter of the Xabago, but the others missed.

"Monet," she yelled, "are you sure you can survive this explosion?"

"No," said Monet, "and you?"

"No," she said.

The doors loomed a few meters ahead. Paige covered her eyes with her forearm and flipped the switch an instant before impact.

CHAPTER SIXTEEN

"*He who is forced to overcome his fear or want of sympathy before he acts, deserves, however, in one way higher credit than the man whose innate disposition leads him to a good act without effort.*"

—Charles Darwin
The Descent of Man, 1871

Though the handcuffs restricted his movements, Jono used his fingers to explore the inhibitor collar they'd put on him to shut down his powers. He and Catfish had been thrown into the cell together with some haste. Judging from the recent rush of activity he'd observed, and now the lack of it, something big was going on out there. He could only hope it was bad for their captors.

The collar was a Genosian model that he'd seen before, during one of Forge's guest lectures back at Xavier's school. Something of a bargain basement model, too. The electronic key lock was the sort of thing that Storm or Wolverine could have picked in a minute flat. Unfortunately, he wasn't Storm or Wolverine, he was Jonothan Starsmore, and they hadn't gotten to that lecture in school yet.

He dropped his hands and looked at his cellmate. This was really the first time the two of them had been in close proximity and alone, but Jono couldn't talk because of the collar, and Catfish just didn't seem inclined. He cowered in the back corner of the little cell, clearly terrified and completely out of his element. From what they'd heard from Smokey Ashe, he'd never been away from the little town he'd been born in. All he knew of the outside world came from video-tapes and satellite TV.

This was a bloody poor introduction to the big, wonderful, wide.

Wish you could hear me, mate.

Catfish suddenly looked up in surprise. He slid closer. "Did—did you say somethin'?"

Jono jumped up off the bunk and moved closer to Catfish. The young man jumped a little, but held his ground.

Jono knew that his powers hasn't been totally shut down, but neither Sharpe nor any of the others here seemed to be able to hear him. He hadn't even bothered to try with Catfish. But maybe he was projecting just a little, and Catfish, for some reason, was sensitive enough to pick it up. Maybe his aquatic mutation somehow made him telepathically receptive. "Can you hear me, mate?"

Catfish nodded. "You're talking in my head. That never happened before."

"I'm a mutant, like you."

Catfish hung his head. "They keep saying that I'm a mutant, but I ain't. Ain't no such thing."

"You're wrong there, friend. Mutants are people like us who are born different. There are lots of us. I'd like for you to meet my mates from Xavier's School some time."

Catfish looked at him with a mixture of suspicion and wonder. "Others? Like me? I thought I was the only one that God made like this." But his eyes dropped. "But I won't never meet them. Won't never get out of here."

"Chin up, mate. My mates are outside with your mate Smokey and his crew. They'll get us out of here."

There was a huge roar and the whole room rocked as though by an earthquake. The light flickered, and they could hear glass shattering somewhere outside in the hall.

Jono looked over to find Catfish trying to climb under the bunk. "Whoa, whoa, calm down! I think that's just our friends come calling. We'll be out of here before you know it!"

Catfish looked up at him hopefully. "Smokey is here?"

There was a sudden rattling at the door. "What are you prattling about, mutant?" It was Sharpe, unlocking the cell door with a ring of keys. That immediately had Jono's attention. He looked closely, and spotted a number of electronic keys like the one that would fit his collar, and others that might work on his cuffs. He also saw that Sharpe had a pistol in his hand. "You, frog boy, come out of there. I need a hostage to get safely past our attackers."

Jono stepped to the back of the cell, and pretended not to be interested in Sharpe. "Sharp is a wanker," he said, as loudly as he could. Sharpe showed no sign of hearing him, although Catfish looked at him with a puzzled expression. "Catfish, do something to get this guy's attention. I'm going to try and get his keys."

Catfish looked fearful, but he suddenly grabbed at the metal mesh wall of the cell and started wailing that he was afraid.

Jono lunged forward, used his shoulder to knock Sharpe's aim safely away from Catfish, then grabbed the keys.

Sharpe recovered quickly, bringing the butt of the gun painfully down on Jono's head. He pushed Jono back, spun and side-kicked him, sending him crashing into the far wall of the cell. *But he still had the keys!*

Jono grabbed one of the electronic keys at random and fumbled it into the lock. If he gave it a little twist, it should either open, or not. He looked up and saw Sharpe, his left arm around Catfish's neck, the pistol pushed against his temple. "Catfish, tell him that if I turn this key, I can blow his head off with a bio-blast."

Catfish hesitated.

"Tell him!"

Catfish nervously parroted Jono's words as his own.

Sharpe laughed harshly. "If that's the right key," he said to Catfish, "and if he doesn't manage to blow *your* head off before I do." Then to Jono. "Put the keys down and slide them over to me. I'm only going to count to three. One—"

He tried to tune out Sharpe, speaking over the top of him. "Catfish, he isn't afraid of you because to him, you're just a *power*, not a person, and he doesn't see your power as a threat."

"Two—"

"But you're a *man*, Catfish, tough country stock, a top woodsman and a crack shot, from what Smokey tells me."

"Three—"

Jono took the key out of the lock and slowly lowered the ring to the cell floor. The gun drifted away from Catfish's head. "You wouldn't be afraid if you were back there instead of here, in this strange place. Make *him* afraid. Show him, Catfish. Show him what you're made of!"

The expression on Catfish's face changed. His wide jaw clenched, his eyes narrowed. He took a deep breath.

Catfish's right elbow smashed back into Sharpe's ribs, at the same time that his left hand pushed the gun up and away from his head. The gun went off and ricocheted off the back of the cell.

Jono felt the bullet whiz past as he frantically shoved the key back in the lock and turned. *Nothing.*

Catfish grabbed Sharpe's gun arm, shoved it under his own arm, turned and twisted. Sharpe gasped, and the gun clattered to the floor.

Jono tried another key. It turned with a click, followed by an electronic beep as the collar turned off. Jono felt the bio-energy furnace in the center of his body powering up. He struggled to remove the collar.

Sharpe turned, saw the collar coming loose. His eyes were wide. For a fraction of a second, he eyed the gun sitting on the floor, then abandoned hope of recovering it.

Jono wrenched the collar free, but Sharpe was already gone.

Catfish stared at the hole where his face and chest used to be, surprised, but not horrified. "You're strange," he said. "Were you in *Hellraiser?*"

Jono rubbed the bump on his head. "We're all strange, mate. Help me up."

As the Genogoth commandos filed past them through the ruined gates of the Foxhole, Jubilee, Angelo, and Ev looked through the rubble for some sign of Monet and Paige. There were only small, almost unrecognizable bits of the Xabago left among the twisted metal, fallen rock, and hunks of shattered concrete. Ev suddenly slapped himself on the forehead. "What am I thinking? Let me see if I can tune in on their auras."

He turned slowly. "There!" He suddenly pointed to a huge pile of rubble at the side of the entrance. He trotted up and studied the truck-sized boulder that had fallen from the ceiling and was now on top of the pile. "Oh, man," he said.

The rock moved. They all scrambled back as the rock wobbled, slowly tilted, and rolled down the pile with a tremendous rumble. Monet emerged from the top of the pile, her costume, hair, and skin caked with dust. She paused, reached down, and pulled Paige from among the piled rocks.

Paige sat up, coughed, and waved weekly.

"I hate," said Monet, shaking her head to cast off some of the dust, "bad-hair days."

Recall, Chill and Pound came trotting up, followed closely by the cyber-hounds. Recall whooped when he saw Paige. Chill reached up and high-fived Monet. Only Pound wasn't distracted. "We gotta find Jono fast," he said, sending the cyber-hounds ahead to look for them.

"I'll guide you," said Recall.

Sharpe ran up the spiral stairs towards the anti-aircraft battery, but stopped half-way up. He swung open a service panel, climbed inside and closed it after him. The narrow passage behind was lit with small service lights at infrequent intervals, and lined with conduits and pipes.

The interior of Foxhole was divided into two roughly equal sections. He was at one edge of the section that held the labs, containment and holding cells, command center, and training areas. In the middle was a huge gallery, with the main entrance at the front end. The gallery was a garage for service vehicles, and allowed trucks with supplies and heavy equipment to be driven completely inside. Beyond was the section that housed living quarters, mess hall, mechanical services, air conditioning, and, of course, the hangar that offered his best chance of a clean get-away.

By now, the gallery was full of enemy troops, and he'd been counting on a hostage to get him across. Now he'd have to rely on stealth and his superior knowledge of the installation. At the top of the gallery, huge overhead cranes moved along heavy beams. He should be able to crawl over one of them undetected, especially if he had a distraction. He pushed open another service panel, one connected to the computers in Namik's office.

Jono and Catfish stopped dead in the corridor, eyeing the cyber-hound that blocked their way. First they were lost, and now this. "Get behind me," instructed Jono, "if I have to blast it in this confined space, things could get dicey."

Then the cyber-hound opened its nasty-looking jaws, and Pound's voice came out of it. "Follow me," he said, and the cyber-hound turned and loped away.

Jono looked at Catfish, shrugged. "Bloody, hell," he said. Then they both trotted off after it.

Black poked his way though the abandoned corridors of the Foxhole, reading the place like a book. Control center *there*, power conduits *there*, microwave wave-guides *there*. Optical data buss *there*. He listened to the chatter in his ear. The technicians had been cornered in the living quarters on the other side of the complex, but the former General Sharpe hadn't been among them.

They'd gone to this much trouble, this much risk, this much public exposure. He wasn't about to let Sharpe get away with the data from this hellish project. Styx's virus should take care of any computer files, but the Xavier children had been right. The information was too dangerous to survive, even in Sharpe's head.

If Sharpe tried to get out on foot or hide in the complex, his people would find him, but Black knew there was another way out. And if he were Sharpe, that's where he'd be heading right now. But he wasn't Sharpe, he was Black, and he had his own destination. He remembered where he'd seen the missile streaking away from its launcher earlier. He stopped in front of the spiral staircase. The surrounding wiring, conduits, and the location all fit. He climbed towards the top.

Smokey Ashe led the troops that surrounded and sealed off the aircraft hangar. They'd already turned back most of Sharpe's people, who were now holed up two floors below in the living quarters. Black had warned them to be expecting Sharpe as well, but if the bad-man should show up now, it would only be to be captured.

Smokey walked past the big VTOL transport plane and the

much smaller helicopter, wishing he could go down to see Catfish, who'd just been found alive and well.

There was a loud, metallic bang. He jumped, but nobody was around except two of his own people, already alert for danger. Still, there was no way Sharpe could have gotten past the people stationed outside.

Then there was a loud whirring of electric motors, and a sudden influx of light into the hangar. Smokey looked up. The hangar's outside doors were opening, and as he watched, hundreds of crab-like defense drones began to clamor over the edge and climb down the hangar's exposed girders.

Jono and Catfish followed the cyber-hound to the central gallery, where the rest of Gen X and the Musketeers were waiting. Everyone cheered when they appeared on an upper balcony and climbed down the stairs to join the others.

One of the Genogoths outside began shouting, then another. The reunion was going to have to wait. The blasted crab robots were back, and they were storming through the front entrance of the base.

Sharpe pulled back the ceiling tile and dropped down into the mechanic's storage room next to the hangar. Outside he could hear the confusion that the defense robots were causing. He only hoped that they hadn't damaged the remaining helicopter.

He slipped out though the door and dashed for the 'copter. The Genogoths ignored him because they were busy. The defense drones ignored him because they were programmed to. He opened the helicopter door and slipped inside, then punched in a random set of coordinates into the autopilot.

Anywhere away from here would do just fine.

Jono kept blasting robots, and more kept appearing to replace them. He shot a bio-blast and scragged another one. It felt good to cut loose, even if he wasn't making much headway.

"Jono!" It was Recall, who waved at him from a stair landing above. One of the robots appeared behind him, but Recall ducked under its lunging claws and vaulted over the railing. He landed heavily next to Jono, stood, and yelled close to his ear so he could be sure to be heard. "There's a conduit up there," he pointed, "just above the bank of yellow pipes."

Jono nodded. "I see it!"

"Blast it," said Recall. "Blast it good!"

Jono complied, directing a sledgehammer beam of orange energy from his chest, taking out at least five meters of the conduit and leaving a sizable crater in the wall behind it.

Suddenly all the robots froze.

Recall grinned. "Some kind of central control circuit for these things. It's amazing what you'll find if you put your mind to it."

Smokey stood on top of a large, rolling toolbox hammering at a robot with a piece of pipe. He was starting to think about the Alamo when the robots suddenly stopped. It would have been very quiet, if not for the roar of the helicopter lifting off through the now completely open doors.

CHAPTER SEVENTEEN

"The puma is described as being very crafty: when pursued, it often returns on its former track, and then suddenly making a spring on one side, waits there till the dogs have passed by. It is a very silent animal, uttering no cry even when wounded. . ."

—Charles Darwin
The Voyage of the Beagle, 1848

Black climbed into the seat of the missile control panel. As he'd expected, it was Soviet surplus, probably another excuse for the government to deny that they knew this place ever existed. Terrorists, they'd say, or super-villains, or perhaps even blame it on "evil" mutants.

Well, it wouldn't matter what they said, as long as this place's secrets died with it. He activated the panel, and as the radar screen came to life, he immediately saw a target, outbound, perhaps two miles away. Fortunately, these missiles should have an effective range of over thirty-five miles.

He fired one. Two. Hell, fire them all. The seven remaining missiles in the salvo streaked across the screen towards their target. One missed. The second one didn't. Or the third. The blip on the screen flared and disappeared. There was nothing left for four through seven to hit.

The kids had seen the fleeing helicopter fly over, heard Smokey on the radio saying that Sharpe was escaping. It was going too fast for Jono to take a shot at it.

Monet looked at Ev. "Come on, baldie, let's go bring him back!"

The helicopter appeared briefly above the distant trees. A swarm of *somethings* shot across the sky with a crackling roar, leaving trails of fire and smoke. The helicopter exploded into tiny fragments.

"Sharpe," said Black's voice in their ears, "has been terminated."

Paige stared up at the spreading cloud of black smoke in the sky. "Yeah, he was a creep," she said, "but Black shot him down in cold blood."

• • •

GENERATION X

The staff at Little Latveria wasn't exactly thrilled to see Generation X and their friends again, but as soon as Black started spreading money around, they weren't exactly upset either. It didn't hurt that the army of Genogoths didn't come with them this time, just a few key players.

Once again they were in the now-repaired Razorback suite, but this time it was just a staging area for people headed out in various directions.

The great majority of the Genogoth army had begun to disperse in all directions the moment the Hound project had been shut down for good. The prisoners had gone with them. Smokey had assured the kids that none of the prisoners would be hurt, but they couldn't be released to the authorities until the Genogoths knew just how much they knew. "Styx managed to rustle one of them memory gizmos before the base blew," he said. "Could be, once he's through figuring it out, even if they remember something, they won't remember nothing."

It was time for Smokey and Catfish to leave. Catfish said his reluctant farewells, especially with Jono, and promised to come visit the school, but only if he could get Smokey to come with him.

"That'll happen when hell freezes over," said Angelo, once they were out of earshot.

"You never know," said Paige. "Times, they are a changing."

Next, it was time for the Musketeers to leave. That was the hardest goodbye. They'd barely gotten their friends back safe and well, and already they were going their separate ways.

"I've got to get back to Chicago," said Recall, chuckling, "before Walt Norman gets our show canceled. You know, the hardest part of this will be going back on the air and not being able to talk about *any* of this."

Paige looked at Chill and Pound. "What about you two? Back to Pacific U?"

Pound shook his head. "Well, long enough to pick up our stuff, then we're headed for Fontane College, outside Boston. They've rebuilt the original M.O.N.S.T.E.R. house there, and thanks to the support generated by Recall's radio program, we're going to help crank up the national organization again!"

Jubilee whooped. "You'll be like, neighbors or something. We can come visit you guys on weekends."

Monet stepped a little closer to Chill. "You have my phone number, don't you?"

Chill just laughed as Espeth slipped in under his arm.

"He's spoken for," said Espeth.

"I have your number," said Pound, helpfully.

"I have *your* number too," said Monet, her tone chilly.

Pound shrugged, and looked down as one of the cyber-hounds rubbed against his legs. "I hope I don't have a problem finding an apartment that takes pets."

Angelo snickered.

"We'll make it over to visit when we can," said Chill, "but we could be kind of busy, what with M.O.N.S.T.E.R. and—" He grinned a goofy grin. "Espeth proposed."

Angelo slapped his head. *"What?"*

Paige giggled. "You don't waste any time, girl!"

"Life is short," said Espeth. "After these past couple weeks, I figure anything can happen at any time. Better make up your mind what you're doing with your life."

Jono raised an eyebrow. "What about the Genogoths?"

"I'm on leave from the Inner Circle. Officially I'm on deep cover assignment, like Smokey." She reached up and tousled Chill's ice-white hair. "I get to keep *him* out of trouble."

He grinned back at her. "Who's going to keep *you* out of trouble?"

Jubilee cringed. "I have the feeling these two are already way down the road to barf-city."

Everybody laughed.

Then Black stepped into the room, and a sudden silence fell. "If you've made your farewells, I'd like to talk to the Xavier students alone, please. Rides to the airport are waiting for the rest of you in any case."

A few more hugs, waves, and platitudes, and the Muske-teers-plus-Espeth were gone.

Black turned to them. If he was bothered by the frosty reception, he didn't show it. "I know that you aren't happy with me, or my methods."

"You basically shot a man in the back," said Paige. "We don't do that."

He nodded appreciatively. "We will simply have to agree to disagree on certain points. I did what I thought necessary to protect the secrets of the Genogoths, and, in turn, of the mutants that we strive to protect."

"Well," said Jono, "we still don't agree. Your secrets have cost too much blood, far as we can see."

"If it's any consolation, we searched the wreck of Sharpe's 'copter. There was no body, but we did find the remains of a highly sophisticated automatic pilot."

"It's the thought that counts," quipped Jubilee.

Black continued. "Sharpe may have tricked us. He could be out there still, perhaps still carrying his secrets with him. Doubtless his employers will want nothing to do with him, but there may be others willing to sponsor a dangerous man like him." He raised an eyebrow. "We'll be looking for him, of course, but I'd watch your backs in the future."

Angelo shrugged. "We're mutants. He can get in the line with the rest of our enemies."

Black took a deep breath. "The Genogoths are a hundred years old," he said, "perhaps it is time for us to change. I am willing to start that change with you. I am trusting you, Xavier's charges, with our secrets. If you don't betray that trust then, perhaps, further reform is possible. I know you don't feel that you owe me anything at this point, but I ask you to do it for Espeth, Smokey, the others, and the mutants like Catfish who depend on us."

Jono stepped forward. "We don't like you, Black, just so that's bloody clear. But yeah, we'll sit on your blasted secrets till the end of time, if that's what it takes to change your ways."

Black nodded. "Then I'll be going. I don't think we'll meet again. The Genogoths will need to go to ground for some time after this spectacle. Arrangements have been made to bus you to the airport, then home. Your itinerary is at the front desk."

Black stopped in the doorway. "Espeth," he said. "Watch out for her. She's all I have left."

Then he was gone, and with him, the last vestige of the Genogoths.

Paige shook her head. "I will *never* understand that man."

Angelo looked up at the boar's head on the wall. "Back to reality," he said, "if you can call this reality."

The satellite phone rang, and everyone jumped about a foot. Paige answered it with a cheery hello. Then her face went white. She put her hand over the mouthpiece. "It's Emma! They're at JFK in New York, changing planes. They finished early, and they'll be home in a few hours!"

"Oh, man," said Angelo, "we are so dead."

Emma Frost hung up the pay phone, a puzzled expression on her face. She walked across the terminal to the gate where Sean, Artie, and Leech waited for her. Thanks to a holographic image inducer, the two kids looked like, well, two kids, of the ordinary non-mutant variety. They were happily arm wrestling with Sean, one on each arm.

He looked up as she approached. "The kiddles doin' okay?"

"I suppose," she said. "It's strange, they were very curious whether we'd seen Gateway recently. Now why ever would they be so anxious to see him?"

J. STEVEN YORK is the author of the second Generation X novel, *Generation X: Crossroads,* as well as two nonfiction books, a zillion or so magazine articles, and a bunch of short fiction that has appeared in magazines such as *Analog, The Magazine of Fantasy and Science Fiction, Tomorrow, Pulphouse, VB Tech* and anthologies, including a novel-on-a-disk included with Sierra's *Outpost 2* (1997) and *Missionforce Cyberstorm* (1996) set in Sierra's *Starsiege* combat robot universe. He lives in Lincoln City, Oregon, with his wife, romance and *Star Trek* author Christina F. York. They share their writer's hovel with his collection of 400-plus toy robots. Interested readers are invited to visit his Web page at www.sff.net/people/j-steven-york.

MARK BUCKINGHAM is presently the artist on Marvel's *Peter Parker, Spider-Man*. Previously he juggled his time among almost every book in DC Comics' Vertigo line (most notably on Sandman's sister *Death*) and Marvel's *Dr. Strange, The Amazing Spider-Man,* and *Generation X*. He is also renowned for his experimental artwork for Eclips Comics' *Miracleman*. "Bucky," as he is often known, is honorary chair of the Comic Creators Guild and co-organizer of the United Kingdom's National Comics Awards. He lives with his wife, Gail, and three cats in the Victorian seaside town of Clevedon, England.

CHRONOLOGY TO THE MARVEL NOVELS
AND ANTHOLOGIES

What follows is a guide to the order in which the Marvel novels and short stories published by BP Books, Inc., and Berkley Boulevard Books take place in relation to each other. Please note that this is not a hard and fast chronology, but a guideline that is subject to change at authorial or editorial whim. This list covers all the novels and anthologies published from October 1994–October 2000.

The short stories are each given an abbreviation to indicate which anthology the story appeared in. USM=*The Ultimate Spider-Man*, USS=*The Ultimate Silver Surfer*, USV=*The Ultimate Super-Villains*, UXM=*The Ultimate X-Men*, UTS=*Untold Tales of Spider-Man*, UH=*The Ultimate Hulk*, and XML=*X-Men Legends*.

X-Men & Spider-Man: Time's Arrow Book 1: **The Past [portions]** by Tom DeFalco & Jason Henderson
Parts of this novel take place in prehistoric times, the sixth century, 1867, and 1944.

"The Silver Surfer" [flashback] by Tom DeFalco & Stan Lee [USS]
The Silver Surfer's origin. The early parts of this flashback start several decades, possibly several centuries, ago, and continue to a point just prior to "To See Heaven in a Wild Flower."

"In the Line of Banner" by Danny Fingeroth [UH]
This takes place over several years, ending approximately nine months before the birth of Robert Bruce Banner.

X-Men: Codename Wolverine ["then" portions] by Christopher Golden

CHRONOLOGY

"Every Time a Bell Rings" by Brian K. Vaughan [XML]
These take place while Team X was still in operation, while the Black Widow was still a Russian spy, while Banshee was still with Interpol, and a couple of years before the X-Men were formed.

"Spider-Man" by Stan Lee & Peter David [USM]
A retelling of Spider-Man's origin.

"Transformations" by Will Murray [UH]
"Side by Side with the Astonishing Ant-Man!" by Will Murray [UTS]
"Assault on Avengers Mansion" by Richard C. White & Steven A. Roman [UH]
"Suits" by Tom De Haven & Dean Wesley Smith [USM]
"After the First Death . . . " by Tom DeFalco [UTS]
"Celebrity" by Christopher Golden & José R. Nieto [UTS]
"Pitfall" by Pierce Askegren [UH]
"Better Looting Through Modern Chemistry" by John Garcia & Pierce Askegren [UTS]
These stories take place very early in the careers of Spider-Man and the Hulk.

"To the Victor" by Richard Lee Byers [USV]
Most of this story takes place in an alternate timeline, but the jumping-off point is here.

"To See Heaven in a Wild Flower" by Ann Tonsor Zeddies [USS]

"Point of View" by Len Wein [USS]
These stories take place shortly after the end of the flashback portion of "The Silver Surfer."

"Identity Crisis" by Michael Jan Friedman [UTS]
"The Doctor's Dilemma" by Danny Fingeroth [UTS]
"Moving Day" by John S. Drew [UTS]

CHRONOLOGY

"Out of the Darkness" by Glenn Greenberg [UH]
"The Liar" by Ann Nocenti [UTS]
"Diary of a False Man" by Keith R.A. DeCandido [XML]
"Deadly Force" by Richard Lee Byers [UTS]
"Truck Stop" by Jo Duffy [UH]
"Hiding" by Nancy Holder & Christopher Golden [UH]
"Improper Procedure" by Keith R.A. DeCandido [USS]
"The Ballad of Fancy Dan" by Ken Grobe & Steven A. Roman [UTS]
"Welcome to the X-Men, Madrox ..." by Steve Lyons [XML]
These stories take place early in the careers of Spider-Man, the Silver Surfer, the Hulk, and the X-Men, after their origins and before the formation of the "new" X-Men.

"Here There Be Dragons" by Sholly Fisch [UH]
"Peace Offering" by Michael Stewart [XML]
"The Worst Prison of All" by C. J. Henderson [XML]
"Poison in the Soul" by Glenn Greenberg [UTS]
"Do You Dream in Silver?" by James Dawson [USS]
"A Quiet, Normal Life" by Thomas Deja [UH]
"Livewires" by Steve Lyons [UTS]
"Arms and the Man" by Keith R.A. DeCandido [UTS]
"Incident on a Skyscraper" by Dave Smeds [USS]
"A Green Snake in Paradise" by Steve Lyons [UH]
These all take place after the formation of the "new" X-Men and before Spider-Man got married, the Silver Surfer ended his exile on Earth, and the reemergence of the gray Hulk.

"Cool" by Lawrence Watt-Evans [USM]
"Blindspot" by Ann Nocenti [USM]
"Tinker, Tailor, Soldier, Courier" by Robert L. Washington III [USM]
"Thunder on the Mountain" by Richard Lee Byers [USM]
"The Stalking of John Doe" by Adam-Troy Castro [UTS]
"On the Beach" by John J. Ordover [USS]
These all take place just prior to Peter Parker's marriage to

271

CHRONOLOGY

Mary Jane Watson and the Silver Surfer's release from imprisonment on Earth.

Daredevil: Predator's Smile by Christopher Golden
"Disturb Not Her Dream" by Steve Rasnic Tem [USS]
"My Enemy, My Savior" by Eric Fein [UTS]
"Kraven the Hunter Is Dead, Alas" by Craig Shaw Gardner [USM]
"The Broken Land" by Pierce Askegren [USS]
"Radically Both" by Christopher Golden [USM]
"Godhood's End" by Sharman DiVono [USS]
"Scoop!" by David Michelinie [USM]
"The Beast with Nine Bands" by James A. Wolf [UH]
"Sambatyon" by David M. Honigsberg [USS]
"A Fine Line" by Dan Koogler [XML]
"Cold Blood" by Greg Cox [USM]
"The Tarnished Soul" by Katherine Lawrence [USS]
"Leveling Las Vegas" by Stan Timmons [UH]
"Steel Dogs and Englishmen" by Thomas Deja [XML]
"If Wishes Were Horses" by Tony Isabella & Bob Ingersoll [USV]
"The Stranger Inside" by Jennifer Heddle [XML]
"The Silver Surfer" [framing sequence] by Tom DeFalco & Stan Lee [USS]
"The Samson Journals" by Ken Grobe [UH]
    These all take place after Peter Parker's marriage to Mary Jane Watson, after the Silver Surfer attained freedom from imprisonment on Earth, before the Hulk's personalities were merged, and before the formation of the X-Men "blue" and "gold" teams.

"The Deviant Ones" by Glenn Greenberg [USV]
"An Evening in the Bronx with Venom" by John Gregory Betancourt & Keith R.A. DeCandido [USM]
    These two stories take place one after the other, and a few months prior to The Venom Factor.

CHRONOLOGY

The Incredible Hulk: What Savage Beast by Peter David
This novel takes place over a one-year period, starting here and ending just prior to Rampage.

"Once a Thief" by Ashley McConnell [XML]
"On the Air" by Glenn Hauman [UXM]
"Connect the Dots" by Adam-Troy Castro [USV]
"Ice Prince" by K. A. Kindya [XML]
"Summer Breeze" by Jenn Saint-John & Tammy Lynne Dunn [UXM]
"Out of Place" by Dave Smeds [UXM]
These stories all take place prior to the Mutant Empire *trilogy.*

X-Men: Mutant Empire Book 1: **Siege** by Christopher Golden
X-Men: Mutant Empire Book 2: **Sanctuary** by Christopher Golden
X-Men: Mutant Empire Book 3: **Salvation** by Christopher Golden
These three novels take place within a three-day period.

Fantastic Four: To Free Atlantis by Nancy A. Collins
"The Love of Death or the Death of Love" by Craig Shaw Gardner [USS]
"Firetrap" by Michael Jan Friedman [USV]
"What's Yer Poison?" by Christopher Golden & José R. Nieto [USS]
"Sins of the Flesh" by Steve Lyons [USV]
"Doom?" by Joey Cavalieri [USV]
"Child's Play" by Robert L. Washington III [USV]
"A Game of the Apocalypse" by Dan Persons [USS]
"All Creatures Great and Skrull" by Greg Cox [USV]
"Ripples" by José R. Nieto [USV]
"Who Do You Want Me to Be?" by Ann Nocenti [USV]
"One for the Road" by James Dawson [USV]

CHRONOLOGY

These are more or less simultaneous, with "Doom²" taking place after To Free Atlantis, *"Child's Play" taking place shortly after "What's Yer Poison?" and "A Game of the Apocalypse" taking place shortly after "The Love of Death or the Death of Love."*

"Five Minutes" by Peter David [USM]
This takes place on Peter Parker and Mary Jane Watson-Parker's first anniversary.

Spider-Man: The Venom Factor by Diane Duane
Spider-Man: The Lizard Sanction by Diane Duane
Spider-Man: The Octopus Agenda by Diane Duane
These three novels take place within a six-week period.

"The Night I Almost Saved Silver Sable" by Tom DeFalco [USV]
"Traps" by Ken Grobe [USV]
These stories take place one right after the other.

Iron Man: The Armor Trap by Greg Cox
Iron Man: Operation A.I.M. by Greg Cox
"Private Exhibition" by Pierce Askegren [USV]
Fantastic Four: Redemption of the Silver Surfer by Michael Jan Friedman
Spider-Man & The Incredible Hulk: Rampage (Doom's Day Book 1) by Danny Fingeroth & Eric Fein
Spider-Man & Iron Man: Sabotage (Doom's Day Book 2) by Pierce Askegren & Danny Fingeroth
Spider-Man & Fantastic Four: Wreckage (Doom's Day Book 3) by Eric Fein & Pierce Askegren
Operation A.I.M. takes place about two weeks after The Armor Trap. *The Doom's Day trilogy takes place within a three-month period. The events of* Operation A.I.M., *"Private Exhibition,"* Redemption of the Silver Surfer, *and* Rampage *happen more or less simultaneously.* Wreckage *is only a few months after* The Octopus Agenda.

CHRONOLOGY

"Such Stuff As Dreams Are Made Of" by Robin Wayne Bailey [XML]
"It's a Wonderful Life" by eluki bes shahar [UXM]
"Gift of the Silver Fox" by Ashley McConnell [UXM]
"Stillborn in the Mist" by Dean Wesley Smith [UXM]
"Order from Chaos" by Evan Skolnick [UXM]
These stories take place more or less simultaneously, with "Such Stuff As Dreams Are Made Of" taking place just prior to the others.

"X-Presso" by Ken Grobe [UXM]
"Life Is But a Dream" by Stan Timmons [UXM]
"Four Angry Mutants" by Andy Lane & Rebecca Levene [UXM]
"Hostages" by J. Steven York [UXM]
These stories take place one right after the other.

Spider-Man: Carnage in New York by David Michelinie & Dean Wesley Smith
Spider-Man: Goblin's Revenge by Dean Wesley Smith
These novels take place one right after the other.
X-Men: Smoke and Mirrors by eluki bes shahar
This novel takes place three-and-a-half months after "It's a Wonderful Life."

Generation X by Scott Lobdell & Elliot S! Maggin
X-Men: The Jewels of Cyttorak by Dean Wesley Smith
X-Men: Empire's End by Diane Duane
X-Men: Law of the Jungle by Dave Smeds
X-Men: Prisoner X by Ann Nocenti
These novels take place one right after the other.

The Incredible Hulk: Abominations by Jason Henderson
Fantastic Four: Countdown to Chaos by Pierce Askegren
"Playing It SAFE" by Keith R.A. DeCandido [UH]
These take place one right after the other, with Abominations *taking place a couple of weeks after* Wreckage.

CHRONOLOGY

"Mayhem Party" by Robert Sheckley [USV]
This story takes place after Goblin's Revenge.

X-Men & Spider-Man: Time's Arrow Book 1: **The Past** by
Tom DeFalco & Jason Henderson
X-Men & Spider-Man: Time's Arrow Book 2: **The Present**
by Tom DeFalco & Adam-Troy Castro
X-Men & Spider-Man: Time's Arrow Book 3: **The Future**
by Tom DeFalco & eluki bes shahar
*These novels take place within a twenty-four-hour period in the
present, though it also involves traveling to four points in the past,
to an alternate present, and to five different alternate futures.*

X-Men: Soul Killer by Richard Lee Byers
Spider-Man: Valley of the Lizard by John Vornholt
Spider-Man: Venom's Wrath by Keith R.A. DeCandido &
José R. Nieto
Spider-Man: Wanted: Dead or Alive by Craig Shaw Gardner
"Sidekick" by Dennis Brabham [UH]
Captain America: Liberty's Torch by Tony Isabella & Bob
Ingersoll
These take place one right after the other, with Soul Killer *taking place right after the* Time's Arrow *trilogy,* Venom's Wrath *taking place a month after* Valley of the Lizard, *and* Wanted Dead or
Alive *a couple of months after* Venom's Wrath.

Spider-Man: The Gathering of the Sinister Six by Adam-Troy Castro
Generation X: Crossroads by J. Steven York
X-Men: Codename Wolverine ["now" portions] by Christopher Golden
*These novels take place one right after the other, with the
"now" portions of* Codename Wolverine *taking place less
than a week after* Crossroads.

The Avengers & the Thunderbolts by Pierce Askegren
Spider-Man: Goblin Moon by Kurt Busiek & Nathan Archer

CHRONOLOGY

Nick Fury, Agent of S.H.I.E.L.D.: Empyre by Will Murray
Generation X: Genogoths by J. Steven York
These novels take place at approximately the same time and several months after "Playing It SAFE."

Spider-Man & the Silver Surfer: Skrull War by Steven A. Ronan & Ken Grobe
X-Men & the Avengers: Gamma Quest Book 1: **Lost and Found** by Greg Cox
X-Men & the Avengers: Gamma Quest Book 2: **Search and Rescue** by Greg Cox
X-Men & the Avengers: Gamma Quest Book 3: **Friend or Foe?** by Greg Cox
These books take place one right after the other.

X-Men & Spider-Man: Time's Arrow Book 3: **The Future [portions]** by Tom DeFalco & eluki bes shahar
Parts of this novel take place in five different alternate futures in 2020, 2035, 2099, 3000, and the fortieth century.

"The Last Titan" by Peter David [UH]
This takes place in a possible future.

MARVEL® Comics
X-MEN®

star in their own original series!

BP Books, Inc.

MARVEL®

❑ **X-MEN: MUTANT EMPIRE: BOOK 1: SIEGE**
  by Christopher Golden   0-425-17275-9/$6.99
When Magneto takes over a top-secret government installation containing mutant-hunting robots, the X-Men must battle against their oldest foe. But the X-Men are held responsible for the takeover by a more ruthless enemy...the U.S. government.

❑ **X-MEN: MUTANT EMPIRE: BOOK 2: SANCTUARY**
  by Christopher Golden   1-57297-180-0/$5.99
Magneto has occupied The Big Apple, and the X-Men must penetrate the enslaved city and stop him before he advances his mad plan to conquer the entire world!

❑ **X-MEN: MUTANT EMPIRE: BOOK 3: SALVATION**
  by Christopher Golden   0-425-16640-6/$6.99
Magneto's Mutant Empire has already taken Manhattan, and now he's setting his sights on the rest of the world. The only thing that stands between Magneto and his conquest is the X-Men.

®, ™ and © 2000 Marvel Characters, Inc. All Rights Reserved.

Prices slightly higher in Canada

Payable by Visa, MC or AMEX only ($10.00 min.), No cash, checks or COD. Shipping & handling: US/Can. $2.75 for one book, $1.00 for each add'l book; Int'l $5.00 for one book, $1.00 for each add'l. Call (800) 788-6262 or (201) 933-9292, fax (201) 896-8569 or mail your orders to:

Penguin Putnam Inc. **P.O. Box 12289, Dept. B** **Newark, NJ 07101-5289** Please allow 4-6 weeks for delivery. Foreign and Canadian delivery 6-8 weeks.	Bill my: ❑ Visa ❑ MasterCard ❑ Amex _____ (expires) Card# _____ Signature _____

Bill to:

Name _____

Address _____ City _____

State/ZIP _____ Daytime Phone # _____

Ship to:

Name _____ Book Total $ _____

Address _____ Applicable Sales Tax $ _____

City _____ Postage & Handling $ _____

State/ZIP _____ Total Amount Due $ _____

This offer subject to change without notice.   Ad # 722 (3/00)